For JimJo, Kate

and the two little

PfoofooblumbyminbowbobsheadsS

Jesse & Erin.

Love you guys !!

Natto

xxx

PS this book... it's kind of a big
deal....

He Played For His Wife . . .

And Other Stories

He Played For His Wife . . .

And Other Stories

Short Stories of Long Nights at the Poker Table

Edited by

Anthony Holden
and Natalie Galustian

**SIMON &
SCHUSTER**

London · New York · Sydney · Toronto · New Delhi

A CBS COMPANY

First published in Great Britain by Simon & Schuster UK Ltd, 2017
A CBS COMPANY

3 5 7 9 10 8 6 4 2

Simon & Schuster UK Ltd
1st Floor
222 Gray's Inn Road
London WC1X 8HB

www.simonandschuster.co.uk

Simon & Schuster Australia, Sydney
Simon & Schuster India, New Delhi

The author and publishers have made all reasonable efforts
to contact copyright-holders for permission, and apologise
for any omissions or errors in the form of credits given.
Corrections may be made to future printings.

A CIP catalogue record for this book
is available from the British Library.

ISBN: 978-1-4711-6228-2
Ebook ISBN: 978-1-4711-6229-9

Typeset in Sabon by M Rules
Printed and bound by CPI Group (UK) Ltd, Croydon, CR0 4YY

Simon & Schuster UK Ltd are committed to sourcing paper
that is made from wood grown in sustainable forests and support the Forest
Stewardship Council, the leading international forest certification organisation.
Our books displaying the FSC logo are printed on FSC certified paper.

Contents

Preface

by Al Alvarez

From Mark Twain to Martin Amis, Somerset Maugham to John Updike, poker has always had a way of moving writers of fiction to some of their finest hours. The writers in this anthology – all of them, without exception, not just the professional writers – know a thing or two about suspense, about surprise, about trickery and, indeed, how to tell a story.

What is it about poker that gets to us like this? In my own case, playing poker was as near as a nice English literary boy without a horse could get to being a cowboy. But slowly I learned that poker wasn't about gambling, and it wasn't about wild narcissistic optimism, either. It was about something in a way much more sober and much more skilful. I mustn't overplay the sobriety card, however, because one of my friends, John, a very smart player, hardly ever played the cards; he played the other players, sometimes in the wildest of ways, and that is a skill that only true mind-games players ever master.

The reader will find plenty of mind-games to keep him going here, several of them played by ghosts, including Shakespeare in Anthony Holden's own story and Billy Bones in Barny Boatman's.

It seems a ridiculous idea, but learning to play poker well can help you grow up. After a particularly shaming two games with a very cool, bored expert from the USA, who could see what chumps I and my friends were, I myself belatedly turned to Herbert O. Yardley's *The Education of a Poker Player*. He writes: 'A card player should learn that once his money is in the pot, it isn't his any longer. His judgment should not be influenced by this. He should instead say to himself: Do the odds favour my playing regardless of the money I have already contributed?' In the end, what he is describing is not so much a game of cards as a style of life. All the stories in this collection are, in a way, lessons in living.

What is extraordinary, too, is how well the debut writers write. Maybe in a funny way they are trained in studying the art and arc of narrative without knowing it. The editors, my old friend Anthony Holden and my comparatively new one Natalie Galustian, have enlisted a diverse array of players and writers both professional and amateur – an engaging combination of poker pros you didn't know could write, professional writers you didn't know could play poker, and neither who could do both. Unsurprisingly, there is a distinctly autobiographical strain throughout; however covert, writing about poker is as self-revealing a process as writing fiction. Whatever else they thought about poker before, their readers are going to find themselves totally absorbed.

Drawing Dead

by Barny Boatman

Am I a good man? I wanna say so. But I am a poker player, old school. It's my job to stick the knife in, step back and smile while your life drains away a buck at a time. And mine with it. Ah, but then there's my charity work. And what a piece of work he is. Was.

I think Billy Bones was there the first time I sat down in a spieler, standing near the table, slapping your shoulder and giving a 'lucky rub' when you raked a pot. Whispering in some bloke's ear and slipping a couple of chips in his inside pocket, quick and slick. A thoughtful, solicitous, charming ponce.

Bones knew. I wanted to be a better man, and that cost. *He's running bad, it's his daughter's birthday, his car's in the pound.* Every time I pull in a pot there's Billy, the ethical rake. And what got me – I mean there was no way on earth that a penny was ever coming back, he got the readies and I got to be the angel – what got me was his little book. *Everything* went in. Every chip,

3

every note, every tournament cash I was due a piece of (if he hadn't run into a bogey or the dice table first). Once I asked him how we stood. He looked so pained that I never asked again.

There had been as many rumours about Billy's health as his criminal record. Those little shits in the Mill Hill game had a book on what was gonna kill him, but no one collected. No one foresaw his deadly ten-floor fall that January night. Down he'd gone, back arched, those long lean limbs flaying and flapping, his pale thin face imploring the heavens. As he saw the stars rushing away from him he thought about what he'd taken from the world and what he'd given it, and he grabbed at his inside pocket. The first policeman at the scene went through the motions of establishing that the man was dead, but the black-red pool around his head already told the story. The corpse had something wedged up below the jaw, clasped in both hands tight to the chest, like it was an access all areas pass to the afterlife. Pulling carefully at those tightening knuckles, the cop saw the book. Neat little rows of names, dates, places and numbers. Currency symbols, percentage signs, sums. And, here and there, a strong straight line of erasure and one word – thicker and clearer than the rest – *PAID*.

It had been a while since I'd seen that little book, when Bones last visited. I'd done a bottle of Chilean red and dozed off watching *Cape Fear*, the remake with Nolte and De Niro. There's something *wrong* about that film ...

4

Tap tap. Something was waking me. The window? No, too high.

Tap tap tap. I rubbed my eyes. Footsteps in the flat? I live alone.

Awake now, I went to the front door.

'Hello, Billy. I thought you were away.'

'Away ... yes.' He breezed through me with casual entitlement. I closed the door against the winter night and followed him to the front room. He kept his back to me and looked out the window.

'What do you want? You know you owe ...'

He raised a hand.

'I'm here to pay you back. All of it.'

He was smart to tell me that right off, because once I believed that Mr W. Bones Esq. was going to pay me what he owed me, I was ready to believe anything.

Never turning, he told his story. There was a woman, beautiful, half his age. *You old dog, Billy Bones, there's hope for us all.* He'd been going back and forth to her apartment in Mallorca for a year. Her husband was a man of importance in the casino industry. He'd met them when working as a driver for an English poker player who travelled to a big game in Marbella. Billy must have been in his late sixties and was long since separated from a wife I hadn't met. I'd never thought of him as a ladies' man and, unlike most of the leering articles I rubbed shoulders with, he never discussed such things. I studied his back. The neat crisp Crombie hanging from his square strong shoulders, the salt 'n' pepper memory of a youthful DA and the yellow silk scarf. He had presence, did Billy Bones, even from behind. I pictured him, chatting easily with the waitresses and massage girls. That big silver ring on a huge slender hand, pushing back his floppy silver quiff or holding a door open for a girl laden with drinks and snacks. Those dark, sad eyes, creasing kindly as he thanked her with a lean-lipped generous grin. He was not a big tipper like me but, come to think of it, the girls did like him. Hope for us all? No, for the suave and charming Mr Bones.

The woman's husband had turned up unexpectedly, Billy was telling me. He'd tried to jump balconies, slipped and fallen ten floors to his . . .

'Hold on, when did all this happen?'

'Now. It's happening now. There'll be something in the papers tomorrow if they connect it to her husband. He's a face.'

'What are you telling me, Billy? If you'd fallen ten stories in Mallorca, you wouldn't be here now . . .'

He was facing me now. And I saw.

'. . . and you'd probably be dead.'

I knew before I said the word, that 'probably' wasn't in it.

I'm a poker player, as superstitious and out of touch with the real world as you'd expect. But we are also the most rational of beings. I was being asked to accept that the ghost of Billy Bones, Billy who lay, still not cold, on a cracked Spanish kerb, had rushed across icy waters and dark fogbound hills to be with me. To make good from the next life what he had never even intended to settle in this.

'How are you gonna pay me, Billy?'

He cracked a weary, disappointed, vindicated smile.

In my world reputation is everything. More important than being good is being thought good. I've got morals, I'll never steal or cheat, unless I'm quite sure I'll get away with it. And only if it's just. I mean, when you absolutely know someone has been pulling strokes on you, when you can taste their disdain, when there's no explanation for how they spank you time after time ... Sometimes you spot a ball bouncing past an open net, and you just lift one hand and help it go where it was meant to. But to cheat? To mark cards, exchange signals, deal from the bottom of the deck? Never.

I guess it, old Dead Billy's plan.

My dreams may be different from yours. You are on stage, lines forgotten, or naked in the playground. I wander lost through vast banks of tournament tables knowing I will never find my seat. Or I push all in with the nut hand, riches assured, look down and see that my pair of aces has transmogrified into a bowl of soup, or a six-legged mouse. The waking fantasies, though, all but the most brilliantly successful must have had them. What if you could read minds, or see what others couldn't? If, just now and then, you simply *knew* the other guy's cards? You wouldn't use it much. But when it really mattered, you'd stop time, go invisible ... whatever. You'd know you were being bluffed. You'd spin it out, make it look good ... and then make that heroic, impossible call. Which maybe, being the great player you are, you'd have made anyway. Come on, I don't care who you are

7

or what you do. Don't be telling me you've never had a waking dream like this.

And here stood the ghost of good old, dead old William Bones, offering me the chance of a lifetime. It was gonna be like *Randall and Hopkirk (Deceased)*. Only me and Billy wouldn't be solving crimes, loading the dice against working villains. We'd be evening up the score at the poker table, solving those mysteries that routinely throw themselves up in the game. There'd be no seeing round corners, mind reading or mirrors. Billy would just lean over, right up close when they peeled up their cards, squint those dark, dead, sorry eyes and call out what they had. Just to me. Evening the score, that was it.

'This is just to clear the debt,' he winced, rubbing his head. 'Don't ask for any more, or ...'

'Or what, Billy?'

'Refusal can offend.'

Even as a spectre, the sweet old bloke struggled to come off eerie and menacing. Good, it was doing my gut in enough having the ghost of poker past rattling around my gaff. This was good old Billy, after all, and he owed me. He said so himself.

To debut our double act I picked a nice safe home game at the Charlotte Despard pub in Archway. Chris the landlord was probably the only other sober player, and if someone had spotted Billy's ghost they'd just have rubbed their eyes and eased off on the ale.

When I play poker what I feel most is control. I make my living from the game. Not a great living, if I'm honest.

Not a great living ... if I'm honest. But, I do get a buzz from playing, and part of that buzz is the uncertainty. We are gamblers, after all. But this was different, the control was a given now, almost total. And the nerves, the excitement, that was heightened too, but in a deeply sickening way.

Bones kind of drifted round the table trying to be in the right place when they looked at their cards. I had to remember what he called out as he couldn't write it in his book, just like he couldn't change his clothes, he said. It's a ghost thing, I dunno. He wasn't much help until, at the end of the night, I won a big pot off Chris when we both had nothing. He bluffed the river and I gave it the Hollywood, saying how his bet didn't make sense, justifying the suicidal call I was gonna make. And I've got to say, even though I take-it-to-the-bank knew that Chris had his fingers in the till, he did keep his cool. 'I know you,' his eyes sneered. 'You're a grinder. A percentage pro who scurries to his lair each morning, cheeks bulging with low-hanging fruit, and creeps out at nightfall, in search of easy prey.'

'Talk away,' he was thinking. 'Make yourself look good in case I show you a bluff. You'll never call without the hand and we both know it, you haven't got the ...'

'OK. I call.'

We went through the motions. He flipped his worthless cards face up on my stack as I shoved it forward. I stared at them. Enjoying the moment, but trying to act like I hadn't known.

'Nine high? I've got that beat.'

'No shit. One pair?'

9

I shook my head and dropped my king and queen of diamonds under his fat pink face.

'Good call,' he managed.

'Good call, good call,' the whole table chanted back, reverent and respectful like an unholy order of gambling monks.

'*Good* call,' jeers Billy for my ears only, and he reaches for his book.

I dragged his chips into my stack, my throat filled with resentment for my 'mate' Chris. Didn't we always have a post-game Guinness, and laugh about the frightened little fishes and the stupid stubborn donkeys who'd fold or call according to our will? *Oh, I'm not going after you without the hand*, he'd say. *No need, is there?* This man had been taking advantage of my good nature. It was easy for him, he had only to open the doors of his boozer and the money oozed into his pockets like syrup off a spoon. This was my living, I couldn't just 'enjoy' the game like he did. And he'd been taking the piss. All those times, late in the game when I was up a nice few quid and he'd bet me off a big pot. Tapping the table, 'good fold, good fold', and giving me that little conspiratorial look, like 'I'd show you the cards if I could, but you *know* I've got you beat.' Don't tell me I should feel bad about this one hand. He owed me.

I didn't stay for the usual drink that night. I went home buzzing from my brilliant call with king high. Class.

The debt was clearing fast and I knew once we'd gotten straight that I'd see no more of Mr Bones. I wanted to give myself a chance of getting ahead on the deal so for his farewell appearance I suggested The Aristocrats Club, a private members' casino which hosts one of the biggest cash games in the country. A couple of years back I was on a hot streak and had been once or twice, but even then it was way too big for me. Just a dead body waiting for the nuts. So Nev Shilling was surprised when I called him to hold me a seat.

'It plays bigger than when you were last here. Sit-down is ten lumps but most start with a pony, and you need a couple of pull-ups. I wouldn't play if I wasn't put in.'

'Fine,' I'd said. I'd had a nice build-up lately and wanted to take a shot at spinning it up. True, right?

Nev was chatting away and stacking chips when I arrived. Next to him was James Skipton, a young pro from Leeds who'd just got back from tearing up the big game at the Bellagio in Vegas. There was Saul the bookie who ran his own game once a month above his shop in Finchley. Gary who'd played in midfield for Millwall, or West Ham, but who'd done far better out of poker than from football. The legendary 'Papa', who has more money than God and has sent hundreds skint on his way to being the game's biggest loser. And Tony. This was Tony's game really, any game he played in was Tony's game.

I'd done a grand in blinds before I played a small pot with Saul. Raise, re-raise, fold.

'So you are here then?' Shilling goaded, and Billy gave me a slow handclap as I placed the chips back on my stack. *Oh, I'm here all right. And Bones is here too. So sneer away, the lot of you, the whole lucky caked-up lot of you. Raise blind to build the pots, tip a tenner for a coffee, laugh and joke as you win and lose tens of thousands in a hand. Fill your smug boots with derision for an honest pro who happens to still respect money, as well as the game. Think you're something special because you've got a few quid and you don't mind chucking it about? Well, have a good chuckle, but tonight's my night. We're gonna do the lot of you, me and Billy Bones.*

Huge pots played out around me. Papa and Saul were losing big and calling for chips, Tony was playing strong and hitting cards, I was picking up small pots here and there, and all the time Billy drifted round the room, calling out hands, checking his damn book and joining in the ribbing and the rub downs. He was laughing too much, and mostly it seemed at me. Imagine, someone has a dig and you're just about to come back with a smart line when Billy lands the second punch, which no one else can hear. I was winning, yes, but he was rattling me. Why?

Around 3 a.m., Shilling flicked his cards in the muck when I caught him in a bluff and Billy leant close into my face.

'Right, that's it. We're done.'

'Just like that?' I hissed as quietly as I could.

'Yes, mate. Good call. Paid in full.'

'Huh?' says Shilling, who had overheard me.

'Yeah, you call and I know my three aces are no good. Easy game, eh?'

Billy was backing out of the room staring intently at his book. Backing out, or shrinking.

I jumped back from the table and whispered urgently. 'Outside ... gotta talk.'

Back at the table, I threw both arms around the chips and scooped them, messy and unstacked. 'Fag break,' I blurted, and darted up the stairs.

From the doorway I squinted into the darkness, panicking. Then I spotted that long, straight back. He was across the road. As I reached him Billy turned to face me.

'What?'

'Listen. Stay with me tonight, just for this game. I can get the lot.'

'Why should I? I've paid you off, it's over.'

'Come on, Billy, what's it to you? What about interest, and the headaches? I've had to work for the money. You still owe me.'

Billy's eyes narrowed.

'I don't know,' he said flatly. 'A deal's a deal, but ... I wanna be fair.'

'Fair, that's it, Billy Boy. I only want what's right. I know you'll ...'

He raised a hand to cut me off.

'I tell you what. It's a big game and you've got almost thirty grand in front of you. We'll carry on until we find one big hand for you to get it in with. One big hand, to the river, against one player, then we're done. But it'll have to be very soon. OK?'

As I walked back in it looked like the game was breaking up.

'Oh, here he is,' laughed Tony. 'Don't tell me, you've

had an urgent phone call from your girlfriend, she's gotta have you now.'

'What? No. It was your missus, Tony, and she can wait. I'm playing on.'

'Well,' he says. 'Good for you, you're what? Twenty up? I was sure you were gonna hit 'n' run. Here ...' He tossed Shilling a hundred-pound chip. 'You win, Nev, he wants to play on.'

'Well, I'm done,' says Shilling. Which had to mean Papa had somewhere else to be. Gary was getting up too.

'You're not going are you, Tony?' I hoped I sounded calm.

'What's it to you? You haven't played a hand against me all night. You never do.'

It was true, Tony was a scary man and a scarier player. If he smelled weakness he would put you to the test, again and again. His style didn't suit me and I always stayed out of his way. But this was different. One hand. One *big* hand. There were five of us, and Tony had more in front of him than the rest put together.

'How much are you playing?' I asked. We both knew that he had played his initial twenty-five grand up to £93,400. He scanned his stack for an instant.

'Ninety? Ninety odd?' Like he was guessing the weight of a pig. 'Why?'

'I want to cover you.'

'Well, pull up then. This I've gotta see.'

Everyone there knew that me and Tony had history, but knew what I thought about money too, what kind of a player I was, and near enough how much I was worth. No one could believe what they were hearing, no one except Billy. He knew what I was up to, I could see it in that sad old handsome face, and he knew I was pushing my luck. But then, like he'd said himself, a deal is a deal and I was gonna get my one hand. My one big, fuck-off, massive hand.

'Don't bother going to the cage,' says Tony, reaching for his inside pocket. 'Can you write me a cheque if you need to?'

I nodded.

He tossed three 25K plaques across at me like he was feeding the ducks in the park.

For a couple of rounds it was raise/fold, raise/fold. The other three, timid townsfolk at a gunfight, were still getting cards, but were no longer really in the game. They were composing tomorrow's story and watching to see which of us would draw first.

I was in the blinds with a pair of sixes and Billy, permanently crouched now by Tony's side – eyes level with the felt – called out the cards to me as he squeezed them up between his thumbs.

'Eight of hearts ... seven of hearts.'

Tony was on the button. I knew the raise was coming. He threw in six hundred pounds without a word. The action was on me and I made it eighteen hundred, regretting it even as I did it. We were playing deep and normally I'd just call and peel off a flop, but this was in no way normal. Yes, I was playing a man whose cards were face up, but I was playing Billy too. If Tony folded now we could play another hand, but if it went to the river it had to be big. I should build the pot now.

Pot building wasn't gonna be a problem. Tony raised again, to five grand. I looked over at Billy and he understood my silent question. 'Yes,' he said. 'I told you right. He's got the seven-eight of hearts.' So, Tony smelled weakness and he was putting the pressure on. This is what he does, why he's so hard to play. I could have raised again, made it fifteen or even twenty to go. That should end it there and then. Against most players it would. But Tony had decided I was weak and I had no guarantee that he wouldn't just push back at me for the whole lot. Then I'd be forced to just flip a coin for two hundred grand. No, I had to call the five thousand and hope he missed. The dealer spread the three flop cards in the centre of the felt: ace of hearts, king of hearts, two of clubs. Good bluffing cards for him, and a possible flush. I checked, and he bet the size of the pot.

Ten thousand pounds.

I hated this. I was still ahead with a pair of sixes but he would win with any heart and – though he didn't know it – a seven or eight as well. I'd have to call and hope he missed the turn. For a man who knew all the cards, I'd never felt less in control. But the turn was OK: king of spades. I was still ahead.

I've thought about this a million times and I know what I should have done. Move all in and pick up the thirty grand. How could he call? But what was it Billy had said? One pot to the river, or one all in? I couldn't ask him now. If it was one all in this would be the last hand and I'd just have won fifteen of Tony's ninety-three thousand. And could I be certain he wouldn't call? The money was nothing to him. I wasn't thinking clearly, I looked down to see my hand check-tapping on the felt. Control? Don't make me laugh. My limbs were acting more decisively than me.

Tony was relentless. He fired out a bet of twenty-two thousand, and even though I knew he was at it, I'd swear he wanted me to call. I saw no choice but to do just that, and to check-call the river when (please God) he missed his hand. The dealer was turning the final card. I stared at the deck, reaching in to influence the outcome with my desperate silent pleading. *Big black card . . . big black card.*

And you know what, I got exactly what I asked for. No seven, no eight and no heart. The dealer peeled the deck and revealed a card as big and as black as they come: The ace of spades.

Yes!

No . . .

No, no, no, no, no!!!

Counterfeited. My hand was now two aces, two kings, and a six. Tony's was two aces, two kings and an eight. He had the better hand. Only just but, in poker, an inch is a thousand miles.

I stared at the board, paralysed. Then I looked up at Billy Bones and his mouth widened into the kindest, most understanding and encouraging of smiles. Of course, I knew what I had to do. It was simple. Tony had the better hand, but he had no way of knowing it. If I moved all in he'd have to fold. I was only going to pick up thirty-seven of Tony's ninety-three grand, but still, thank God I'd pulled up the extra money and could use it now to buy the pot. As clearly, as calmly and as deliberately as I could I said the two words that can never be revoked or retracted. More fateful and irreversible than 'I do'.

'All in.'

I waited for Tony to have his moment, to put me through the wringer and make me sweat. I stared dead ahead. And I waited. Something was wrong. He wasn't showboating or saving face. He wasn't folding, he was thinking. My breath was getting shallower, my heart was beating faster and I fought the strongest impulse to swallow as Tony studied me.

'It don't make sense, could you have an ace? Ace what? To call before the flop? To check-call flop and turn? Nah, you'd check the river to catch a bluff. A king? Nah, I know you don't have ace-king and you don't take all that heat with less. You never played it like a picture pair, except quad kings? But you were *scared*. You still are. You don't want a call, do you?'

This was nauseating. I knew his cards and it did me no good to know them. Knowing them was what had got me into this mess. Tony was looking straight through me and it felt as if I was the one exposed, as though it were *my* cards that were face up. Where's the justice in that? But he had nothing, he could talk as long as he liked, he was never going to call.

18

He was still trying to put me on a hand.

'A flush draw? No. It was five K before the flop. I know you've got a pair. But how big?'

Fold, you weasel. Fold and I'll never bluff again. I'll take up religion, become a flaming monk, so help me, just stop being a hero and throw your cards away. Should I put the clock on him? No. Don't speak, don't move.

Below Tony's sharp interrogative tone I became aware of a second voice, full of syrupy concern.

'Oh dear, mate.'

It was Billy. 'He's reading your soul, he's gonna call us.' Us?

What did he mean, 'Oh dear'? Did he know I was bluffing too? Was I so transparent?

Still Tony talked it through. 'Jacks you'd check. Nines, maybe? I think it's bigger than fours. No, it felt to me like sevens, sevens or sixes. I think I've got to call. Whatever you've got, good bet.'

And with that, he pushed his chips forward, and brought my world to an end.

I didn't move or speak for a few seconds. My mouth was dry, my throat and lungs were awash with mustard gas and my gut was boiling. Greed, fear, indecision and animosity. Four headless horsemen had ridden me over a cliff.

I spoke, faintly. 'I had you. I had you to the end.'

I pushed my cards a few inches forward and kicked away my chair as I got slowly to my feet.

I looked around, where was he?

'Billy Bones,' I said. 'Billy Bones. Ninety-five grand.' I

was yelling now. 'I've just done ninety-five grand ... to eight high. That fucking Billy Bones ...'

'What's that?' asked Tony softly. 'Billy Bones? Funny that you should mention him. He died last week and he owed me ninety grand. They were gonna break his legs and I helped him out. Poor old Billy. I knew I'd never get it, but he swore to me. So many times he swore to me, that he'd pay me back. If it was the last thing he did.'

Jack High, Death Row

by Grub Smith

The skinny black padre, Malley, had been working on the prisoner for a long time. The closer it got to his date, the more Malley thought he could turn him around. He'd sit next to him on his bunk and talk about the scriptures, his eyes shining behind his gold-rimmed spectacles, saying how Jesus could forgive anything. Going on and on about it like a car salesman.

The prisoner let him talk. It made a change from staring at the walls. But he wasn't looking for an easy way out from Malley, or from anyone else. He knew he was guilty, and if that meant he was going to hell, so be it. Eight years on the Row would count as pretty good practice.

He'd murdered his wife, just the way they said. Ginny. Squeezed her soft neck until she went limp. The crazy thing was, he couldn't picture her face any more, or her smell, or even the way she wore her pretty black hair. Dating for two years, married for ten, but all the details lovers take for granted were blurred or forgotten. Only

21

his hands retained an essence of her. He could still feel her throat, pulsing and fighting for air in the nerve ends of his fingertips, if he shut his eyes and thought about it, which he did pretty much every day.

'Is there anything you need to tell me?' Malley asked.

The prisoner looked around the waiting cell, at the half-eaten cheeseburger and the half-drunk strawberry shake, at the armed guards sitting a yard beyond the bars. He shrugged. Malley lowered his voice to a whisper.

'Son, you only have a few minutes now. If you repent, the Lord is sure to forgive you. Don't go before him with your pride intact.'

The prisoner had seen plenty of men break on the Row, stone killers caving in as Malley spun and tightened his web of words and hope around them. On their last day, they shuffled away in double irons, weakly muttering prayers. Broken by belief. The cons would discuss it the next day: 'You won't see me wailing like Bob did ... who'd a thought that Davis would pussy out, he was almost holding the Warden's hand ...'

Staring through his own familiar bars on those melancholy occasions, the prisoner had never tried to judge the condemned men, or to catch their eyes. He'd studied Malley instead, the little padre walking backwards in front of the procession of guards and officials, reading a prayer from the black book. His voice was always the same, hushed and slow and solemn, like the words were made of iron. But under the glint of his glasses, the prisoner reckoned he could detect a hint of something else in the padre. A smirk he couldn't hide, like he'd won a prize.

'Well, there is maybe one thing.'

Malley leant forward, eager. 'Tell me, son.'

'How long do I have exactly?'

Malley checked his watch. 'The Warden will be here in ... just over sixteen minutes.'

The prisoner nodded calmly, then it was his turn to lean forward. He whispered into the priest's ear, up close, seeing the whorls of flesh as a delicate purple-black.

'Padre, are you a betting man?'

Malley twisted away, looking confused for an instant, then plain wary. But still interested; the first time the prisoner had wavered an inch in all these years. 'I suppose that depends on the bet.'

'I've got a wager for you.' He opened the last carton on the table, and loaded his plastic fork with a slice of cheesecake. 'All you've got to do is play me at one hand of poker.'

The priest shook his head. 'You know as well as I do that Warden Swift has banned gambling for prisoners on the Row.'

'No gambling, smoking, spitting, TV, dirty magazines and swearing. I know the list. Like things weren't hard enough for us already.'

'He has his methods. I can only respect them.'

'Him? He's a sick man and we both know it. The first day I got here, he hauled me into his office, sitting there behind his big old desk, said he'd never let me see a woman again. Never. Not even a picture in my cell. No movie stars, no centrefolds, no works of art. I wouldn't get to read a paper that hadn't been cut up first, case I caught a single glimpse of a female. Can you imagine what that's been like? I haven't even seen a photograph of my wife in eight years.'

'You raped and killed your wife.'

'It wasn't rape. Not that it matters. I made love to her, then I killed her for what she'd done.'

'The jury said different. And the Warden likes the punishment to fit the crime. It may seem cruel to you, but perhaps he's done you a favour, keeping your mind off bad memories and temptations. Not seeing a woman, it allows you to concentrate on what matters right now, which is ...'

'You know I'm not even allowed a picture of the Virgin Mary.'

'Then let's pray to her instead. She is known to comfort us, a gentle mother to all men ...'

The priest clenched his hands in prayer, but the prisoner put down his fork and leant back in his chair, the shackles around his ankles jarring noisily against the table leg.

'Yeah? Well, where was she when the Warden put the cold hose on me, every day for a week last winter? When the hacks kicked me so hard I nearly lost an eye? The guy enjoys it. He's a sadist.'

'He believes strongly in reformation of character, and suffering is part of that. It's a very Christian approach, in a way.'

'Well, I'll tell you my approach.' The prisoner's raised voice caused the guards to look up from their chairs, ready for trouble. He nodded at them to show he was calm, and reverted to a near-whisper. 'You're right about one thing, I am a proud man. So here's the deal – one hand of stud. Five cards each. If you win, I'll promise Jesus whatever he wants. I'll go into that chamber singing "When the Roll is Called Up Yonder". I'll do it on my knees if you like.'

'It will take more than that. You'd have to feel genuine remorse.'

'I can do that. Hell, you think I'm *not* sorry? I loved her. '

Malley seemed to waver.

'Even if you don't trust me, can you really deny me the chance?'

Malley paused. He took off his glasses and polished them on his sleeve, weighing the matter up. Finally, he spoke. 'And if you win?'

'Simple. You delay the Warden on the walk. Give me one extra minute on the way to the chamber. Go long on the words when you give me the last rites, tie your shoelaces, anything. I know you can do it.'

'The execution is scheduled for 7 a.m. I can't change that.'

'Sure you can. The only thing the Warden fears more than upsetting the State is riling God Almighty. And who dies on time, anyway? Remember Ted Forbes from Bartram? The Jackson Lake killer? He fainted twice on the walk before they strapped him in, and then it took three squirts of gas to finish him off. They were in there more than an hour before they got it done. Or the time Doc Walker went into the chamber too early, and they had to call another medic to give him CPR? What have you got to lose?'

25

Malley replaced his glasses on the thin bridge of his nose. He raked his fingers back through the shallow grey hair on his scalp.

'Here's what I don't understand. You've had eight years to wait for this day, and I've never met a man who seemed less worried about dying, leastways one who I'd consider sane. So why is one more minute suddenly so important now?'

The prisoner loaded another slice onto his fork, the blueberry topping smelling sweet and artificial in the stale air of the cell.

'Padre, I've been a liar and a conman all my life. I've stolen cars, robbed stores, been in and out of jail cells since I was fifteen years old. About the only thing I ever did right was loving my wife. I never cheated on her, not once, and I wish with all my heart I hadn't killed her. But now I can't hardly remember what any woman on earth looks like, let alone the girl I was wed to.'

He brought the cheesecake to his lips, but changed his mind, putting it back into the carton and pushing it away.

'But I do recall the times we'd get up early just to roll around in her daddy's corn crop on June mornings up there in Kansas. The dawn sun warming our faces just right, and her laughing and joking next to me.' He closed his eyes for a moment. 'There's a window faces east on the way to the chamber. I want to look back into it for one bare minute and feel the rays and imagine her close to me. To think about maybe seeing her again. In heaven, if Jesus can redeem me like you say.'

'You know the guards will be armed? And that

window you're speaking of must be twenty feet off the floor? If you're planning anything dumb . . .'

The prisoner gave a wry chuckle.

'It's never been done. And I can't even jump six inches in all this jewellery they got me wearing. I'm not playing you, padre. It's just a dying man's simple wish. So, how about it? One hand of poker? For my soul, you might say. You win and I promise you this, I'll pray so loud they'll hear me in Gen Pop.'

Malley smiled for the first time.

'It's a nice idea, but you're forgetting one thing. We don't have any cards.' He looked at his watch. 'And you have less than five minutes.'

'The hacks have a deck. How do you think they pass the time? Ask them. Hey, Sullivan? Lend the padre your cards.'

The head guard gave him an icy, see-nothing look, but Malley told him it would be OK, just this once. A battered, blue-backed deck was passed through to him.

'You want me to deal?'

'That sounds fair to me, padre. But to keep things on the straight and narrow, how about I shuffle them first, 'less you mind?'

He took the cards and pulled them from the pack. The bicycle pattern was grained and faded from use, and there were small sweat stains and creases on every one. He hadn't split a deck for nearly a decade, but at once it was like speaking a language he'd grown up with. All those road games and tobacco bets in County lock-up, the ten-dollar grifts with drunks in bars. Barely looking down, he riffled the fifty-two then clasped his hands around them, passing them back to the priest.

'Let's do it if we're going to.'

Malley's eyes were shining, caught up in the game now. He dealt slowly, like an amateur, a hick player. A hole card each, then the ten of diamonds for the prisoner and the seven of clubs for himself.

'So far so good. I almost wish we were betting money too. I might clean out the collection plate.'

Malley cautiously bent down towards the table edge and peeled up his hole card for a peep. He tried to keep his face a mask, giving nothing away. 'Aren't you going to look?' he asked.

The prisoner shrugged. 'I'm in no hurry, remember.'

Malley dealt third street. Three of spades for the prisoner. He got the four of clubs.

'You flushing on me, padre?'

In the distance, there was a heavy clatter of steel as doors were slid open. The guards stood up and began to straighten their tan uniforms.

Two of hearts. Jack of diamonds.

'I guess you're in front now. Go easy on me, padre. Come on, pair me up. Ten, three or deuce. Or a bullet even. This is getting to be fun, ain't it?'

Nine of spades. Ten of hearts.

'Ouch. You stole that ten from me.'

Keys rattled and were inserted into the lock of the inner door. They could hear the Warden's voice barking orders. Hurriedly, the padre showed first, flicking over his hole card to reveal the six of hearts.

'Jack high, son. That's all I've got. Can you beat it? Hurry now.'

The prisoner slowly moved his fingers towards his

28

hidden card, pausing to gauge if they were shaking. His nerves were good, but his hands suddenly seemed old and ruined. The battered knuckles, the chipped nails, the thick, faded jailhouse tattoos. The hands that had killed her, ugly mitts, like they weren't part of his own body, the hands that had choked a rough purple necklace around her sweet neck.

'Well, let's see.' He squeezed the corner upwards and glanced for a long time, seeming not to believe what he saw. Malley could sense the Warden standing behind him, but he couldn't look away. After what seemed like minutes, the prisoner finally spoke.

'Padre, your jack's good.'

He pushed his cards into the centre with a sullen swipe, splashing the whole deck and sending them skeetering off the edge of the table. He pulled his hands back to his chest and looked up to see the face of his tormentor scowling down at him. Behind him were two hacks holding shotguns, and the rest of them were lining up into formation. He took a deep breath, like a man preparing to take a long dive underwater.

'Warden Swift. And there was me thinking this wasn't my lucky day ...'

'I've got to hand it to you, that went better than I'd hoped.'

At the back of the witness room, the Warden was talking to Malley.

'I had him down as pure trouble, but you seem to have tamed him like a lamb. I won't even ask about the card game you were playing.'

Malley allowed himself a smile. The prisoner had kept

his word, repeating the Lord's Prayer loudly and clearly as they led him down the hallway, not even glancing back for a second at the red dawn flooding through the skylight. It had gone like clockwork.

'I'm sure your methods had something to do with it all, Warden,' he added, modestly.

'That's good to hear. I knew we'd bust him between us in the end.'

The small curtain was drawn back, and they took their seats alongside the other witnesses, five or six journalists and lawyers, and the crew from the Coroner's. Behind the curtain, the chamber looked like a small submarine with four large portholes.

The prisoner could not hear them through the glass, and nor did he seek their gaze as he was efficiently strapped down by the silent guards. Sullivan checked his bonds one last time, then nodded to the Warden. He backed out and the door closed behind him with a dull metallic shudder.

The second hand on the clock climbed implacably round to the hour, the telephone on the wall stayed mute, and then the lever was pulled. Two tablets dropped into the trough of water behind the death seat. The gas began to curl upwards, cloudy and slow. The Warden watched it, satisfied, through the glass.

'Did he say anything raw about me in there? Don't spare my blushes, padre.'

'No. Not at all.' There was no point in ruining a decent morning's work. 'Mostly he just got sentimental about his wife, the way they all do near the end. How he loved her, how he regretted what he'd done, how they used to lie together in her father's corn fields in Kansas before it all went wrong.'

The Warden turned to look at him.

'Cornfields? Her daddy was a bartender in Miami. Died when she was a baby. Never went near a field in his life. Poor chump must have been raving at you.'

Unnoticed, the prisoner turned his left hand under the thick leather strap, getting just enough of a twist that he could glimpse the object cupped secretly in his palm. It was a crumpled card, bent almost double by the tight grip he'd held it in.

His hole card, the queen of spades, smiling back at him. Plump cheeks and big dark eyes.

He grinned, then sucked hungrily at the almond-smelling air.

Ginny. Ginny, with the pretty black hair . . .

Once More, Into the Abyss!

by Jennifer Tilly

The phone call from Binky should have been an omen. Binky never calls me. He only texts. Binky is in charge of procuring people for the biggest cash games around town. He gets five hundred dollars for every fish he brings in and, needless to say, I am one of them. Before Binky discovered the poker world he served a similar function, getting paid for each hot girl he delivered to the clubs. He also deals occasionally, but he is a little erratic, sometimes showing up drunk and falling asleep on the sofa, while Noah who runs the games fills in for him.

When I met him, he was a big, cheerful, not very bright bodybuilder. The famous poker phenom Andy Lamas discovered him in Brooklyn and brought him out to Vegas to sort of be his personal pet. Binky slept in Andy's guestroom for about four years. Being around a top-tier poker player like Andy, Binky developed a bit of a gambling problem. When Andy finally kicked him out, he owed him about thirty thousand dollars.

I always liked Binky. He was uncomplicated and simple. I had a dark period in my life when my brother was slowly dying from cancer. During this time, I would constantly lose, and Binky would meet me in the hallway with tears in his eyes and plead with me to go home. Once he walked me out to my car after a particularly bad night, and we stood under the bright lights of the parking lot and talked. He told me he had lost his dad to cancer and knew what I was going through.

He gave me some advice to curtail my losses.

'Look how Lee always leaves at midnight, win or lose. He's not obsessive about poker. There's always another game. I see you play and you don't know when to quit. Sometimes you're almost back to even, but you'll have about 100K on the table and then you lose it all. When you've got a big stack at risk it's good to just call it a day. Also you should have a stop loss ... Tell the host to cut you off after a certain amount.'

To hear him telling me these things in his thick Brooklyn patois, looking at me with those sad puppy dog eyes of his, made me feel like someone cared about me. Feeling like someone cares always makes me cry. And when I cried it made Binky cry. We stood there in the cold under the fluorescent lights at 5 a.m. and cried about our mutual losses. I'd always known him as Andy's goofy friend but to have him show such compassion made me feel there was more to him than just a big dumb body-builder that liked to chase girls.

Still, we were never close. That's why it surprised me when he called me that day.

In the recent months, the poker world was all abuzz

with Binky's crazy exploits. As a lark, some of the guys in one of the big cash games fronted him money one night when they were short-handed. He managed to run twenty thousand up to two hundred thousand in less than twenty-four hours!

With his winnings, he made some wise investments – a ten-thousand-dollar pair of sneakers and a time share in NetJet. Not to worry, a week later he ran his two hundred thousand up to a million, and then three days later won another million at the big private game at the Aria. Binky! Binky who used to deal drunk, and sleep in Andy's guestroom!

Of course, then it all started going south. Just as quickly as he won, he began to lose. Apparently he played like a maniac and the whole poker gang wanted a swing at this particular piñata. When Andy invited me to his game, the lead billing was given to Binky.

'Binky will be there!' Andy promised. 'All he does is lose now! He plays horribly!'

Yes, Binky is Andy's friend, but Andy has a business to run and if Binky is going to lose his money, Binky would prefer he did it at his game. Andy prides himself on having the best game in the world stocked with the biggest fish. He's like those people who go on hunting safaris that fill their property with semi-tame wildlife and then charge people to come and shoot them. Easy pickings.

I played with Binky that day and it made me sad. At that time, he only had about 200K left of his two million. In the beginning, he was jovial, cracking jokes, and being the life of the party, but as he steadily lost, he grew more sullen and desperate. He looked like a total degen. He was sweating profusely, his face was puffy and red, and his once-chiselled body soft and flabby. I remembered the advice he had given me once about moderation and wished he would take it.

That was the last I heard from him until the phone call. I was driving in my car, and when I looked down and saw my phone flashing 'Binky', I knew something was wrong. I hardly ever answer my phone but on a whim, I picked it up. He sounded so down I barely recognised his voice.

'Binky,' I said. 'Is everything all right?'

No, everything was not all right. He had lost everything, and worse owed upwards of six hundred thousand to various entities all over town. The guys staking him had all turned their backs, and now he'd had a falling out with Joey Martinez who'd let him play his game.

A complicated story followed of how Binky was gambling, gambling, gambling, but he had the key to his mother's safety deposit box where her jewellery was stored. He knew if he lost, he could pawn his mother's jewellery. She was sick and would not notice. Anyhow, of course he lost, but when he went to his mother's box, it was empty! Unbeknownst to him, his brother, who was an even bigger degenerate, had a key as well, and had already sold the jewellery to pay for *his* gambling debt! I was horrified by this story, but tried not to show it. His poor mother.

'Well, Binky,' I said authoritatively, 'there are genetic markers for gambling, just like alcoholism.'

When my dad died, I found out that he'd had a huge poker problem. It was a family secret, and I had no idea.

My mom and dad divorced when I was very young and I didn't see him much after that. My sister Beth, who grew up with my dad, admitted he used to play poker all the time.

'He would come home occasionally with a jade ring or some paintings. Those were his poker winnings. But usually he lost. Then one day Sally, our stepmom, gave him an ultimatum: Poker or me!' He chose his marriage.

That always made me sad to think of the many poker-less years that stretched ahead of him after that. He had a little rinky-dink Casio seven-card stud game he would play before he went to bed, to 'unwind'. When he died Sally gave it to me, along with his dog-eared Sklansky book and his fake watch collection.

After he passed away I asked my mom about my dad, and her eyes opened wide as she recalled the trauma of living with a gambler. When she would take the children to Disneyland or to visit her parents he would jump in his car and drive straight to Las Vegas without passing Go.

And she would say 'Las Vegas' in a horrified whisper, like it was catching. Once he took my mom there for a vacation. He presented her with a hundred dollars and said 'This is to gamble with.' My mother was very proud of the fact that she took the money to the mall and bought a pair of shoes instead. She sure showed him! He never knew. Of course, my dad lost his hundred dollars, but my mom had a fancy new pair of Las Vegas shoes to show for the trip.

Because we grew up with our mom, it was always deemed a bad thing to have any of our dad's traits. If we were competitive or liked games we were being 'Stan-ish', as if my dad's name was a pejorative to convey extreme irresponsibility. Once I met a woman who was about to marry my dad's brother. She took me in a corner and went on a diatribe about how he didn't warn her about my dad. 'Stan came in the room at a party and said he needed to borrow some money, and everyone ignored him. I reached in my pocket and said, "Sure, how much do you need?" He never paid me back!' she huffed. I wondered why she was telling me this. I was seven. I hadn't seen my dad in years.

I don't remember him much from when I was little. But the memories I do have I carefully catalogued so I wouldn't forget them. Once I was three and my throat hurt and I was crying, and my dad came in the room and gave me some chocolate lozenges, and read to me. He was a big warm presence. Even though he couldn't take away the pain he somehow made me feel better.

After my dad died, I started playing poker, and was just as obsessive about it (or Stan-ish about it, as my mom would say). I started out with 25/50 cent at the kitchen table, then 1dollar/2dollar, now 100/200. No matter what level you play at there is always a more interesting game just beyond your bankroll.

'Poker is a huge swirling sinkhole,' I said to Binky. 'You go to the edge, just to take a look, and the ground gives way beneath you and it starts to suck you in. You and I can't just stick our toes in ... we have an addiction. It's in our genetic make-up.'

Binky was in no mood to listen to my bad analogies.

'I've just had a bit of bad luck,' he whispered hoarsely. 'I'm going to pull myself out of it.'

And as he starts to outline his plans for restitution, my car is driving under the palm trees of LA, and reception is dipping in and out. It doesn't matter. Everything Binky is saying is just sadness, and I don't want to hear it.

Tonight, I am finally returning to Dan's Big Game after several months' absence. I have been training for my comeback. I have a new cautious style. When I arrive, I announce I have to leave by 1 a.m. I have an important meeting in the morning. I tell the host to cut me off at a certain amount (one hundred and thirty-one thousand dollars . . . the exact amount I have in Aria chips that I've been carrying around with me in a small embroidered Lulu Guinness pouch, which has proven to be my lucky talisman: in three months, I have never had to dip into it once). Finally I will try to only play in position, and if I go on tilt, I get up and walk around for ten minutes. This seems to be working for me. In the smaller games, I have been steadily winning. I feel I am ready.

Now, Binky emerges from the void like a harbinger of doom. It seems like a bad omen. When his melancholy voice pauses for validation, I give it to him.

'Well!' I say kindly. 'It sounds like you are really doing your best to make things right. There's a lot of money in home games; I think you will be able to get back to even in no time.'

I am lying and I know it, but Binky doesn't seem to notice.

'Thanks,' he says tearfully. 'I just don't want you to think I'm a bad person.'

'Of course I don't!' I exclaim. Another lie.

And then a third lie.

'Whoops, I'm approaching my destination! I'll talk to you later!'

I hang up and continue to drive, feeling uneasy. The desperation and crazy play Binky exhibited during my one game with him was like holding a mirror up to myself. It's so easy to fall into that vortex.

Binky's sad phone call has created a sense of unease. It is daylight saving time and it gets dark early. As the sunlight fades so does all my confidence. I go home and organise my whole house, as if the tidiness of my environment will reflect in a disciplined game. I put on make-up and my lucky rings. I dress in layers for the fluctuating temperatures throughout the night. I put my pouch of Aria chips in my purse. Bob, my boyfriend, is hovering in the background trying to give me 'space'. I am grateful for this. Last thing I need is a Nervous Nellie throwing bad vibes my way. I hear him making fidgety busy work in the kitchen while I gather my stuff to go.

I love Bob very much. He is a screenwriter like me. When he folds me in his arms it dredges up a long-dormant memory of my dad. A faint, faded recollection of being adored, and understood. The only thing he doesn't understand is why I have to play poker. He hates poker. Hates it. He can never join me in celebrating the wins, because he knows they will be followed by crushing losses. The losses lead to long periods of mourning where I look around for someone to blame and decide it's his fault. I try to remember the feeling of being a winner, casually dropping into conversation how much I won, like it's no big deal. The proud glow of accomplishment that lasts almost a week. Before I leave the house, I take a deep breath, look in the mirror, and say, 'Tonight I am going to win a hundred thousand dollars.' The words sound hollow to me. I think of saying it again with more conviction, but decide against it and head out the door.

'Bye, honey,' I call over my shoulder.

'Bye, sweetie,' Bob replies, happy to be acknowledged. 'Don't forget to . . .'

The rest of his sentence is muffled as the door slams behind me. Don't forget to . . . what? Straddle? Raise the button? Come home?

I haven't been at Dan's house for so long I almost forget where it is. I walk in the living room and am greeted with the smell of perfume. There are about eight massage girls in five-inch heels and tight, revealing dresses. These girls are here to massage and otherwise service the players. I try to avoid letting them do anything for me, 'cause anything they do, you're supposed to give them a chip. The smallest denomination is a hundred dollars. They bring you a bottle of water: a hundred bucks, a plate of food, a hundred bucks . . . I don't know what the going rate is for other services. Suffice it to say every now and then a player disappears with a girl and returns twenty minutes later.

They are very sweet. They talk in little girl voices, and lean on the men, and pout when they're ignored. Ned Jenson once complained the girls cost him thirty thousand in one hand. They know nothing about poker so they don't know when to back off. A million-dollar pot was developing and this girl was playing with his hair and blowing in his ear, so he gave her a 5K chip to go away. He realised his mistake almost instantly. He looked around the table, and all the other girls were pouting and giving him a sad face so he felt he should give them all a chip. There were six girls so ... thirty thousand dollars.

Dan's house is big and modern and filled with excruciatingly ugly but expensive art. All these players are heavy into art investment and try to outdo themselves with acquisitions. Dan's sister and her friend deal this game. They don't know how to split the pots, count down stacks or call the action. If there is a complicated procedure, they look helplessly to the nearest savvy player. Obviously there is no dealer abuse allowed. The dealers have a sense of entitlement because they are related to the host. Sometimes they push the pot to the wrong player. You just have to be on your toes.

Tonight, the players are Max, an entrepreneur who owns a string of strip clubs, Dan the Art Collector, a Hollywood director, two producers, a restaurateur, a small-time pro, and Connor, a 'businessman'. I'm not sure what 'business' Connor is in but I'm pretty sure it has something to do with money laundering. He always seems to have unlimited funds. Max has flown out from Vegas with Connor on his plane.

We start out with a 40K buy-in. I double up right away, and then again. I win every pot. I start to feel very pleased with myself. I don't know what I was worried about. I'm up about 90K, and I feel easy and in control.

Then the following hand happens: I look down at

pocket aces. All the worst stories seem to start with pocket aces. There are already three people in the pot so I re-pop it to fifteen thousand and everyone folds but Max. The flop is seven, seven, jack, rainbow. I bet. Max calls. Turn a five, I bet. Max calls. River, a two. I check. Max goes all in. I hate it now. I fucking hate my hand. I don't know how, but he has me beat.

But then, you know, Max bluffs a lot. And maybe he put me on ace/king, ace/queen. Maybe he was floating for when I checked the river? He knows I'm scared money, he knows he can move me off my hand! I am standing up now and the whole room seems to be receding. One part of me notices my involuntary rise from my chair. That's usually a bad sign. When I stand it's usually an indication of, 'You call, baby, and it's all over.'

'I call,' I hear a small voice say.

Max seems surprised.

'You call?' he repeats.

He seems to be reluctant to expose his cards, and for a second I think it will all be a bad dream and I will have doubled up. Then he flips his cards over gleefully and the dream shatters. 'Pay up, suckers!' he chortles, and then feigns surprise. 'Oh, we're not playing the seven/deuce game? I thought we were!'

White-hot rage crawls up between my eyes. Seven/deuce? Seven/deuce??!!! He called my fifteen-thousand-dollar raise just to fuck with me? Grimly I sit back down. Gone are my dreams of an early night, and playing within my bankroll.

'Noah!' I yell. 'Give me a hundred thousand dollars!'

Now the polite careful girl waiting for aces has

disappeared. In her place is a raging maniac on a suicide mission. I am Binky on crack: I play every hand,
I double, triple straddle. I play in position, I play out
of position. I continuation bet, I check-raise, I do
everything but win.

A few hours later I am stuck balls. In poker as people
get even or up, they start to drift away. Eventually
everybody has gone home except me, Connor (who is
also deep in the red) and Max (who is up, but has to
wait for Connor). One by one the girls leave, draping
a fragrant arm across my shoulder on the off-chance I
give them a parting gift of a hundred-dollar chip as I
am wont to do. But I am too stuck and too miserable
to be Lady Bountiful, and I don't even look up from
the table.

Max disappears upstairs with one of the remaining
girls, and the game pauses. I can tell Connor desperately
wants to get unstuck through me.

'I don't wanta play heads up,' I whine.

I have been able to exploit Max's desire to hold on to
his new-found wealth by chipping away at him slowly.
He himself recognised it was slowly dripping away from
him, and now he wants to fuck.

We wait uneasily for him to return. The dealer is impatient. The sun is coming up. She wants to go home.

'We're taking a break until Max gets back,' Connor
explains. 'He said he was going to be two minutes.'

'He said *ten* minutes!' she snaps.

She's seen these breaks before. She knows it takes time
for a coked-up guy to get off.

*

The minutes tick by. In the harsh morning light every-body looks like a Boschian nightmare. Connor's skin is the dull grey of a cadaver, and I can see holes in the dealer's face covered with thick caked make-up. I imagine I look horrible too. My lips are cracked and I feel greasy and gross. Connor and Max's plane takes off at noon.

'Let's just play a few hands until he gets back,' suggests Connor hopefully.

Connor labours under the delusion that he is better than me. He is wrong. Everybody is better than Connor. That, and his bankroll, makes him welcome at any game. I reluctantly sit down. Heads up is very volatile, and I am sleep deprived.

'Might as well make it 500/1,000,' says Connor cas-ually. I recognise the hustler move, upping the stakes to accelerate action but as I said, I think I can beat him.

'OK,' I say in a tired little girl voice like I don't know I am being manipulated.

Twenty minutes later I have managed to extricate one hundred thousand dollars from Connor. The dealer is getting pissed. She flicks the cards out disdainfully. I ignore her. I am on my way back to getting even. I stack the chips in a business-like way, putting a hundred-dollar chip at every 10K interval.

I barely hear the doorbell ring. Noah, who runs the game, had ordered some burgers. He wanders over to open the door, and suddenly all hell breaks loose. I hear yelling and things being broken. Then one of the girls screaming. I turn my head and see a mad scrambling man in a ski mask hustling Noah in front of him, bran-dishing a gun. Noah is white but trying to maintain equilibrium. His hands are in the air in a placating manner.

'There is no money here,' he is saying. 'We play on credit.'

The intruder is having none of it.

'On the floor!' he screams harshly in a strange indecipherable accent.

The girls hit the floor like they are used to it. The dealer, Connor, and I stare open-mouthed at this surreal scene. In our gambling haze we are unwilling to abandon our game. It's only when he waves the gun wildly at us that we drop also. The girls' purses are lined up on the coffee table, and as he riffles through them, he screams, 'The safe! The safe!' Obviously, he knows Noah's claim of a cashless Utopia is not accurate. Then he discovers my pouch with the Aria chips, unzips it, stops, and slowly turns his head to look directly at me.

I reel in shock. Under the ski mask I am staring at Binky's puffy red-rimmed eyes. I suddenly realise why his accent sounded so strange. His native Brooklynese kept leaking through. He stands holding my chips and looking at me sadly for what seems like an eternity, and then he stuffs them in his pocket and starts to follow Noah out of the room.

As he does there is a popping sound, and he jerks backwards in a grotesque stutter step. An explosion of blood, like a bright red firework, shoots out of his shoulder and hits one of Dan's priceless paintings.

Max has returned. He is naked from the waist down and raving like a lunatic.

'I will kill you, motherfucker! That's right! You come

to my game and try to fuck with me! Fuck you! Fuck you! Fuck you!'

And with each 'fuck you' there is a pop, pop, pop, and holes appear in Dan's paintings. Apparently there is a silencer on his gun. Aside from the initial contact he totally misses. He is a terrible shot. Binky starts crying like a baby and runs out the door holding his shoulder, as Max chases him.

'That's right, you motherfucker, you pussy, you snivelling coward! Get the fuck out of here!'

Dan and two half-dressed girls appear as he re-enters.

'What's going on?' says Dan. The girls hide behind him in exaggerated damsel-in-distress mode. Max ignores him. He runs to the kitchen, and dumps out the silverware drawer. Grabbing a spatula he drops to the floor and starts frenziedly trying to scrape the red stain off the red carpet. It is not a pleasant sight. I can see his balls swinging frantically below his butt as he works.

'We've got this motherfucker's DNA!' he screams triumphantly. 'We're gonna track him down and put him away!'

Dan wanders out to close the open gate, and the girls cling to each other and cry prettily, enjoying the drama.

Of course, nothing comes of it. Dan is running an illegal game, and does not have a permit for his gun. They can't report it. Aside from my 131K in Aria chips, nothing much was taken. The girls didn't have much money on them, and Max started shooting before Noah managed to open the safe.

The next time I showed up at Dan's game, he had an

iron gate and expensive and ostentatious security cameras surrounding the property. As for me, I couldn't say to Binky, 'Dude, I know it was you, give me back my chips.' He would just deny it. Besides he knows where I live. Many times, he has dropped off checks at my property. Who knows what a desperate person is capable of. So even though I almost got even, I ended the night with a big loss.

Through the poker grapevine I heard rumours that the mob Binky owed money to threw him down the stairs and dislocated his shoulder. I guess I'm the only one who knows that Binky was the intruder and what really happened to his shoulder. Then a month or so later I heard he tried to cash in my Aria chips, and when they asked where he got them, like the dumb lunk he is, he claimed someone gave them to him to pay off a debt. Of course, they were confiscated. It is illegal to use casino chips as currency.

Anyway, that morning after the robbery, I drive home in a daze. It is almost noon. On Sunset Plaza I see girls just like me, meeting their friends for lunch or shopping, carrying Starbucks in little cardboard trays. They are normal girls, like I used to be. They are just starting their day, maybe they went for a hike or to Equinox earlier. Soon they will go to the office and type, or do whatever people do in offices these days. After work they will meet their friends for Happy Hour or go bowling or something. None of them stayed awake all night in a room full of hookers and blow, losing hundreds of thousands of dollars and getting shot at.

*

Bob is waiting up for me.

'I couldn't sleep,' he says anxiously.

He knows it's a bad sign when I come home after the sun has come up. Now he just has to find out how bad. I always play down my losses to him. When he says, 'Was it a bad night?' I'll just nod, and sometimes he'll query casually, 'How much did you lose, five thousand? Ten thousand? More . . . ?'

And I'll just say, 'More.' I don't say 'About one hundred thousand more.' I don't want to frighten the kiddies. To a civilian, ten thousand dollars is an obscene amount of money. Likewise, I can't tell Bob I ran into Binky and he was wearing a ski mask, and Max shot him. I just say, 'Rough night.' And we leave it at that. Bob says, 'I'll make you some eggs,' like that will fix everything. And even though he can't take away the pain he somehow makes me feel better.

I dreamt I saw my dad that night. I was heads up against the billionaire Andy Beal in a super-high-stakes game. I wasn't properly rolled to play that big, but I had taken my last most precious diamond off my finger and put it in the middle. It was going to be OK. I was all in with the nut flush on an unpaired board. And Andy called and rolled the straight flush. Just like a bad James Bond movie.

As my entire net worth, along with my last diamond, went cascading towards Andy I looked up and my dad was standing there smiling. A wave of happiness rolled over me. I felt like we were sharing something infinitesimally special. 'Isn't it fantastic?' he whispered like he was in church. His eyes were shining. 'Poker is a fucking fantastic game!'

Good Luck, Everyone

by James McManus

Twenty minutes after the dinner break I'm quietly belching iced tea and chorizo, nursing an above-average stack of 985,000. Feels good. My stack has been yo-yoing since this time last night, though I've won more big pots than I've lost. It's Day 2, Level 26, with blinds of twenty thousand and forty thousand, and five thousand-chip antes. I peek between my knuckles at the eight and six of hearts, flick them back to the dealer. I'm waiting for decent pairs or big aces to raise with, not splashing into every damn pot, trying to out-flop or out-play folks with drawing hands. My opponents all know this, and I know that they know that I know it.

This is the third table I've been high-carded to since the 1 p.m. restart. It's neither soft nor especially terrifying. Five pros in their twenties or thirties, a nervous orthodontist who licks his upper lip before check-raising, and three tight but experienced geezers: me, a Brit with a short stack to go with his posh Oxbridge accent, and a good old Oklahoma boy on my left. The pros, with their big beards and logos and watches, all seem plenty tough, though there's no Fedor Holz or Jason Mercier four-betting eight-seven suited. Not that these guys are incapable of such moves, but they aren't relentless about it. At least not *gulp* so far.

The kid in the Run It Once hoodie raises to 95,000 from early position and gets a call – not a shove? – from the Brit on the button, so I'm happy to call in the big blind with sevens. On a flop of 9-A-Q with two diamonds, the kid continues for 185. The Brit looks tempted to shove the 425 he has left, but after ten or twelve seconds he folds with a sigh and a wince. I just fold.

I pull my own hoodie higher up on my neck. This part of the Amazon Room is breezy, with highs in the low to mid sixties, as the Rio's AC overcompensates for the Mojave, where it's still in triple digits, plus all of us humans radiating 98.6. I started the day in Brasilia, where short sleeves were in order, but you always have to pack a sweatshirt or fleece for these events, to be ready for what can be a fifteen-degree difference between Brasilia and the briskest corners of Pavilion or Amazon. A plastic sign hangs from the lamp above each table, and ours, Purple 422, isn't the only one swaying in the zephyrs. The good news, the best news, is that while this might not be the final table, it is the final room. Only ninety of us are left of the 7,213 who bought in one or two days ago for $1,500. The money bubble popped a few hours ago, so even if I get busted next hand I'm good for $8,860, my first non-mincash in a couple of summers, not that it's all that colossal. The last nine survivors will slug it out tomorrow in the Thunder Dome, the brightly lit arena on the other side of this cavernous room, where an Omaha eight-or-better final table is down to four players. The families and friends whoop and holler whenever their boy scoops a pot. Once they calm down again, pretty much all you can hear is the clicking of hundreds of thousands of chips in the rafters and shadows above us. There's no place on earth I'd rather be.

With a raise and a call to me on the button, I reluctantly fold the J-9 of spades. No doubt that's way, way too tight, unless you're committed to surviving at least two more pay jumps. It sure ain't the best way to win a tournament, but the difference between $8,860 and the $12,370 I'd earn by outlasting nineteen more players is roughly the difference between a family vacation next month in the Rockies or, say, Wisconsin. I admit the seven grand I husbanded for the Series could've simply paid for Jackson Hole, Yellowstone, the Beartooth Highway, maybe even Glacier, but I really didn't want to break my streak. Since finishing fifth in the 2000 Main Event, I've played at least three bracelet events every year. I've already broken my vow to never skip the Main, which provided 247K and the material for the *Harper's* cover story and *Positively Fifth Street*, which led to other good things. But when that single event started requiring eight days by itself, on top of the two you spent flying, scheduling our family vacations got harder and harder in the shrinking gaps between recitals, soccer and softball seasons, trips our daughters took with their friends, ACT prep, and my poker – and I could *still* get knocked out on Day 1. (Getting broke in the second hand of '09, with queens full losing to quad treys, was particularly inconvenient.) Now I come out in early June, when the two younger ones are still in school. In the same eight days, with the same 10K bankroll or less, I can play half a dozen three-day events and be home in time to hit a few places my girls want to see.

This afternoon I sent them all a picture of a brindled bomb-sniffing pit bull, a near dead ringer for our Jessie, except for its tactical vest. Jennifer gave it her big-kiss bitmoji: *MUAH!* Grace texted, *Awww bring her home this very instant!* Bea wondered, *Soft serve butterscotch on the poker room carpet?*

Folding K-10 to a raise, I wish there were more dogs in vests. We're in a venue, after all, with thousands of mostly jihadi-age men, with backpacks that haven't been checked or passed through a metal detector, let alone an EDS machine. The ceiling cams would ID them, but not before it's too late. Pressure cookers, TATP, AR-15s broken down to fit in a North Face . . . What target represents decadent capitalism better than the World Series of Poker?

Bea will be in London for the fall trimester, which will run us a few extra grand and plenty more sleepless nights. Bridget, our oldest, is building her nanny-placement business and can always use a C-note or three for a phone or an ad. We're lucky their kid sister, Grace, makes enough babysitting to pay for Lollapalooza and thirty other concerts, and her last two years at New Trier will be covered by property taxes. When we had three of them in public schools, the taxes were never the knee in the balls they'll become when Grace graduates. We'll have to move to a way cheaper town, even if Jennifer's teaching job is two blocks from where we live now. So maybe I *should* play more suited connectors, since first prize would solve in one stroke what we only half-facetiously refer to as our housing crisis. We lived in a modest ranch before *Fifth Street* but moved into a three-storey brick in '04. Assuming it would be the first of a string of bestsellers, we took on a bad mortgage, trading a jumbo for an interest-only Mutombo. That and the taxes come to $8,278 a month. When I turn sixty-six in March, I'll be old enough to retire, but I can't even consider it before I'm seventy-one, when Grace gets out of college.

I open for 100 with eights. The orthodontist lick-calls, and handsome Jake Donellan squeezes to 345. As I think about whether to smooth-call, there's a thrum at the back of my throat, the kind that often blooms into angina. Not now, for Christ's sake! But here it comes anyway, the dull throb beneath my sternum, not painful enough to scare me, but enough to make me not want to play for what could be the rest of my stack. So I fold, though it kills me to reinforce a principle Jake was already committed to: three-bet tight old men every time. It even says as much in raised red and white stitching on the sleeve of his navy blue hoodie.

Angina hits me maybe six times a year, but it usually fades after five or ten minutes. When I first described the attacks to Matthew Lee, my cocky but smart cardiologist, he put me through a stress echocardiogram, about as much fun as slogging up Kilimanjaro with a noose around your neck. The verdict was 'stable angina', for which he wrote me a scrip for nitroglycerine.

I unzip my backpack's top pocket for the bottle of .4mg tabs. Pinching the little white pill, I pretend to scratch my nose while slipping it under my tongue. The bitter sting means it's working. When I get home, I'll ask Lee for the spray, which works faster, or the patch, which delivers a continual dose. You can also take it as a suppository, I think, if you really want to ruin your table image.

The clanging headache also tells you it's working, as the pain basically leaps from your chest to your forehead, where it feels way less life-threatening. After making sure they're not kings or aces, I fold seven hands in a row, since I might not be able to handle the stress if a big pot develops and I'm facing a staredown with less than the nuts. I finally raise to 110 with the A-Q of clubs. Tulsa seems happy to call, and we stare at the 2-K-A flop.

Lee has been on at me to lower my BMI and LDL cholesterol, and he's got me on Tricor, fish oil, and aspirin. The stress echo showed no ischemia or arrhythmia, only some mild regurgitation of the mitral valve and trivial regurgitation of the aortic valves. I'd never been happier to be deemed mild and trivial. But another thing I need to discuss with him is that you're not supposed to suck nitro after popping Viagra, though that's when you're most likely to need it.

'Your action, Jim,' says Buz, the new dealer.

I bet 195. Tulsa groans and goes into the tank, cutting out raising chips, but eventually mucks. I exhale and pull in the pot. Inhale. Stack some chips. Breathe.

*

By 9.45 the angina and headache have both disappeared, maybe because I'm up to 1,535,000, over half of it from busting the Run It Once pro, whose A-K got out-raced by my queens.

Tulsa's third postprandial Corona has just been delivered. And to go with his OU windbreaker, he has donned a red *Make America Great Again* hat.

'Change my dang luck,' he said, pulling it out after losing a pair of small pots. It's a foppy little number, not rounded like a ball cap but rising like a suspension bridge to a peak, with a matching scarlet braid across the bill. First one I've seen from this close. When you teach at an art school and live on the North Shore, you can go weeks without seeing a Trump supporter, at least not one willing to sport the regalia in public. Part of the beauty of the Series is that it brings together folks of every political stripe, income and education level, from every state and free-market country. Much more like real life than academia is, no doubt about that.

Tulsa meanwhile has called the Brit's all-in shove with A-K. With a sigh, the Brit rolls over A-Q and stands up. When Buz puts a queen and a king on the flop, Tulsa thunder-claps his hands and yells, 'Have some!' The turn is a blank, but a second queen spikes on the river. 'Freakin' kiddin' me?' he asks Buz, who's busy counting down the Brit's stack, before taking 315,000 from Tulsa's.

'I folded a queen,' says Jake. Rubbing it in, or the truth? Maybe both.

'Really well played,' Tulsa drawls sotto voce, as if he or anyone else wouldn't shove seven bigs with A-Q. 'Hits a fuckin' one-outer on me?'

'Must've been the lucky hat,' says the Brit, who is back in his chair now, restacking. A fair rejoinder to the sarcasm. Then: 'Your man is a pathogen.'

'You mean Mr Trump?'

'Indeed,' says the Brit, breaking the unwritten rule that the poker table, especially when playing for long money, isn't the place to debate religion or politics.

'This woman's a pig, that one's no longer a ten, says he wants to date his bleeding dough-tuh . . .'

'What he said, all he meant, was blood was coming out of her *eyes*.'

'On his very best day, he's an insta-left swipe.' This from Lan Nguyen, a young LA pro who replaced Run It Once in seat seven. 'Loud, obese, looks like he's having a stroke. I mean—' She chuckles and hugs herself, shivering.

'Man's jest bein' himself. What can I tell you?'

'Too much banh bo at the Phat Phuc Noodle Bar,' says Lan. She puffs out her cheeks, or at least makes them less concave.

'And what's with the piss-tinted Fauntleroy hairdo?' asks the Brit.

'Hey, chomp a brown pickle,' says Tulsa. 'Or try one a these.' He pulls the wedge of lime from the mouth of his latest Corona, cocking his wrist as if to fire it across the table. A droplet of lime juice or beer zings my left cheek. 'You limey blokes love these, I hear.'

'He likes people who weren't captured,' I say, against my better judgment. 'He likes draft dodgers born into nine-figure fortunes.'

Attacked from all sides now, Tulsa turns and glares

at me, though he must know throwing a punch gets you banned from the Rio.

'Ain't you the guy called down that crazy black dude with jack high?'

'I am,' I admit, relieved by how eager he sounds to change the subject. 'Except it was queen high. His name was Ellix Powers. He died last September.'

Tulsa replaces the lime, pushing it down through the neck. After wiping his fingers on his jacket, he gathers his cards.

'What'd he, OD or something?'

Finding kings between my knuckles, I raise to 110. Tulsa folds, but Lan and the orthodontist both call.

'Heart attack,' I say, triggering a new burst of chest pain. I hope it's just psychosomatic.

Tulsa has no response. Maybe he's respecting that I'm in a hand, though I doubt it. When the flop comes queen high without any obvious draws, I bet 225. Both of them fold pretty quickly, thank God.

As I stack green and orange, the Brit says, 'Will he take his forked tongue out of Putin's mauve arsehole any time soon? Though we hear—'

'Sounds like you're all on the rag, like your pal Crooked Hillary.'

Lan laughs out loud at the notion.

'Hot flashes, maybe.'

'That's a tell, right?' says the Brit. 'The Tom Thumb non sequitur?'

'What're you 'tards even talking about?' says Tulsa. Taking a pull of Corona, he mumbles in the direction of Lan, 'Nice little stack you got there.'

*

The table has chilled by the time the action kicks up to 25/50/5. The third hand dealt at this level gets folded to me, and with the A-J of spades I open from middle position for 135. Tulsa snap-calls. When no one else wants in on the pot odds, I have to wonder how many 2-7 off-suits there can be in this deck.

The flop comes A-6-5 with two baby spades. He expects me to continue, so with top pair, third kicker, and the nut flush draw I'm tempted to cross him up. Before I can act, though, he puts both meaty hands behind his five towers and leans into the cushion in a kind of drunk push-up, while making real sure his chips don't budge even a millimetre forward. I decide to let him stay in this angle-shooting pose for a while. Comfortable like that? I sure hope so.

I used to wear sunglasses but got too many headaches straining to see the suits of the board cards, especially from seats at either end of the table. This year I'm wearing my 2013 Stanley Cup hat. The back two-thirds is mesh, so it's cooler and lighter than the other two Cup hats. When Tulsa turns to look at me, I tilt the bill six degrees lower. He can't see my eyes, while I can see everything from his greying red stubble to his hairy, sunburned mitts. Only when he finally leans back do I tap the felt once with one finger.

'OK,' he says, pushing out all his chips, about 650K, into a pot half that size.

OK, you're crushed, or OK, I'ma bluff your lamestream-media-watching ass? He's given me a terrible price to draw to the flush, and top pair ain't likely to be good here – unless he's drawing himself. I'm tempted to call just because I don't like his attitude, though making it personal is one of the biggest mistakes you can make, especially deep in a tournament. If he's got a bigger ace or two pair, I have twelve outs twice; if he's flopped a fucking set, only nine. Not having seen him get out of line even once, I can't really put him on a naked bluff, unless it's payback for mocking his candidate. If I call and hit a spade I'll have well over two million chips. If I lose, less than twenty big blinds. I'm good for $17,819, but I'd be out of the running for the really long money. My heart bangs and wobbles as I recheck my cards, hoping my tinsel memory made me forget I've got aces down there. No such luck. I also remind myself of all the times I've berated myself for playing too passively, that no one folds their way to a bracelet.

'Clock,' he says.

'Are you serious?'

'Clock.'

'Fuck the clock,' I tell him, before Buz can summon a floorman. 'I call.'

Tulsa snaps down pocket sixes, making me a 3-1 dog. I'm in even worse shape when the turn is the trey of clubs, though my skittering pulse and imperfectly progressive bifocals made me see it at first as a spade. So that when the river is the spade trey, my heart almost clears a high hurdle, before it trips and collapses. Tulsa starts whooping it up.

'Drawin' dead and gettin' there,' he finally says, pulling the chips in.

'Sure wasn't dead when the money went in.'

He doesn't seem to follow my drift, but he does have

over 750K of my chips. An All-American Dave's girl in a tank top and shorts arrives one table over with someone's late dinner in a white paper bag, but I'm too rattled, too nauseated to watch her walk away with her tip. Down to sixteen bigs, I pretend to check my phone, as if everything's still copacetic. The fist in my chest clenches tighter.

A new dealer, Tessa, settles into the chair, reaching for the lever to raise herself up a few inches. She spreads a fresh deck in a long face-up arc, making sure every card is where it should be, then flips them over like fifty-two acetate dominoes and washes them vigorously against the Uber logo. She shuffles four times, cuts fairly thin, burns the top card and starts pitching.

'Good luck, everybody,' she chirps.

Most of the table, me not included, says thank you, though we can't all be lucky when the goal is to take everyone else's last chip. Yet almost every dealer says this upon sitting down, leaving, or both.

'Aw, Tessa's jes' bein' nice,' Tulsa flirts.

It's a zero-sum contest, I think but don't say. What we need isn't good luck, but avoiding the bad kind. Heart attacks, second-best hands, Oklahomans.

'Aren't ya, doll?' one continues, nothing if not persistent.

Tessa nods and keeps pitching, making her hazel eyes round for a beat, already tired of us. She starts me off with 2-6 for not saying thank you. And for the next five hands I don't see a pair, or even a card above eight. At least folding's easier on the cardiovascular system.

62

Breathing carefully, avoiding stress, I manage to keep the discomfort at 5 or 6. I'm tempted to call a raise with Q-10, but not while in fold-or-shove mode. With only fourteen bigs, I'm shipping any pair, any ace, any king with a face or a ten. As I'm anted down further, my range will have to get wider, so c'mon, Tessa! The Royal and Ancient Gods of Randomocity know who will win my next race, but you're the one burning and turning. And maybe she heard me, since she's just pitched me nines. Here we go. After Lan calls my shove with A-K, Tessa puts a beautimous nine on the flop, along with an ace and a king. Lan is dead to four outs, but my scrotum and pulse are sure one will spike. The jack on the turn helps a little, but only the deuce on the river allows me to exhale. Thank you, Tessa.

More than anyone, of course, it's the dealers who determine who wins these events. Not that poker skill isn't a sizeable factor, but the difference in skill between the very best players and the rest of us isn't quite big enough to overcome three days of rungood. The sample size is too small for the variance to flatten out. Over two or three years, the wizards get most of the dough, but not over three days. That's why so many people buy into these things. If the top twenty pros kept taking them down, they'd be the only ones playing, for ever more minuscule prize money.

Three hands later, after calling a min-raise with the A-Q of hearts, I flop the nut flush draw, check, call an almost pot-sized bet on the flop, hit the third heart on the turn, and get it all in against a pierced, tatted kid who just moved here with a stack slightly smaller than mine. He shows me a king-high flush.

'Nice hand, sir,' he says, standing up. 'Lotta hearts.'

'Lotta hearts. Thanks. You got coolered.'

It takes over a minute to stack what turns out to be 1,995,000 in chips. I'm smoothing my towers of green when Tessa pitches me aces. My raise gets called by two shorter stacks. On the 3-A-8 rainbow flop it goes check, check, check, but they *both* shove into me on the turn – dead man's hand for the orthodontist, set of treys for the Brit. When the river blanks off, the Brit mutters, 'Let that be a lesson to ya,' an old line of Devilfish Ulliott's.

Jake and I laugh.

'Ni han, sah,' he says.

For decades I've watched dealers put out boards giving one player the nuts and one or two others strong enough hands to lose all their chips with, shipping them to the same unworthy luckbox again and again and again. In the last dozen hands, in four massive pots, I've been the luckbox. 'Bout time! The endorphin rush of sextupling up is harshed by the tingle running down my left arm. If I'm having a heart attack, could the timing be any more vicious? I mean, I almost have to laugh. All these years itching for another shot at a bracelet and now I have to call 911? Lie in some chaotic ER while my stack gets blinded down to nothing? Though if it gets any harder to breathe, I'll be lucky if it's not the ICU. Or the morgue.

Twenty-one of us are playing seven-handed as Level 29 boosts the price of poker to 40/80/10. The buzz in my arm's getting bad. Even worse, Tessa's gone, though her replacement, Tim, has been kind enough to make me wait only a couple of hands before slinging me Big Slick.

Jake makes it 220, and the new guy in seat three smooth-calls, as do I, though a better move might've been shoving. After a flop of 9-6-7, all diamonds, I recheck my cards. (My worst range of memory is the last thirty seconds, though I remember some hands, down to the suit, from decades ago.) Neither of these is a diamond. But who says either New Guy or Jake has even a single big diamond?

After making it 500 straight, I feel like I've had seconds of Jennifer's tagliatelle before running up six flights of stairs, as they both stare me down. I'm about to pass out when Jake folds. When New Guy folds too, I have over four million – four times more than I had as the chip leader late in the 2000 Main. After I won a huge pot by calling T. J.'s bet on the turn with no pair, just A-K, Slim Preston drawled, 'That boy's got the heart of a cliff-diver.' All I need now is one that will keep beating till we bag up tonight. If I'm not feeling better by then, I'll go get a shot of Thrombolyte, or have one of those balloons inserted through my groin, then try to get some sleep at the hospital and be ready to play in the Dome.

There's a break while they redraw for seats at the final two tables. Sitting off to the side by myself, I slide another nitro pill under my tongue. They work faster if you lean forward, inhale, and bear down like you're passing an XXL turd. Boom! Nothing like sucking an explosive to get your blood flowing again.

But now that I'm breathing easier, my brain is shouting, 'Call 911!' Maybe I could persuade the EMT guys to carry me on a stretcher the sixty yards to the john, insert the balloon on the way back, then stand by till play ends tonight. My bladder is yelping, along with everything else, but I don't feel quite up to the stroll. I barely have the energy to open Jennifer's text: right fingers pressed against her cleavage, focus on the three-diamond ring I bought her out here sixteen years ago. *Can't wait to c u on Wednesday,* i.e., don't be bad in the meantime. As if.

If this were a cash game, I'd Uber to the nearest ER. I have no idea where that is, but I do know that once the docs get their hands on you, they can practically bring you back from the dead. Whether they kept me in the hospital for an hour or a week, my chips would be waiting for me when I got back. Whereas all a tournament player has is equity in the prize pool. The whole time I was gone the dealers would be taking 150K in blinds every round, plus 15K in antes per hand. But. Do I want to risk dying here, surrounded by poker degens, eighteen hundred miles from my girls? I sure as hell don't want to prematurely exit my favourite, my better-than-sex, situation: sitting behind a big stack late in a bracelet event. I'd rather die as a chip leader than live in a tangle of IVs, EKGs, beeping monitors. Once they start tying you off with those rubber strips, stabbing the crook of your elbow and the back of your hand, they've got you. Plus I've never been able to not watch my thick, yellowish blood slowly filling up the glass vials.

If Lee or Jennifer were here, they'd've already called

911, even though Lee likes to say, 'Hospitals make you sick. The trick is to stay the hell out of them.' Jennifer would simply ask what I thought our girls would want me to do.

The monitor I prefer, the one right above me, shows fifty-two seconds left in the break, between twin scrolls of prize money.

1	$1,065,304
2	$807,402
3	$612,419
4	$366,787
5	$276,632
6	$210,121
7	$160,734
8	$123,831
9	$96,082
10–12	$75,119
13–15	$59,136
16–18	$46,909

I hoist myself out of the chair and walk as unlike a dying old man as I can twenty steps over to my new table. Seat seven, between Eric Chobani and Viv Pontchartrain. We're still playing 50/100/15. With 3.685 million, I'm basically tied for third with four other players, including Viv, who I'm lucky to have on my right. Tulsa's at the table behind me.

My stack does not suck. Nine twenty-chip towers of orange support five towers of dark green 25,000s. The two pretty lavenders on top, with grey-on-grey chevrons daubed onto their sides, are each worth 100,000. NO CASH VALUE indeed. The whole thing is fun to caress. I washed my hands before dinner, but there's already greenish-black schmutz under my right middle finger-nail, from riffling short stacks together. Time to run it up and ship this damn thing, then write *Positively First Place* hopefully with a less obvious title by the time I turn it in.

Black tens is the first hand I open with, attracting two callers, neither a player I recognise. I lead into the 3-Q-7 flop. When the Middle Eastern dude in seat one says, 'All in,' my chest pain spikes high enough to make me literally piss in my pants. I try to look normal while folding. There was 900K in that pot I might've won by bristling up or getting lucky, but so now ...

I must've blacked out. My arms thrum with current, and I can't turn my head. If I could, I'd sneak another Nitrostat under my tongue. No, no, not sneak! Who cares now who's watching? I try to text *luv ya* to Bridget but knock my phone off the cushion and onto the floor. Bending over that far wouldn't end well. Too dizzy, for one thing. Ask Viv to, or Eric? No way. Even funnier, I'm still pretending to be A-OK.

A card spins into my knuckle.

'You solid, man?' says Eric, with pesto on his breath.

'Clearly not,' says the guy to his left. 'Are you kidding me?'

A second card pings off my thumb. My hands just don't work well enough to block out Viv's or Eric's view as I thumb up the corners. Red kings.

A guy to Viv's right opens, I can't see for how much. The awl through my ventricles scrapes away what was left of my will as the dealer, Allah, shifts his gaze: action on me. I had him yesterday in Pavilion, but I can't remember if I lost or won any big pots. Same round face and wide smile, same black wire frames, dark wrists still too slender for his glowing white cuffs. If only I could write about this! All I can do is knock some lavenders and greens off my stack, not on purpose. One is still rolling past the pot when someone says, 'Call.' Allah tosses the all-in disc towards that player.

'So Jim's all in too?'

I'm doubled over, paralysed in a hug of the white-hot bolt being screwed into my thorax. Desperate to breathe, I'm coughing and gagging instead.

Carpet grit burns my left cheek. Glasses half-off. Slender ankle, grey sock.

'He's choking, for Christ's sake!'

'No Heimlich, man, unless you wanna kill him. Here comes the stretcher.'

'They've been letting him *play*?'

'Sir, can you hear me?'

Huge bearded face above mine. Dark pupils, kind. Doing my best to make eye contact, to tell him he has my permission to take me away from the table and please tell my four girls I love them so much, trying to name them as he pulls away, repositions himself. To do what?

Miles above us, Tulsa looms over me.

'Wow. Talk about a bad beat.'

Thumbs yank my mouth open, slimy teeth clack against mine. Can't see but can't shut my eyes. Compared to this latest sledge jolt to my heart, beard hairs across my bulging eyeballs are a kind of relief. But not really.

Can't even scream now as chip crickets click in the darkness.

Five Tables

by D.B.C. Pierre

Everything has its DNA, and poker must have its DNA, but it's harder to decode when there's a gun pointing over the table. Who knows if the code is in the cash or the cards, the coiling smoke or the crocodile faces. You'd expect the gun if this were a movie but it's not, it's your common-or-garden Friday night with pizza that also found the flair to mix a .38 Special revolver in a scene with alcohol, weed, testosterone and poker. To top it off, the owner cheats and still has worse cards than you.

If I played chess there would be no revolver. If I played bingo – still a game for money – there would be no revolver. If I played backgammon, bowling or darts, even for money, for cars and houses, against cheaters – no revolver.

So what the fuck is it with poker? Where did this gangsta gene come from? The reason we don't take a gun bowling, for instance, apart from the chance that we might use it, is that we don't want to put anyone off their stride. Once a gun comes out there's no unseeing it, the shadow stays cast and speaks for itself.

'Shall I fix some more dip?'

'Thanks, I have a revolver.'

'Little refill there?'

'Thanks, I have a revolver.'

'I just saw you palm that king off the table.'

'Bang.'

Did Western movies cast this long a shadow or was revolver DNA there all along? Let's say this guy routinely packs a gun: why pull it out for poker and not for Happy Families? Come to that, where are all the gun-slinging heroes of rummy and bingo?

I look back to try to break the code.

My favourite aunt introduced me to poker on a dark wood Victorian dining table. She did it without a revolver because she was the revolver and her range was all your life long. No one ever tested it, you knew by looking down the barrel. She played with a couple comprising an Italian and a Spaniard who could scream at each other just for being an Italian and a Spaniard. On top of that they played hard. My uncle was also at the table smoking cigars and keeping things honest. At a certain point a lock of silver hair would fall over his face and he would be funny for the rest of the night, although he was generally a solemn man. I was at the table. Nine, ten years old. This aunt was the kind who bullied and usurped your parents till you found yourself living it up past two in the morning. God-sent favourite aunt, we played for money and tasted wine and yelled in broken English to make the foreigners understand through lianas of smoke trying to coil up to the light between our flailing hands.

'Look the jet pork.'

'*What?*'

'Look the money in the jet pork.'

'Ah – *jackpot!*'

'Ha ha ha.'

'Ha ha ha ha!'

The Italian made authentic pizza and it was deep-fried, not baked. Handful of tomato and herbs, plus parmesan from the days when it still reeked of vomit. All this could happen at midnight. It was the life for me, oh yes. Both couples took the game seriously enough to end up yelling at each other, you'd feel the tension rise and rise till one of them found something hilarious and the air would collapse in bricks. They were always yelling and always finding something hilarious. It acted as a bellows that fanned you till you popped. I'm sure the poker was merely a Ouija board for it, one strand in the gene for something bigger and probably dinosaur-shaped. French doors to the living room were shut, which only happened for poker. The door to the kitchen was also shut, which sealed us in a crucible. Glasses clinked, faces grew edgy and cash morphed around like a splattered amoeba, blobs of it attached by invisible stalks to your brow that met and writhed over the table. Five-card draw was our game, no jokers. Life or death once the deck was shuffled. Then:

'Jet pork.'

'Ha ha ha!'

The first night popped my brain for good. After that the endorphins didn't even need a game to take place,

73

I got a rising buzz just waiting for the right conditions to gather, like a puppy waiting for a leash to rattle. The phone rings: could be the Italian. Glass of wine: could lead to two. Two could lead to poker. The phone rings: Spaniard, could lead to Italian. Good mood could lead to wine, wine could lead to poker. Occasionally the stars would line up, right mood, right wine, ring ring, Italian. Then the table sloughed its salt and pepper and cloth to become a vortex, a court of miracles where the laws of maths spun dust-devils up through your hands. I didn't know at the time how unlikely it is in the history of the world that a deck of cards has ever shuffled into the same order twice, nor how remote the chance is that it ever will; but you could feel that maths swirling. It was a voltage. And there was violence in it. Play-violence, but violence, until laughter broke through like a bomb in a vase. Even the laughter was violent.

Everything was lit up so high, that's the thing.

The light stayed with me till years down the line when friends who'd also felt the buzz joined me in magical thinking about it, and we tried to invoke it from scratch. We hunted that DNA as a surfer hunts waves, finally doing what the surfer would do if he was made president: drop a bus in the sand two hundred yards offshore to cause the right nature of waves. Our method was to invest the table with the sanctity of a shrine, a monument to the maths and the light and somehow even the yelling. We created a table of miracles before the fact, a real court of miracles by simply calling it one and wishing on it, although in another life it was the kitchen diner of a bungalow in the suburbs where the wood-effect Formica was more accustomed to children. Still it seemed to work, we bent the laws of probability with poker and other games, but it was impossible to say how much of it came from the game and how much from our worship. Not that it pretty much mattered at the time: the cards were a doorway to the sacred in everything, and it wasn't long before we were celebrating the absent dead from the table by reciting obituaries with our first drink upraised, Steady Teddy, Doris Elliot, Billy No-Legs, Mr King, fifty souls in the end, and some of their dogs.

It also showed that the buzz could survive without violence. At this level the DNA was like a toy piano, you could make it go plink but you couldn't play a tune. We just plinked and partied and built a church for the thing.

Worlds away at a rescued office table in another time above a mechanic's shop on the seamier outskirts of a town, I rode the court of miracles again. All the old strands were there, the barking, the laughter, but the wine was now rum and the pizza was baked and delivered by any place we could find that would still service that address. Two Vietnam veterans ran the table, having practised in the jungles where they also grew their what-the-fuck smiles. They were physically half a generation older than me but something in their lives made them younger by that much and ten years more. They had ungrown-up at a certain point. Ungrown-up or maybe given up. However it was, they had come back with a taste for mellower times than choppers and napalm. Occasionally they borrowed my belt to try and spawn mellow times in a vein. It meant there was no gun at this table. There was no violence in the buzz, but there was still a buzz; it crackled at a lower voltage with drawled punctuations of 'Shii-it' from one of us who slept under cardboard sheets on the street after having disgraced himself at the Salvation Army hostel. We didn't know how he'd done it exactly. Probably didn't take much, he seemed affable enough under his whiskers. One of the table's jobs for the night was to see that he left with enough small change to take a bottle of Thunderbird back to bed, although after the first hand we often had to stake his kitty anyway, sometimes stake the whole night and still advance him the Thunderbird. We worked it out among six of us. Again the violence/DNA theory took a hit at this mellow table, but here's the interesting thing about it compared to other tables: everybody cheated. Everybody cheated and everyone knew that everybody cheated. Which is a different game.

Cheating was accepted by a consensus of crocodile smiles and dirty chuckling. It was accepted that cheating was fun and could still be honourable. Deceit was already in poker's DNA, went the logic, so this was no quantum leap as far as the table was concerned. As I watched and learned, it occurred to me that maybe they had invented an anti-gun. If you bring a gun to a table to guard against cheating, then endorsing cheating not only removes the gun but the need. There was nothing to guard against, and the table did rejoice. If you got busted you just forfeited the hand.

Cheating, I saw, is as much an art as poker, probably the bigger of the two. Perhaps in the hunt for mellow times these boys still needed something in the sound of choppers, an edge, because cheating is hard work and the effort doesn't run concurrent to the game but on top of it. You bend the laws of maths for the poker then bend them again to cheat. After three drinks the main game is the cheating and not the cards, invisible partnerships start to form under the table which then drag politics and management into play on top of everything. It's a slippery slope. Before long, antes and stakes are complex deals with hedges and each-ways and interest on credit. Then after that, as with any free market, the poker soon isn't a big enough platform. I was present at the first free-market Monopoly game some time later. A Dadaist spiral to nothingness where someone soon made a deal to buy Go and dock wages, someone bought Jail and ran protection rackets, another bought Chance and Community Chest and finally the bank, at which they sat out the game to become a loan shark, and then quickly won.

Not violence but abandon was the strand in play.

As luck would have it, abandon wasn't a problem for me at the time. Although I never played that table again, it wasn't because I wouldn't have. It was like not only watching Rome burn but burning it down yourself with a Zippo. I moved on armed with three strands of DNA so far – violence, sanctity and abandon – without knowing that this gunmetal grey table would be the last court of miracles I'd ever see around poker. DNA is just a code, of course. The trick is how it expresses.

Far south there was a table that expressed it all worse. It seemed to tick some of the boxes, with weed, with rum and beer and tequila and a dog. No women, but there was mighty talk of them; you either get one or the other, and oftentimes the talk treats you better. But everything else seemed wrong. For starters the place was like your rich grandmother's house in Coral Gables or something, all white marble and palms, the only edgy thing was a cross on the wall. Even the dog was wrong, a white lap-dog right out of a calendar. It was *Dr No* meets *Benji* and *Scarface*, and the table was run by an acquaintance called Wilson who was a nice guy apart from being all wrong for poker. White-skinned and rich and scrubbed and trimmed, a tennis-playing King Arthur with cashmere over his shoulders and a good line in the kind of ultra-hospitality that's used for agendas other than wanting you to accept what's offered. Outrageous excesses like a Latin child's, offering you their car if you can prove you really asked for rum and not beer, offering cars and houses and firstborn sons to other witnesses, until suddenly you have six people round a table who all heard you say, 'I'll take a rum,' but none can admit it because the stakes are through the roof. So there was abandon there. Abandon and something else, personality politics or something. You sensed that some of the statements were short steps away from a gun. And in truth this was the first table that would have had a gun anywhere nearby. But there was no gun at the game, and it didn't matter, the only telling thing about the game was how wrong it was, given how many boxes it ticked on the court of miracles menu. Rum, beer, smoke was there. Cards, ashtrays, people, a dog.

Violence, abandon.

But we were like sky-blue suits in a retirement home, safari suits on testosterone.

The court didn't fly, it wasn't going to survive, we

could tell at the first game. Wilson put the last nail in the coffin by rolling out an anecdote where he took his girl-friend, a spotless fashion girl, up against a tree in a vacant lot and then dashingly whipped out a silk square to wipe her clean. 'Then,' he said, 'I just dropped the silk right there, in the scrub, out of privacy and courtesy for her.'

We could only take a last look at the cashmere, the loafers, the earnest Pimpernel gaze. And say, 'Shit, that the time already?'

'Bye, Wilson.'

'Later, Wilson.'

Even so, as if all roads lead to Rome, especially when it's burning, one thing did come out of Wilson's game that led to the final strand of poker DNA in this calculation. It was a face I bumped into again, another player that day, friend of Wilson's called Nestor who reminded you of the cookie monster, or anyway one of those puppets that pop up out of dustbins with furry brows. I don't know how friendly they were, buddies moved fast in that neighbourhood where honour and bullshit flowed like lava. They may have only known each other a week but it was impossible to tell because they played this lifelong soul-mate card the moment you met. Nestor had the type of face that can grin without any warmth creeping into his eyes. Straight, black, firewalled eyes with big tufts of lash and brow sprouting around them.

Nestor was from Independencia but didn't want to be. Independencia is a clump of towers on the other side of the ring-road from our leafy patch of life. He came over the highway like a rat and wore leafy-patch clothes and said leafy-patch things in order to fish in our richer waters. We didn't know at the time that he came from there, not that it would matter per se. But it was the tip of an iceberg of stuff we didn't know. He drove a brand new Lincoln without registration plates, which in our part of the world meant he was either a federal cop or a minister's kid. Something untouchable by law, anyway. I also drove without plates at the time, because the protocol was honoured by traffic cops who wouldn't risk pulling over an untouchable. But I was only bluffing, whereas Nestor had a whiff of real untouchability about him, and the car also looked the part, with heavily tinted glass and all the bells and whistles of a bullet-proof limo. It took some balls to bluff untouchable because if your arrogance wasn't flawless or the car didn't live up to the scam, real untouchables would seize it and keep it for themselves without even passing your cigarettes back out of the glove box. So there was a sense in which the city's fancy unregistered cars were a moving kitty like the mobile stakes of a poker table. Nestor looked the part. His rangy, spider-like swagger, his outreach and his impact on the surrounding world didn't let his shtick down. And like all that crew he behaved like a lifelong soul mate within ten minutes of meeting you, which on one hand you took with a ton of salt, but on the other could be hard to override.

It at least called for the benefit of the doubt. That was the clincher.

We discovered that Nestor carried a gun after one of us on a tourism and hospitality course took exception to a teacher at a hotel reception desk where they were training, and launched a typewriter at his head. That genuine soul mate of ours decided to test the lifelong brother card with his new acquaintance Nestor, who flew over brandishing a gun before any cops arrived. We gave double benefit of the doubt after that.

Then we started playing poker with him.

My position in life at the time was that I was cashing up to move away. One of the things I was selling was a professional film rig, five grand's worth of camera and monitor with accessories, almost mint in its box.

Nestor liked it. 'Let's play for it,' he said.

'No way,' I said, 'I'm cashing up to move.'

In the meantime we played poker on a round wooden table in an apartment on the third floor of a building in the city. Although Nestor was the only player I knew who cheated at that table, it was he who pulled out the revolver one day. A gun at the table is disquieting enough by itself, it's even hairier when it belongs to the only cheater. He first passed around the cylinder loaded with one bullet to see if we would prove our lifelong soul-mate status over a game of Russian roulette. Then he purposefully loaded it and laid it in the middle of the table where it spoiled the fun.

One thing I can tell you about being the gun owner at a table: your cheating skills suffer. He was stuck between abandon and finesse, the place where one inner voice warns not to call up four aces every time but to make it look credible, and even lose occasionally – and another says fuck it, you have the gun. In the end he played this way and that but his timing was way off. We were getting lucky by natural causes. He ended up cheating his way into worse hands than we were honestly dealt. Tension rose and rose. No laughter came to break it. He found nothing hilarious.

'Fuck this,' he finally said. 'Let's play for real.'

'What do you mean?'

'Sudden death or something, double or nothing.'

He was lining up for one master stroke. We could see the night's pot disappearing before our eyes. The best we could do was argue him round to a hand of Blind Baseball, the vicious nine-card face-down stud game where threes and nines are wild and four earns an extra card. A game that can make you rich or poor before you even know what happened. A drain unblocker like a nuclear bomb.

After three hands he was poor before he knew what happened. We had to play the lifelong soul-mate card in earnest, blowing an ozone-layer's worth of smoke up his ass just to get out of the room alive with any winnings. In the end he must have earmarked us for a rematch, because although he fondled the gun, cocked and uncocked it, used it like a finger to point at us all, he still let us out alive.

It was the last time I ever saw him, save for one glimpse years later in an airport, a glimpse of him by me, not me by him. Which is just as well.

My camera rig soon sold to a shiny guy from a good family whose cheque went on to bounce across the country. Then I discovered he was a Nestor soul mate. The cheque turned out to be stolen. Nestor liked that rig all along.

I rang around our crew trying to track him down, even tried Wilson. But he was gone. Then after a while, talk filtered back that Nestor was in bigger trouble than just the rig. Whatever it was led him to hide his beloved Lincoln with a soul mate while he left town. But he picked our soul mate, the one he saved at the hotel. I phoned him straight up:

'Give me the keys,' I urged. 'I'll take full responsibility.'

'You crazy? He entrusted them to me as a brother.'

'But who was your first brother?' I said. 'Him or me?'

I picked the car up and stashed it out of town in a garage that belonged to a nice girl we knew. Nice innocent girl unknown to guns and poker.

For all I know the car is still there.

In return Nestor left me with a final key to poker DNA. Obvious when you think about it, but poker is the one game you can win even when you're losing. A bullshitter's game. So on one side you find it's a valve for happy children, as I was at my aunt's table, the child bastard in us all who wants to be celebrated for his deceit. But on the other side you find the mass of players who play because they know they're going to hell anyway. You know who they are. In a milieu beyond your simple non-smoker who can rout a pack of your tabs during a night lies a deeper world of the truly empty. The empty, damaged and haunted. Not professional hustlers but the untrustworthy fucked-up middle classes, the ones who've figured hell out and are just killing time between purgatories. Maybe the court of poker miracles is as close as they can get to love, to achievement.

Maybe that's close enough.

A game you can still win when you're losing. A border between the real and unreal, between loss and gain. Good winners, bad winners, good losers, bad losers.

Place to see who we really are, and maybe why we really are.

And why we so badly need a court of miracles.

So cut that deck and deal the cards.

Lady Luck

by Lucy Porter

About an hour out of Paddington, the refreshments trolley came clinking down the aisle.

'Green tea, please,' said Steph.

As the guy poured out her hot water, Steph glanced sideways at the little bottles of wine and vodka, tantalisingly within reach.

'That'll be two pound ten please, madam ... hey, Steph, it's you! Oh my God, listen, I know it's probably really annoying, but can I have a selfie?'

As he was getting his phone out, Steph slipped a few miniatures off his trolley and into her bag. She gave the guy a massive kiss for the photo and he grinned shyly.

'So are you going all the way through to Cardiff, Steph?' he asked.

'Yeah, babe, I'm doing a telly thing? It's for the Lad Channel? Some poker game? I dunno what it's all about. Make sure you watch it, though? I'll blow you a big kiss through the screen!'

Steph winked at the guy as he wheeled his trolley away.

Steph picked up her bag and went into the toilet. She sniffed the cherry air freshener, which wasn't bad at first, until she noticed the stench it was trying to conceal. She wrenched the top off a tiny bottle of gin and sniffed that instead. Her phone started ringing. JESS OFFICE flashed up on the screen.

'All right, gorgeous,' she answered. 'Yeah, chill out, I'm on the train now ... No, I'm in the bog as it goes. I've just gotta wipe ...'

Steph covered the mouthpiece, downed the gin in one and continued.

'Babe, I'm not sure doing this show is a brilliant idea ...'

Her agent sighed and said, 'Listen, Steph, you know I would never make you do anything you don't want to do, but you *have* to do this. You've only been on TV twice this year, and both of those appearances were complete clusterfucks.'

It was true. In January, Steph appeared on BBC1's *Tonight's The Night*. Though she couldn't remember much about it, she'd seen the YouTube clip of herself falling down the stairs. Then, in June, she'd gone on a Channel 5 reality show where celebrities had to learn circus skills. It'd started off OK, but then an unfortunate incident with a troupe of Chinese acrobats got her kicked off the series. Steph winced with embarrassment as she recalled it, then tuned back in to hear Jess saying, 'I've pulled so many strings to get you this poker gig. It's your last chance. You have to prove that you can do live TV without being drunk or racist. How did you get on in rehab this time?'

Steph took a miniature vodka out of her bag and opened it quietly.

'It was great, thanks, honey. Really nice bunch of people, lovely rooms, much better than that place in Sussex. They had Maunder and Parry toiletries in the bathroom, which was nice.'

'Well, Steph, we're all rooting for you here, you know that,' replied Jess. 'I wasn't sure if I should mention this right now, but the UK Beautiful Homes Channel have been in touch. I know it's only a shopping channel, but they have a huge, loyal viewership and there's a decent amount of money in it for you. They want to offer you a weekly slot.'

Steph zipped her handbag shut.

'I *love* the Beautiful Homes Channel. I'd be perfect for it!'

'I know!' Jess laughed. 'You might have gone bankrupt twice, but you decorated both the houses you lost really nicely. And everyone loved those magazine spreads you did. Even if you are a spendthrift junkie, you've got great taste. When you were being evicted from your last place, loads of people wrote in wanting to know where you got that antique rug you were trying to wrestle back off the bailiffs . . .'

Steph was thrilled.

'It was gorgeous, wasn't it? Nineteenth-century Persian. Cost me a packet.'

'... and when you were on the front of the *Sun* for smashing that vase over the head of your last boyfriend,' Jess continued, 'Heals sold clean out of them in a day. The Beautiful Homes Channel just want you to coo over their soft furnishings and appliances.'

Steph's heart was racing.

'It's the job I was born for, babe, I'd be amazing at it – and imagine how much free stuff I'd get! Just tell me what I have to do.'

'They just want to see that you're not a total liability,' Jess said. 'You're still incredibly popular with the public, despite everything, and God knows you've had an amazing journey ...'

Steph knew she'd been lucky. She was just an ordinary girl from Croydon, drifting between bar jobs, getting drunk, having a laugh, and sleeping with awful men. Then her mates persuaded her to go on *Speedmatch*, the late 1990s Channel 4 dating programme. The nation saw her as an idiot with a heart of gold, and immediately fell in love with her. Jess signed her up after just two episodes. Over the next five years Steph appeared on endless reality shows and panel games, had a novelty pop hit, put her name to a ghost-written kids' book and even launched her own fragrance.

Everything had happened so fast. Steph couldn't pinpoint when it started to go wrong, but in the last few years the wheels had come off. The tabloids blamed the booze and drugs, but Steph worried there was something more fundamentally wrong with her. She was still getting drunk, having a laugh, and sleeping with awful men, but having the world watching had taken all the fun out of it.

Back in the bog, Steph realised that Jess was still talking to her.

'This poker show is a really easy way to prove that you've still got it.'

'But I don't know anything about poker,' Steph said, downing another miniature. 'There must be something else I can do to get back on television? What about a weight-loss DVD?'

'No, no,' Jess replied. 'When you lose weight everyone knows you're back on the coke.'

'How about a sex tape?' Steph blurted.

'Not again!' Jess snorted. 'The last one killed off the family audience for your kids' book. I guess there were a lot of porn lovers who wanked off to it, then felt too creepy reading your book to their kids.'

Steph took her vape out of her bag. 'But everyone loved me back in the day. Can't we get a reality TV gig again? Milk the whole "she's so stupid but lovable" angle?'

'Listen, Steph. *Absolutely everyone* on TV is stupid but lovable these days, it's not a USP any more.'

'But surely there's something I haven't done yet?' Steph whined.

'Well, I suppose you could kill someone . . .' Jess said flatly.

After a few moments' silence, Jess laughed. 'I am joking by the way,' she added. 'Look, I don't care what you do, just don't drink on the job tomorrow. It doesn't matter if you win or not. In fact, better you don't win – we don't want people thinking you're actually smart. Just comment on the decor in the studio ... slag off the lighting and the sofas ... that way the Beautiful Homes people will know you're on board.'

Steph pulled hard on the vape and exhaled languorously. This sounded quite easy.

'Yep, got it, babe! Can do! Go us!'

She rang off, sat back down on the toilet, unzipped her handbag and downed a miniature rum. Then she went back to her seat and snoozed lightly, woken by the voice of the train guard over the Tannoy saying, 'Ladies and gentlemen, we are now approaching Cardiff Central, our final destination.'

A nice man at the station holding a sign drove Steph to her hotel, where someone from the show was waiting for her. The young production runner – he couldn't have been older than seventeen – told her to come to the hotel bar at eight o'clock to meet the other contestants for a poker tutorial. The show was going out live at one o'clock in the morning, so they would only have a few hours in the hotel before the cars arrived to take them to the studio.

By eight o'clock, Steph had hit the minibar pretty hard. She weaved her way down the stairs with some difficulty. The other celebrities taking part in the show were playing cards on a table in the corner of the bar.

The production runner showed Steph to an empty seat at the table. She'd really rather have sat at the bar on her own, but she found herself in between Carly and Denise, a couple of comedians from a Channel 4 all-female sketch show. They told Steph how much they liked her outfit, but given that they were both dressed like homeless men Steph found it hard to believe them.

Still, at least they had a bottle of wine, and they got an extra glass for Steph.

There was an older, quite handsome guy opposite Steph, who handed her two playing cards and said, 'OK, kiddo, let's see what you can do with these!'

Steph recognised him vaguely; she thought he had been a snooker player that her dad liked. He held out his hand for her to shake.

'Martin,' he croaked, in a smoky Cockney accent. 'Although I do also answer to "The Cyclone".' He winked at Steph.

Next to Martin there was another older guy, although this one was a lot less handsome. He was wearing a ridiculous trucker's hat and lots of gold jewellery. This guy held out a hand with a load of gold rings on it.

'Clive, although I do answer to "Donkey Dick".'

Everyone at the table laughed politely, and Steph realised that she'd seen him before on the BBC1 show *Men on the Job*. He was a builder from the North East who'd become a national treasure because he always cried when they built a conservatory for a sick child or a loft conversion for a war veteran.

The young runner said, 'Right, now that you're all here, we can begin the tutorial.' Martin, the snooker player, stood up to leave, grabbing Steph by the shoulders as he walked off.

'No offence, sweetheart,' he said. 'It's just that these tutorials are for beginners, and I don't want to give away anything about my play in case you're smarter than you look! Mind you, that seems bloody unlikely!'

He laughed maniacally right in Steph's face and, although it annoyed her, she found herself laughing along.

The young runner handed out bits of paper with the values of all the poker hands on them. He talked about big blinds, little blinds, slow-playing, check-raising, family pots, heads up and going all in. Steph tried to work out the difference between a flush and a straight, but she was already starting to feel a bit tired. Clive the builder took it all very seriously. Carly and Denise larked about, trying to make everyone laugh. Steph suddenly became unbearably weary. She didn't care about poker, and it felt like she was trying to learn the language of a country she had no interest in visiting.

The tutorial ended at about nine o'clock, and they were all told to go to their rooms and freshen up. Cabs would arrive at midnight to take them from the hotel to the studio. Just as Steph was about to head off upstairs Martin, the snooker player, reappeared with a bottle of champagne. This she was happy to see, as she'd been holding back on the drinking until now. She wasn't sure if everyone knew she'd just come out of rehab, but if they read the tabloids they would all be aware that she had been 'battling her demons'. She realised it would look bad ordering a double vodka lime and soda but she got one anyway, to go with Martin's champagne.

Martin was so, so kind to her, she thought. He didn't judge her at all. He told her how brave he thought she was for doing TV again so soon after the fiascos of *Tonight's The Night* and *Chinese Circus*. He told her how nice she looked, and how much he'd enjoyed her novelty pop hit. He'd even bought Steph's perfume for a young friend of his, and his friend really loved it, despite the nasty rash it caused. Steph was starting to think that Martin was the nicest guy she'd met in ages, so when he suggested that they go up to his room to carry on chatting, it felt like a good idea. Especially when he mentioned the bottle of port he had up there.

As soon as they got into Martin's room, he started kissing her and took off her dress. He pulled out a wrap of coke and started chopping out lines on the glass top of the writing desk.

'I just got out of rehab, so ...' Steph confessed toothlessly.

'Oh, of course, darling, no worries,' Martin said. 'Just do half a line then. I cut them pretty fat.'

Handing Steph a rolled-up bank note, Martin poured her a glass of port while she snorted the half-line. Martin took his shirt off and stood in front of her, licking his lips and sucking in his stomach. Steph then snorted the rest before they went and lay down on the bed.

Martin was quite a wet kisser, and quite stubbly. After a few minutes Steph's face was damp and sore. He was very heavy when he lay on top of her, but Steph quite liked how reassuringly solid he was. She curled her legs around him and squeezed. Steph realised that she really needed to do a shit, so she rolled out from underneath him and went to the bathroom.

She sat on the toilet for so long, she thought she might

have fallen asleep for a bit. But when she came back out Martin was still wide awake. He clasped her to him very tightly. They were both sweaty. Steph's mind was racing, but she felt heavy-limbed. She was wondering whether it was too late to get a train back to London tonight and meet her mates in Camden. Maybe she could get a cab? She couldn't afford it, but if she called Ben he might offer to pay at the other end.

Steph saw that Martin was staring at her very intently.

'What's up, baby?' she said. Martin leapt off the bed and started pacing up and down the room. His face had gone really red, and sweat was dripping from his forehead down his nose.

'Darling, I don't think I've ever told anyone this before, you won't think I'm stupid, will you? This is mad but . . . oh God, no, I can't say it . . .'

Idly, Steph found herself saying, 'Go on, you can tell me. You can tell me anything, babe.'

Martin came over and stood by the bed.

He tilted her chin up towards him. 'I just . . . oh God . . . I just . . . I just really want to buy a boat. A totally massive boat.'

'Yeah, I went on a boat once, it was nice. It was a ferry to France . . .'

Martin shook his head. 'No, I don't mean a ferry, I mean like a yacht . . . or a super-yacht, that's what I want. I want an enormous one, a huge, gigantic one.'

Steph suppressed a giggle, but Martin carried on.

'It's just so free. The ocean. You can go wherever you want. Not like on the roads, where you just have to go where they tell you. Like, say you're on the A303 and you suddenly think you'd like to go to Axbridge, but you can't, because that's on the A371, but you're on the A303 so you have to carry on until Axminster, you know?'

Steph nodded vacantly and applied some lip balm. Martin was spitting as he spoke now.

'At sea, no one could tell me where to go or what to do, I'd be free – finally free. Cannes, Monte Carlo, the Bahamas, that island Richard Branson owns in the Caribbean ... I mean obviously I'd have to ask his permission to dock, but I reckon that would be OK because I met him once in a poker tournament. Anyway, I could go anywhere. And you could come with me. You'd look amazing on a super-yacht. You would, you know.'

Steph nodded and lay back sleepily on the mound of white pillows. Martin waved the rolled-up bank note in her face, so she sat up on one elbow and snorted a massive line of coke off the bedside table.

Martin hopped back onto the bed beside her, and slipped his trousers and pants off. Steph wasn't bothered about having sex with him, but she was a bit surprised when he angled his bottom towards her and handed her the rolled-up bank note.

'Listen, darling,' he whispered, 'could you just blow a little bit of the coke up my arse? I get more of a hit that way.'

Confronted with Martin's hairy bum hole, Steph was disgusted, yet intrigued. She'd never done this before. At first, she struggled with the mechanics of how, but her teachers at school had always said she was good at problem-solving. She sucked some coke into the rolled-up bank note, but stopped when she could taste it on her tongue. Then she inserted the tip of the note between Martin's cheeks, closed her eyes, and blew out of her mouth as hard as she could. The bank note flew out of her mouth, lodging itself inside Martin. The coke must have hit the target, because Martin sighed with pleasure.

Pulling the bank note out of his cheeks, Martin offered, 'Do you want me to do the same for you?'

Steph shook her head. He was obviously keen to do something for her in return. It was quite sweet, really. Men didn't often consider her feelings.

'I know,' Martin said. 'I'll just rub a bit of coke in for you, down there.' Steph looked on, slightly bewildered as he set about her nether regions with his coke-covered fingers. After a short while, Steph said, 'Thanks very much, you can stop now.'

Martin grinned at her. 'Do you want to have sex, love? I mean, I find it a bit hard to come when I've done coke, but I'm happy to give it a go!'

'No, you're all right, thanks,' Steph replied. 'My fanny's quite numb now, anyway. I might just head back to my room.' The coke had had no effect on her brain and she was starting to feel bone-tired.

Martin held Steph gently by the shoulders and put his face really close to hers.

'Before you go, there's something I need to talk to you about.' Steph braced herself for more boat chat, but instead he started talking about the poker game.

'It's really important that I win this tournament tonight. The guys from Poker Blast really want to sponsor me, and if they see me win a high-profile telly game I reckon that will really seal the deal. So I need your help, sweetheart. It couldn't be easier. If you just play tight to start with, let the others knock each other out, and then when we're heads up, fold anything decent and play any old crap. It'll be sweet as a nut.'

Steph must have looked even more confused than she felt, because Martin started laughing.

He ruffled her hair. 'You don't know a lot about poker, do you, angel?' he said caringly. 'All I'm saying is don't play many hands until it's just you and me, and then let me win. OK?'

This sounded brilliant. She basically had to do nothing, and then play badly.

Martin went to the bathroom and got some pills out of his wash bag. He offered one to her.

'I brought some downers. I might get an hour's sleep now, it'll help me be on form for the game. Do you want one?'

Taking one of the pink capsules, she put her clothes back on and motioned to leave. Martin gave her a big hug, and she nearly fell asleep in his huge, comforting, sweaty arms. She managed to crawl down the corridor to her room and collapsed on the bed.

She woke up and the phone in her room was ringing.

The young runner said, 'Hi, Steph, the taxi to take you to the studio is downstairs now.'

Feeling surprisingly well-rested, she replied brightly, 'Yeah, it's all good, babe. I'm just doing my make-up now, yeah?'

She put the phone down and looked in the mirror. Having slept soundly on her back for the last hour or so, her make-up still looked fine. She just added a bit more foundation to cover the stubble rash, and another coat of mascara.

Carly, Denise, Martin and Clive were waiting with the runner in reception downstairs. Two taxis were outside, and Martin engineered it so they were alone in the second one. He reminded her of the plan he'd made earlier, and she promised him she would do exactly as he'd said. Martin held her hand and Steph enjoyed the way he gently stroked her fingers as they sat in silence. Cardiff looked so romantic in the moonlight, she thought. She'd never been to Wales before, and she wondered if she'd get a chance to look around in the morning.

Once at the studio, they were rushed in to have their hair and make-up checked. There was a big green poker table in the centre of the room, with glass panels cut out of it and cameras underneath, so that the people at home could see what cards the players had. Other cameras were placed around the table to cover the players' chat and reactions. The studio was cold, and Steph shivered when the sound man took her cardigan off as he was fitting her microphone.

Carly and Denise, the comedians, were clearly very nervous.

'We've never done anything on live TV before,' said Carly.

'I've done loads of live telly, babe, it's no big deal!' Steph said. She intended to be reassuring, but she was sure she heard Denise snort with laughter. Clive the Handyman had put on a ridiculous outfit. He had a sweatshirt with the hood up, some sunglasses and massive headphones.

'He doesn't want to give away anything about his play,' said Denise, and she and Carly collapsed into hysterics. Martin the snooker player looked a bit purple in the face and was very sweaty, but he was chatty and happy, posing for photos with the camera crew.

Steph was still feeling very sleepy. As they showed her to the poker table it felt like she was watching all this happen to somebody else. The young runner explained that they had to leave their cards on the table, because the cameras underneath would show the viewers what cards they had. The floor manager told everyone they were about to go live in five minutes. A dealer came to the table and did some funny business with a deck of cards to decide who would sit where. He was a handsome bloke of about twenty-five, and Steph flirted with him to relax.

'Babe,' she pouted, 'you obviously know about all this shit, yeah? I don't have the first clue what I'm doing. Look after me, will you?'

He laughed and nodded, and told her that he was a big fan of her work. He explained to Steph that she was on the big blind, so she would be the last person he asked what she wanted to do when they started playing. The floor manager counted down to the live broadcast. The TV monitors in the studio played the theme tune and opening credits for *Poker Nightz* before turning blank again.

Some pundits in a studio next door would be commentating on the game. Steph couldn't see them, but the floor manager said they were doing a bit of a preamble and the game would start when they'd finished. Everything was deathly silent around the table, apart from the odd bit of giggling from Carly, or was it Denise? Steph had forgotten which one was which. Martin was fiddling with his poker chips and Clive the Handyman had his eyes closed and his hands in his lap like he was praying.

Steph felt sleepy again and had nearly nodded off, when suddenly there was a kerfuffle in the studio, and all the cameras started moving around.

The floor manager said, 'OK, ladies and gents, we're about to go live in three ... two ...'

The *Poker Nightz* theme tune kicked in again and the cards were dealt. Steph looked down at hers – the five of hearts and the two of clubs. She was glad because she knew this was a rubbish hand, so she watched the others doing stuff with their cards and chips until the dealer raised his eyes at her, and she realised it was her turn. Steph tried to remember what she was supposed to do.

'Erm ... Fold?'

The dealer said quietly, 'You can just check.'

'Check,' Steph said decisively.

The dealer laid three cards out in the middle of the table – a queen, a jack and a nine.

Clive the Handyman sat bolt upright in his seat. One of the comedians put her hand over her mouth, and the other one started bouncing up and down. Martin didn't do anything. Everyone started putting cards and chips in the middle of the table, until the dealer raised his eyes again in Steph's direction.

'Check?' Steph said.

To which the dealer replied, 'Bet or fold?'

'Fold?'

The dealer motioned for her to put her cards in the

middle of the table before laying down another card – a queen. More chips went in and Steph could see that Clive the Handyman was getting very excited indeed behind his sunglasses because his bushy eyebrows were raised.

The dealer laid out another card. Another queen. Clive the Handyman put all his chips into the middle of the table, so did Carly . . . or was it Denise? The comedian and Clive both stood up and put their cards face up on the table. The comedian had a jack and an eight. Clive the Handyman had a king and a queen.The comedian had all her chips taken away, and they were given to Clive the Handyman. The comedian laughed and walked away from the table, shaking her head. Steph heard the *Poker Nightz* theme tune again and the floor manager came in to tell everyone that they had gone to an ad break.

The camera crew disappeared, and Martin and the dealer commiserated with the comedian who'd just lost. They were all talking about potential straights and three of a kinds. Steph didn't have a clue what they were on about. The make-up people came back in to put some powder on everyone – it was a very small studio and they were all getting a bit sweaty. The losing comedian was taken outside to do her 'exit chat', and the rest of them were offered a drink of water or the chance of a toilet break.

Steph didn't really need the toilet, but she wanted to get out of the tiny studio. She was taken down the corridor by the young runner, and went into the loo to splash some cold water on her wrists. She looked a little grey. Just as she was about to leave, Martin poked his head around the door. He handed her a wrap of coke and whispered, 'Well played, love, just keep doing what you're doing.'

Steph went into a cubicle, scooped some coke out with her long fingernail and stuck it up her nose. She sauntered back into the studio just as the floor manager was ushering everyone into their seats.

The next section of the show seemed to last an eternity. Steph folded whenever she could and checked when the dealer told her to. Everyone else moved their chips around, stood up, sat down, cried out in anguish, punched the air. Clive the Handyman had ripped off his headphones and taken off his shades, and was at loggerheads with the remaining comedian. Steph was the only one who kept completely calm, largely because she had no idea what was going on. Although Steph didn't understand what was happening with the cards, she had seen enough drama to know that Clive and the comedian were locked in furious, personal combat and Martin was anxious about the outcome.

Eventually, the other comedian lost all her chips to Clive the Handyman and left the table. Clive was exultant and Martin looked relieved, if a bit pale.

At the next ad break, Steph took the opportunity to revisit the toilet. Carly and Denise were in there smoking, giggling as she came in.

'Ooh, looks like your boyfriend's having a hard time,' Denise said.

'Martin's not my boyfriend.'

'Not Martin,' Carly said. 'Clive! I thought you must be shagging him because you folded that pair of kings and let him win the hand. He only had queen-three off-suit. I could see it all from the green room. You really screwed Denise over there.'

Confused, Steph started to panic.

'Oh, no, sorry,' she said. 'I really wasn't trying to screw anyone over, babe?'

The comedians laughed. 'It's fine, we're really not bothered. We're happy just to let the old blokes get on with it. They're so competitive, it's tragic. We're only doing this because our agent made us.'

Steph was so glad that they weren't really angry with her. She laughed and said, 'Me too. I just want to get on the shopping channel.'

'Yeah, we're trying to get a sitcom away with Channel 4,' Denise said. 'It's nuts that we have to do this poker bullshit, isn't it? But apparently it's "raising our profile". To be honest, we can't really be arsed. We know we're going to look like sneering dickheads, but we're totally out of our comfort zone.'

Steph felt bad for judging them earlier. Even though they did look like homeless men in their jeans and big jumpers, they were clearly on her side. She sat up on one of the sinks, taking the wrap of coke Martin had given her out of her handbag. She offered it to the comedians. They chopped out some lines for themselves and one for Steph. There wasn't much left, so Steph told them to keep the rest. They had a group hug, before one of the comics produced a little plastic bag of pills.

'Want one of these?' she said. 'It might get you through the cockfight between Martin and Clive.'

*

Back in the studio, the young runner asked them if they'd like anything to drink. Clive asked for a fizzy mineral water. Martin said he'd like a red wine, which made Steph feel bold enough to ask for a double vodka, lime and soda. The floor manager was trying to get them back into their seats, and as soon as they sat down the *Poker Nightz* theme played again and the dealer went into action.

Steph could pinpoint the exact moment that the ecstasy kicked in. She'd folded her first hand, and was watching Martin and Clive play against each other. Suddenly she felt her whole body tingling and a rush of warmth radiated from the base of her spine up to the top of her head. She felt deeply sorry for Clive because she could see how sad and lonely and bitter he was. She experienced a massive rush of love for Martin. He was sweaty and desperate too, but he had been so kind to her and he so wanted to win, and now that was all she wanted too. Steph kept folding her hands like Martin had told her to. Soon enough he had knocked out Clive the Handyman, who stomped out in an absolute fury. As he left, he hissed in her face.

'This is pathetic. What are you playing at? I should have won this!'

Steph beamed up at him and tried to put her arms around his neck. The floor manager dragged him away, while Steph sat there smiling at Martin, who just looked back at her quizzically, mouthing, 'Are you OK?'

There was no time for a toilet break this time, so the floor manager counted them back in to the live broadcast.

'Three … two …' Steph swayed in time along to the *Poker Nightz* theme tune as the camera rolled again.

The dealer hurriedly gave her some cards as he said, 'You're big blind, shall I take the chips?'

She laughed at his anxious little face and said, 'Chill, baby, it's all good.'

She looked at the cards she had been given. She saw a three of hearts and a seven of the black bobbly thing. Steph had totally forgotten what she was meant to do, but she was feeling supremely confident and happy.

'So, Steph,' the dealer chimed, 'you're big blind and Martin's called, so let's see the flop.'

The dealer put a king, a three and a five on the table. Steph vaguely remembered that she was meant to play a crap hand, and she was pretty sure that a three and a seven weren't very good. Steph was now completely at ease with herself and her surroundings. She tossed some chips into the middle of the table. She didn't know or care what they were worth, she just enjoyed throwing them. Martin did the same. Steph chuckled, her fingers were looking really funny and she couldn't stop stroking her nail varnish.

The dealer turned over another card. It was another three.

Martin allowed himself an encouraging smile and raise of the eyebrows at Steph. There were three threes on the table but Steph had no idea whether that was good or bad. All that she knew was Martin had smiled at her and it was making her feel *amazing*. She threw some more chips – the really pretty red ones – into the middle of the table. Martin threw some lovely green ones into the mix and Steph thought that she really must get out into nature more – she used to love walking in the Forest of Dean when she was a girl. She wondered if Martin liked trees and leaves and animals and all that shit.

The dealer turned over another three.

Steph looked at it. So many threes! It must be a sign. She thought to herself, what could 'three' mean? She pictured her and Martin with a baby. It felt good. She looked at Martin and he was positively radiant. Steph thought he must also be imagining life in a cottage in the woods with their baby. She wanted to give him everything. She pushed all her chips into the middle of the table, as if to say, 'Here you are, take it all.' Martin did the same and Steph felt a rush of connectivity.

They turned their cards over . . .

Steph saw the dealer's eyebrows shoot up and his mouth fall open. She looked down at the table. Martin had a pair of kings.

He shouted 'You *bitch*! You should have folded! Why didn't you fold?' He clutched his chest, and staggered back from the table. Martin's mouth fell open just like the dealer's had, except his lips were turning blue and his eyes were rolling back in his head.

Steph rushed over to him, screaming.

'But we were going to buy a boat together! And live in a cottage in the woods with our baby! I love you! Martin, I love you!'

She held him and wept through the *Poker Nightz* theme tune until the floor manager came and prised her away.

*

The next morning in the hotel, Steph was woken by her phone ringing. It was Jess.

'Did you see it, babe?' Steph croaked. 'He died. He actually died. I killed him. I didn't mean to.'

'Yep, awful, isn't it?' Jess lied. 'What an awful thing ... Anyway, you need to get back to London ASAP. There's a car coming for you now, so get up and get dressed. You're on *Back of the Sofa* on ITV this afternoon and then it's wall-to-wall TV and radio appearances for the rest of the week.'

Steph sat bolt upright in bed.

'But I'm a murderer now,' she said. 'Won't that kill my career?'

'Are you *kidding*?' Jess laughed. 'It's the biggest thing that's ever happened on the Lad Channel! Usually, it's just Italian soft porn and documentaries about benefit cheats! You held a man as he was dying and showed your tender side – that clip has been seen all over the world and now you're a tragic heroine who's just lost the love of her life.'

Steph bounced out of bed and immediately started doing her make-up. She hadn't taken it off for two days now. It was still looking good, although her mascara had run a bit from all the crying.

'I've got you a meeting with BBC2 about a home make-over show,' Jess continued.

'Babe,' Steph interrupted, 'I'm not going anywhere near BBC2. It's BBC1, ITV or nothing. Now, can you get onto a few designers and line up some free clothes for this week's telly spots? Tell Darren to meet me at ITV and he can do my roots in the make-up room there. Just email me the schedule ...'

'That's more like the old Steph I know and love. Oh, and Channel 5 want to know if you'll do a poker tournament for them?'

She pondered for a moment before replying.

'No, I don't think I'll play poker again. I guess I'm just not a lucky person??'

The Old Card Room

by Patrick Marber

I was winning that night. I'd walked in at three in the afternoon with two hundred pounds and turned it into three grand. This was a lot of money in those days, enough to live on very well for a month or two. I'd been lucky; I played hands I shouldn't have been in, made wild calls and got paid, ran bluffs people believed. My play was eccentric and seemingly unreadable. I made myself look nervous when I wasn't, I kept my mouth shut and faked a tremble with the nuts. I was loose. Alone and loose. I played blackjack too. Won at that and then roulette. My numbers were magical: zero one two, eight eleven, thirteen, twenty-seven. I imagined being approached by a house manager and accused of having a system. I'd rehearsed my response: 'Sir, I'm a lucky idiot. Check my bank statements. I'm in to you for thousands.' This was true.

I was younger then. Just twenty. But no one called me 'The Kid'. I didn't have the flair for that. I played like a novice: tight and scared with occasional bouts of bravado provoked by boredom. Sometimes they said, 'Your deal, young man,' but they never called me 'The Kid'.

It was 2 a.m. in the old upstairs room. In those days the game was seven-card stud, pot limit. We were playing six-handed. On my right was a smartly dressed man they called 'The Chauffeur'. I'd not seen him around before. He was in his sixties, pale, with quick, careful hands. He never made a mistake on the shuffle or the deal. Opposite him was an old Indian gent. Always wore a dark suit and sober tie. The regulars called him Dr Patel but I didn't know if that was his real name or even if he was a doctor. Whenever he won a hand the man to my left would murmur, 'The Doc's got the lot.'

I cupped my hand over my two down cards and saw two black ducks. I glanced up and the two of diamonds was dealt to me. I hadn't caught a wire up in weeks. Dr Patel spoke first with an ace. Two guys passed and The Chauffeur raised, showing the Suicide King. I figured he was trying to get a quick read on that ace. I called with my best fool face on – along for the ride, a lunatic limping in. The Doc raised again and The Chauffeur called. Almost as an afterthought I called too. By now there was a good four hundred in the pot and we all had a few thousand in front of us. I vaguely considered that I was facing bullets and a pair of kings – possibly with an ace. I didn't much care. I'd decided I was winning this pot. The only question was how much money I could make.

The fourth card came. No help anywhere as far as I could see. I got a useless eight of diamonds. The betting went as before. The Doc opened big, The Chauffeur raised, I affected to think about it a while and then called. The Doc raised again. We both called. At that point The Chauffeur looked at me for the first time. He smiled. He gave me a look so benign and gentle I wished he was my father. It could've been a warning, it could've been a blessing.

The guy dealing was two to my left. He whistled as he flipped a red ace to The Doc. The man next to me murmured, 'Got the lot.' The Chauffeur hit a ten of hearts. I saw he was flushing and pitied him. Me? I got the case deuce. Two of hearts. How pretty it looked on that blue baize. Dr Patel looked at my up hand over his glasses. Deuce – eight – deuce. Then he flicked a look at The Chauffeur's king – seven – ten – suited. He shrugged and lobbed a single chip into the pot. A thousand. The Chauffeur took a sip of his lemon tea. I lit a cigarette and tried not to shake. I was reading – if I read at all – the poor old Doc for a full house aces over who cares. And I reckoned The Chauffeur had been running a bluff with the vague out of making a house or a flush. So I was surprised when The Chauffeur put his tea down and raised another grand. I took a drag. I glanced at his cards and took in those three hearts. I knew I had four ducks. At least, I thought I knew. With fingers like custard I checked my hole cards. Two black twos. They hadn't morphed into threes. I was home. I looked at The Chauffeur.

He smiled again. His eyes lively with pleasure. I called two grand.

Dr Patel scratched his temple. He frowned a moment. He sighed. He took his glasses off and put them back on.

He leant forward from his seat and studied my hand and the chauffeur's hand. Then he said, 'I don't know what madness is occurring. Good luck, crazy men.' And he passed his cards. The dealer said, 'And then there were two.' He rapped the baize and dealt the final up cards: The Chauffeur caught a king and I paired my eight. I was showing two pairs. My bet. I looked at his cards again, pretending to think, a procedural nicety. And then I felt a strange heat flare through me, as if someone had turned the gas up to full inside my body. It occurred to me that I was looking at four kings. I was looking at two showing but realised he had two more in the hole. His smile had been a warning, 'Get out while you can.' He'd been dealt a wire up, same as me. No, impossible. What are the odds? No idea. The dealer, from some other planet, murmured, 'Your bet.' I panicked and checked.

The Chauffeur nodded. As if to suggest, 'Smart move.' In a sense it was true. I'd slow played the hand from the off and a check here seemed consistent. And then he surprised me again, he said, 'Check is good.' My entire system melted with relief. No decision required. No humiliation necessary. Yet.

I watched the dealer pass the hole cards across the table. I watched The Chauffeur pick his up and squeeze. I studied that profile, the eyes, the ears, praying for a flicker of disappointment. There was none. Can't you just shed a tear? I pulled my useless card towards me, nearly flipped it. I put it on top of my dead deuces and cupped my hand over all three. I squeezed. Two of clubs – two of spades – king of diamonds. I looked again. The fabulous old dude was staring at me. 'Yes, I'm the king of diamonds, I really am. The fact that I am the king of diamonds means that The Chauffeur on your right does not have me in his hand.' Unless they'd invented a new suit it was impossible for him to have four kings.

It was my bet. I had him locked up. I glanced at him. Still twinkling, enjoying his night. He responded with a slight movement of his head, a kind of shrug and bow on an angle. A 'do what you must do'. I stared at the pot. Hard to tell, four or five grand in there. The biggest pot I'd ever won. And I still had a grand in front of me. Now ... how to get him to call? Maybe lob a playful five hundred in there? Show 'weakness' and he might even raise and set me in? Then again, the poor man's pot committed. If I shove my grand in he has to call it anyway. He's beaten. Beaten by a lucky kid. I saw him driving home in another man's flashy car. I saw him smarting with sadness he called that final bet. I thought and thought. I saw his disappointed wife, I saw grandchildren with lousy Christmas presents. I saw a front door needing new paint. I said, 'Check.' The dealer exhaled. Dr Patel stared in surprise. The Chauffeur made a tiny movement with his tongue, I saw his cheek move a touch. He said, 'Check is good.' I showed my cards. He nodded. The man on my left muttered, 'Huh, kid got the lot.' I kept my head down, avoided their eyes. They knew I'd spared him. I didn't want their admiration nor their scorn. The game continued. I passed most of my hands. The Chauffeur played a few more, lost the rest and scooped up his jacket. 'Gentlemen, you'll find me in the bar. Good luck all round.' He bowed to the table. He didn't look at me.

*

A while later I'd lost a few hands, given back a few hundred to the table. I was exhausted. I took my chips and got up. The other players nodded amiably when I said goodnight. I took my chips to the desk. They gave me six sealed plastic bags with a thousand in fifties in each. A year ago I'd never seen a fifty-pound note. They gave me another eight hundred in fifties and twenties. I went to the gents and locked myself in a cubicle. After some effort I was able to put the bags in my suit pockets without my winnings being too obvious. Alone and unseen in that cubicle I celebrated. My arms aloft, a brief dance of victory. Nearly seven grand from two hundred.

I headed downstairs for the exit. Not tempted to risk a penny more on the gaming floor. I was thinking about The Chauffeur. He'd been on my mind since he'd left the table. I wanted him to be OK. I wanted 'it' to be OK. At the exit I turned round and made my way to the bar. He wasn't there. A waiter told me he'd just gone. I ran downstairs and out of the building. The car park was to the left. If I stood by the ramp I thought I might see him driving out. I waited. I lit a cigarette. A minute later a black Bentley appeared at the foot of the ramp and headed up towards me. I peered in as it passed. Not him. A stern-looking man with a velvet collar on his coat. I took a drag. Patted a pocket, felt the little crackle of plastic. A silver Polo appeared. I ignored it and pulled on my cigarette. As the car hit the top of the ramp it slowed. The driver's window was open. It was him. He stopped when he saw me. We looked at each other a moment. Him slightly confused, me amazed by his vehicle.

'Need a ride?' he said. I told him I didn't. 'Least I can do,' he responded.

'I'm sorry about that pot,' I said. 'If I should be.'

'You took pity on an old man. Don't do it again.'

He stared at me, the engine ticking over.

'Are you upset I didn't thank you?'

I thought about this.

'Maybe a little.'

He nodded. 'It wasn't the place.'

Another car was heading up the ramp. The Chauffeur said, 'See you around, kid.' He drove away. I never saw him again. No one did. Someone said he stopped playing. Another guy said he spent his whole time chauffeuring his daughter to various hospitals and doctors.

It's gone now, the old upstairs room. I don't even know where it was, I mean in that building. The game changed, the casino changed. The smokers got shunted outside to a heated terrace. The dress code went too. I used to like putting on my poker suit. But it wouldn't fit me now. I'm too old.

Heads Up

by David Flusfeder

At moments like this, when time was being pulled so tight that she felt impossibly stretched and narrow herself, she would add to her mental list of Things She Hated About Dealing.

She hated players who helped themselves to change from the pot.

She hated bets that were barely pushed forward so she had to reach for them, putting even more strain on her lower back and shoulders.

She hated players who had to keep being reminded to put in blinds and antes.

She hated players who took advantage of her enforced proximity to leer at her and flirt.

She hated card-room managers who filled out rotas without any regard for the personal lives of their staff.

She hated the pains in her shoulders and neck and back.

She hated herself for giving up on having a personal life.

She hated players who blamed her for their losing hands.

She hated players who took out their disgruntlements, with themselves, their lives, their luck, by not tipping her.

She hated card-room managers who stole her tips from her.

She hated being treated as part of the furniture of the card room, which meant that any passing man with power could rest his hands on her shoulders.

She hated moments like this one, still waiting, the deck held up in her left hand, as she was poised to pitch the first card, as the speeches went interminably on, and the players hadn't even been introduced yet, and she had forgotten how not to smile.

She was already hating Kenneally, who was still making his speech.

His hair was grey, what was left of it, and he wore a grey suit, and was the President of the Federation, which had set itself up to be the organising body for all tournament poker. He was telling this shiny room about the Federation now, and how far it had come in a very short time, and thanking his broadcasting partners and his corporate partners, as two other members of the Federation's steering committee, Lucio Tambini, who was slick and handsome in a vacuous sort of way, and a red-haired man called Robinson, whom she would never hear speak, adjusted the position of the screen that displayed the names and logos of all the Federation's sponsors so it would fit in the shot with Kenneally.

They were in the ballroom of the South Bank Hilton.

If the lights hadn't been quite so dazzling she might have been able to see across the river to the green and red canopies of the outdoor terraces of the Houses of Commons and Lords.

'One day,' Kenneally was saying, 'poker will be recognised as a sport, which will eventually be invited to participate in the Olympics. Think of that, gentlemen!'

There was some applause but not that much, probably because no one believed this and maybe because everyone was getting as bored as she was.

'Without any more ado, let's introduce the players!'

He passed the microphone to Tambini, who went onto her hate list too as he initiated some comedy squabbling over whose idea this all was, before thanking Kenneally for his inspirational leadership, and coaxing the room into another round of applause.

There had been a gala event the night before when all this, she felt, could have been got out of the way.

Finally, the introductions were being made.

'And here they are! Mike Bridges is thirty-eight years old and has won eleven WSOP bracelets but we all know him as the most feared high-stakes player in Las Vegas and Macau for over a decade. Let's hear it for Mike Bridges, ladies and gentlemen, from Atlantic City, New Jersey, USA! Mike Bridges!

'And Rainer Gottschalk, he's twenty-one, an internet sensation. Rainer won his first WSOP bracelet this year, when he was finally old enough to be allowed inside an American casino. Rainer Gottschalk, from Weimar in Germany!'

She wondered if she would be introduced (*A-aa-aand*

let's big it up for your dealer, without whom none of this would be possible, ladies and gentlemen, Ms Wendy Valerian!), but she knew she would not be, and instead Tambini was now introducing Xi Tianxi, who had flown out from their watch manufacturer partners in Geneva. Finally, Wendy was able to move away from the table, to shut her eyes, to stretch and relax the muscles of her face, to slowly lift and roll and lower her shoulders, as the players were presented with new watches.

Mike Bridges, wearing beige chinos and a New York Mets sweatshirt, stood beside Rainer Gottschalk in jeans and a heavy metal T-shirt. On either side were Tambini in his white dinner jacket and Xi in a black evening dress. Xi slid the watches onto the wrists of Bridges and Gottschalk. Bridges, who did everything, apart from poker and baccarat, somewhat languorously, glanced down at his watch in a slow, unimpressed appraisal. Gottschalk giggled, as if the touch of a woman's hand upon his arm was a novelty, and then showed it to his retinue of supporters, who looked just like him, with long greasy dark hair, heavy metal T-shirts, and jeans and trainers. One, whom she assumed was his father, was distinct by his grey straggly hair.

Kenneally tapped his own watch and nodded at Wendy to sit back down. He took the microphone again.

'Thank you, Xi, thank you, Lucio. Thank you, players! The game is Texas Hold'em, heads up. This is a winner-take-all hundred thousand pound event. Players will start with ten thousand chips, and blinds will be at 25-50, where they will remain. Poker is a game of skill, and this is a demonstration of that fact. Pressure of blinds and antes will not be a factor influencing the outcome. The action will be broadcast and streamed on a fifteen-minute delay, so that there is no possibility of either player being informed of the other's hole cards. Let's shuffle up and deal!'

Finally now, she pitched the first cards, and there was a physical relief to be doing so.

Bridges was leaning twisted against his chair, one arm over the seat back. He lifted the corners of his cards very slightly, glanced down at them. Otherwise he gazed at his opponent with his mouth slightly open.

Gottschalk was sitting squarely at the table. His arms surrounded his chips. His hair fell in front of his eyes.

The action was on Bridges. He threw in two chips, making it 125 to play.

Gottschalk re-raised immediately. There was a jerky quality to his actions as he put in the chips, as if the messages from brain to limbs passed through more complicated channels than was usual.

Bridges's mouth closed, then opened again as if he wanted, mildly, to warn his opponent against this heedless aggression. Instead, he shook his head very slowly and solemnly, and four-bet, making it 1,100 to play.

There were excited murmurs from the crowd. Some people clapped.

Kenneally had told her he anticipated play lasting much of the day, at least until after the lunch break. But the players' aggression was making it seem that it might all be over on the first hand.

Gottschalk giggled and called.

She dealt the flop: ace of hearts, queen of clubs, two of clubs.

Gottschalk led out. Bridges, staring at him throughout, slowly tossed in the call.

Alerted by the action, Tambini had come towards the table. He rested a hand on Wendy's shoulder.

The turn card was the king of hearts.

'He checks now,' Lucio whispered.

Gottschalk bet. Bridges called again. Each player had just over half their starting stack left.

Wendy waited an extra beat, tapped the table, burned the next card, and exposed the river card, jack of diamonds.

Kenneally seemed oblivious to it all, off to the side, talking to Xi Tianxi.

Gottschalk bet, Bridges raised. Tambini's hand became heavier on her shoulder.

And Gottschalk folded. He slid his cards over towards Wendy. He looked at his opponent's chips – Bridges now had over four times as many.

Tambini released his pressure. He was wearing one of those watches too. It had a gold bracelet and a gold face with no numbers or markings. Wendy wondered how many Xi had brought over from Geneva.

Gottschalk folded the next hand, and the next, to Bridges's raise. He won the one after that, taking the blinds with a raise, and the next, re-raising Bridges's button raise.

An hour had gone by, and Gottschalk had won a few chips back, but Bridges still held a significant lead.

Spectators drifted in and out. The urgency created by

the first hand diminished, the precipice that had been waiting for Gottschalk receded. Finally the first break came. Wendy went out of the ballroom, which had once been the chamber for the Greater London Council, and into the green room to find coffee. Some of Gottschalk's crew were here, the straggly-haired heavy metal fans. Most of them were playing internet poker on laptops and tablets.

She drank her coffee looking up at the monitors. There were two, one showing the live feed, and the other, on a delay, which showed the hole cards in a lower corner of the screen. Bridges was unchanging in both, his lower jaw slightly open, staring at his opponent. Gottschalk sometimes had his arms around his cards, sometimes he slumped in his seat, like a boy waiting for permission to leave the supper table. Bridges did everything methodically, but he made quick decisions. And Gottschalk's mind moved so much faster than the rest of him. That's what accounted for all that nervous energy, Wendy thought. It was the effort of the body to keep up with his thoughts that sent everything fizzing and skipping. His hands were by far his best feature; on another man they would have looked capable and refined. On him they were rather incongruous, and flapped. She wondered what it would be like to have sex with Gottschalk. Presumably a quick paroxysmal frenzy and then over.

Kenneally was fielding congratulations from other balding men in grey suits.

'I know, I know! I thought it was all going to be over in a single hand!'

He drew the back of his hand across his forehead to

mime the wiping away of sweat. Kenneally's fingers were short and plump and very pale, like a family of overfed worms.

Gottschalk was pointing at the screen of one of his friends, advising him how to play the online hand.

Bridges was sitting by himself looking at his phone. He glanced up at Wendy, perhaps because he had felt her scrutiny upon him, and smiled. Mike Bridges's smile was open and uncomplicatedly boyish and at odds with his slack-jawed persona. She wondered how much of that was performance.

The monitor was replaying the first hand. Gottschalk had ace-jack, Bridges queen-ten. Gottschalk had been ahead all the way to the river, which had given him two pairs and filled Bridges's unlikely straight.

'Amazing laydown, can't believe he got away from that,' Tambini said. He seemed to have a skill for gliding silently in behind her.

'They're very evenly matched, aren't they?' Wendy said. 'Who do you think's going to win?'

'Bridges. It's what he does. The kid's great, but he's going to overreach himself eventually,' Tambini said.

When play resumed, Gottschalk adopted the opposite of his usual style. His customary game was hyper-aggressive, three-betting often, regardless of his cards, to put pressure on his opponent. But now, he was folding more, and calling often. This new strategy was pushing Bridges off balance.

At the next break, Kenneally interrupted her route to the coffee machine.

'When do you think this is going to be over?' he asked.

'It could be any time,' she said.

'I know that. I want to know when you think.'

'Not today,' she said.

'Really? You think it's going to run into tomorrow?'

'I'm sure of it.'

She had said this to annoy Kenneally, but as soon as she had spoken the words, she realised that she believed them to be true. It was something to do with the changes in gear that the players were making – because Bridges had adjusted now to Gottschalk's passive-aggressive style, and was mirroring it back at him, gathering more chips, which meant that Gottschalk had had to loosen up again in response, and there was an intimacy between these two players that was growing, and which wouldn't be content with a speedy ending.

If the blinds had risen at every break that would have changed the rhythm of things, but as it was, the players continued to play and the dealer continued to deal, without respite apart from the scheduled breaks, until ten in the evening, when Bridges had little more than a slight lead and the game was suspended until noon on the following day.

As Day 2 was about to begin, Bridges reached across to shake his opponent's hand, a gesture that surprised Gottschalk but then he grabbed hold of Bridges's hand with both of his and energetically shook it up and down.

Play at first was tentative. Maybe they were tired. According to Tambini, Bridges had spent the night playing baccarat at the Ritz in the company of Xi Tianxi. Chips passed in small amounts back and forth. Nothing decisive occurred or threatened to. Gottschalk's father dozed in the front row, with his hands folded over the belly bulge of his Metallica T-shirt.

And then came the big hand. Gottschalk raised pre-flop, Bridges re-raised and Gottschalk called. One of the chips from his call, an orange 500, rolled on its side away from the rest on a stuttering lonely route. Wendy had to stretch to gather it in, and this was, she realised, the first time that she had had to do so, and she wondered if she would ever have an opportunity to thank the players for their good manners. Bridges checked the flop, Gottschalk bet, and Bridges called. Both players checked the turn. Bridges led out on the river and for the first time in the match, Gottschalk delayed his action.

Bridges leant back against his chair. He riffled some chips together, clacking two stacks into one with thumb and little finger opposed. He stared at his opponent all the while. Gottschalk was looking down, his elbows on the table, his hands clasped into fists supporting his face, pushing his narrow cheeks into little pouches. His body swayed to a rhythm discernible to no one else in the room, or, maybe, just perceptible to his opponent.

He must have felt the force of his opponent's attention upon him, which would have devoured a weaker man. He dwelled up, he hesitated, he dwelled up some more. Wendy had gathered the unused cards in the deck. She had nothing left to do. She imagined a soothing blue light moving up from the base of her spine that would radiate out, making the bad red light at the top of the spine shrink and fade and disappear.

And Gottschalk went all in. Decisively, he pushed all

his chips towards the middle and crossed his arms and stared at the table.

Now it was Bridges's turn to dwell up. Kenneally, who must have had some instinct for catastrophe and triumph, was standing behind her. He placed both his hands meatily on her shoulders.

'Is this it?'

'It could be,' she said. She didn't want it to be over.

The board was 4-5-8-J-K. It was the eight of hearts that had hit on the river, making a flush available as well as a straight. She guessed that Gottschalk had the straight – 6-7 was the sort of hand he liked to play – and the decision he had been struggling over was whether Bridges had the flush. With the flush, even a low one, Bridges surely would have called straight away. Or maybe Gottschalk would have bet the same way with the nut flush, to entice a call. Eventually, reluctantly, Bridges tossed his cards into the muck.

'Nice hand,' he said.

'Thank you,' Gottschalk said, building his chip stack into high towers.

Gottschalk now had the lead. He went to work at increasing it, but Bridges fought back, fighting for every pot, scrapping for every chip.

She watched the hand replayed during the lunch break. It was nothing like she'd pictured: Bridges had a very thin piece of the board; with A-8, he had been contemplating calling the all in with third pair. And Gottschalk, with 2-3 of diamonds, had absolutely nothing. He'd made the bluff with the nut low.

Bridges had known. He'd heard the rhythm that

Gottschalk was moving to. But he hadn't been able to act on his knowledge. There had been just enough uncertainty to prevent him from making the hero call and winning the match.

Bridges and Gottschalk were watching the replay too, from opposite ends of the room with plates of food balanced on their knees.

Kenneally was in conference with Tambini. Wendy joined them.

'We need another dealer,' she said.

'You quitting?'

'No, but the way this is going, it's too much for one person. You'll need two dealers to alternate.'

'We'll raise the blinds.'

'Can we do that?' Tambini said.

'I'm not paying for another day of this.'

'Check with Robinson, but the rules I think say the two players have to agree to any change in conditions.'

'Well, we're going to have to make sure they do, then, aren't we.'

Gottschalk didn't mind. Bridges did.

'It's just starting to get interesting,' he said.

Kenneally asked Gottschalk to persuade Bridges.

'He would listen to you, I'm sure of it.'

'He doesn't want the blinds to be bigger?'

'But unless they are, this might run on for another day. We're not sure if we can hire the venue, and the TV people and so forth. So we thought you might have a word with him.'

'If he doesn't want the blinds to be bigger then neither do I.'

'Well, thank you, thank you very much,' Kenneally said.

The contest resumed, and the players were finding new ways to excel. Play was aggressive, ferocious, and elegant. Wendy had never seen poker played as well as this, and in such a sustained way. Sometimes, the action went to too dizzying a level for her to entirely comprehend what she had just witnessed – it was intimate, extraordinary, like watching two great minds opening up to each other in public.

Kenneally had to rent the venue for a third day, and most of the TV crew.

'Just to hire these lights is killing us,' he said. 'But here,' he said, passing over a watch to Wendy, and pulling down his shirt sleeve. 'A bonus.'

Wendy went to the Ritz hoping to find Bridges there, and she did see Xi Tianxi at the high-stakes baccarat table, but Xi was gambling there alone.

Watching the TV crew set up for the day, Tambini told her Kenneally's latest idea.

'He wants to ask you to work out a way to stack the deck, deal them a cooler, you know? Kings versus aces, straight flush against quads, that kind of thing.'

'I didn't hear you say that.'

'I said, he's going to ask—'

'I know. I heard. It's a figure of speech.'

'I know that. I was making a joke. But he's desperate.'

'I thought this was what he wanted to demonstrate? Poker, the ultimate game of skill.'

'No one wants an event that goes on for ever.'

No one, that is, apart from the players. It wasn't that they soft-played each other, Bridges was as aggressive as ever, Gottschalk as analytically ferocious. Each was playing to win. When the lunch break came, they both made small sighs of disappointment.

'We're going to have to downsize,' Kenneally said.

Day 4 took place in Bridges's suite. The players sat on sky-blue upholstered low chairs with frilly silk skirts at a bridge table that the hotel provided. To make way for the lights and the camera, the rest of the furniture was moved the other side of the dividing doors into the bedroom.

Day 5 was also in Bridges's suite.

'Doesn't anyone have somewhere else to go?' Kenneally said.

He had called a meeting after Day 5 had wrapped up.

'Look, why don't we split the prize money equally? Declare a draw. This has been fabulous, there's been all kind of press attention. Both of you I know have been offered new sponsorship deals. It's win-win-win.'

Bridges shook his head.

'We play on,' he said.

'Rainer?'

'What Mike says,' he said.

'Tambini?'

'There's nothing in the rules about us being able to call a premature halt. Natural disaster or act of God only. Maybe you'll get lucky.'

'There's no such thing as luck,' Kenneally said glumly.

Wendy did wonder, on a rain-stormy Day 6, when Kenneally disappeared for a large part of it, whether

130

he had worked out a way to harness lightning or flood. But Day 6 concluded with Bridges having regained the chip lead and no natural or unnatural disasters having afflicted the hotel.

'Look,' Kenneally said, 'why don't we declare a draw and give you both the winner's prize money? I think Robinson has found some wiggle room with the sponsors. We can make this happen. Guys?'

Bridges and Gottschalk didn't have to look at each other to agree upon their answer. They both shook their heads, at the same time.

'You don't really understand much, do you, Mr Kenneally?' Bridges said.

The hotels were downsized after Day 7.

Day 8 was a rest day. Wendy lay on her bed for the first part of it, listening to the sounds her flatmates made preparing for work and then the noises that the street made, which she had never heard before. She took a shower. She picked up her white shirts and black trousers and waistcoat from the dry cleaners. Her shoulders and wrists burned. The vertebrae in her neck felt as if they were becoming unmoored from the spine. In the evening she went out for dinner with Bridges.

She told him some things about herself, because she chose to interpret his silent attention upon her as curiosity. She listed some of the things she hated about poker players. She thanked him for his good manners at the table.

'No one's splashed the pot, there's been no grandstanding or Hollywooding, your manners have been impeccable.'

'If you hate poker players so much, you should get away from us.'

'Probably. I should go back to university. Finish my degree ...'

'Or?'

'Maybe become a poker player myself.'

'Why would you want to do that?'

'Because I think I might be good at it. Maybe one day I'll be brave enough to try. What about you? What would you have done if you hadn't found poker?'

'I don't know. Maybe something with real estate? Is that not a good answer?'

'No, it's not that. I just thought you'd say philosopher or monk or assassin or something like that.'

And then he turned the conversation to some of the more notable hands of the previous day.

At the end of the evening, as she was about to step into the cab he had ordered for her, he told her that she had very nice hair, which was said, she thought, in lieu of a goodnight kiss.

Day 9 took place in a corner of the poker room at the Victoria Grosvenor casino on the Edgware Road. A red velvet rope cordoned off the area of play from spectators and slot machines. The cameraman was a friend of one of Kenneally's children from film school. He was cultivating a moustache or maybe he had never shaved.

Day 10 continued at the Vic. The event had gathered to it its own devotees of bloggers and enthusiasts. The TV interest had long ago abated, and most of Gottschalk's original retinue, including his father, had returned home, to Weimar and Leipzig and Dresden, but others had replaced them. They also wore heavy metal T-shirts and denim jackets. Xi Tianxi had gone back to Geneva, and sometimes Mike Bridges would remain at the casino after the contest had finished for the day, and play a few rounds of baccarat, but he preferred to eat Japanese food with Gottschalk and to return to the small room that Kenneally was now renting for him.

Before play began, the opponents always greeted each other with their traditional double-hand clasp and the warmest of smiles.

On Day 12, their spot was occupied by a craps table. The cameraman was there, looking disconsolate.

Wendy called Kenneally but neither he nor Tambini were answering their phones.

'We'll find somewhere else,' Bridges said.

Days 12, 13 and 14 took place in an upstairs room of a pub decorated with pictures of race horses and World War II fighter planes.

Day 15 was a rest day.

Day 16 was conducted in transit: a train from St Pancras to Paris; a second train to Frankfurt; a third to Leipzig. Bridges had never been to Germany, and Gottschalk was keen to show him some of the sights he had grown up with.

Wendy saw them off from Paris. She contemplated dropping the watch she wore into the hat of a busker ineptly playing an accordion in the Metro, but decided she had earned it. Maybe she would use the money the players had tipped her with to stay over in Paris for a few days. There was a card room that had used to be the

Aviators' club on the Champs d'Elysées that she went to, thinking she might pick up a couple of casual shifts. As she waited for the manager to return she joined a no-limit cash game at the 1-2 table.

If there had been one thing that she had learned from her time as a dealer, it was that Kenneally was right about luck, and yet, throughout her session at the 1-2 table, and then 2-5, it was as if her recent proximity to Bridges and Gottschalk had touched her with some wild charm.

The session was close to miraculous. She heard, at least for a while, the rhythm that Gottschalk moved to.

She didn't see Kenneally again, but she heard that the Federation had folded. One night in the card room in Paris, she caught sight of a photograph of Robinson on a news programme, projected behind the head of the presenter, but the sound was down and she never learned what he was said to have done or to have had done to him.

And nor did she see Gottschalk or Bridges again. There were supposed sightings of them, in Munich, Leipzig, Warsaw, Vienna. Someone who called himself Mike Bridges entered two Omaha events at that year's WSOP but didn't arrive to claim his place. Gottschalk's online avatar went broke, but it turned out that it was his father who had been playing.

She heard rumours that the contest had finally ended in a bar in Kathmandu called The String of Pearls. In this version, Gottschalk had won, and returned home to Germany, where he was studying chess and karate, while Bridges had entered a Buddhist monastery.

Or the bar was in fact in Moscow, or Milan, or in one

of the Florida Keys – and it was only in the last of these that Bridges was said to have won.

Once, Tambini materialised behind her during a tournament she had come over for at the Vic. She was making a bet, moving her chips towards the dealer, when she had to shrug a hand away from her shoulder. She looked up, away from her opponent, and closed her mouth, which she sometimes left open as a sort of private joke, or act of homage.

'I'm working for a new Federation now,' Tambini told her.

She was more interested in the news he had of the latest sighting: in a café in Kinshasa an obese German had been seen with a slim older American gambling at cards that people thought might be Gottschalk and Bridges, perpetually at play.

Primero Face

by Anthony Holden

It was a bold bet, quite out of character – deliberately so, of course. Normally I play as tight as a nun's whatsit, as dear old Alvarez used to say in the long-lost days of the Tuesday Night Game. Now, first to act, I've bet the max. It's a rash move, I know; OK, I've been dealt pocket queens, but the board is showing a king and an ace. I am all too aware of the whole table staring at me, sizing me up, looking for a nervous tell. It's not like me to play loose-aggressive – if that is what I've just done. I'm not sure. I never am. I have no idea if this was a super-cool move, or a super-dumb one.

But I'm surely about to find out. Don't speak, I remind myself. Don't look anxious. At the same time, though, don't look too confident. Don't look anything.

I had raised before the flop, naturally, and the first two players folded. Now I raise merely my eyebrows as the next two seats also fold, then look down the other end of the table to find myself caught like a terrified rabbit in the stare of the most elegant pair of all-seeing, all-knowing Elizabethan eyes.

'Thou wretched, rash, intruding fool ...' he intones, with a mischievous grin all over his scarily intelligent face. Oh shit, methinks he's got a king. Or an ace. Or both. Or even a pair of either. He's going to raise the bejesus out of me.

I try to maintain eye-contact of an unflinching order as he openly re-checks his cards while idly riffling his chips. Then he scratches his beard and opens his mouth, as if to speak, and I grow ever more determined to make no response, to give nothing away. Eventually, with a rueful smile, he says simply '... farewell!' – and slides his cards into the muck.

Will Shakespeare has just been toying with me. Now the fidgety adolescent to his left says 'Pooh!' He scratches under his wig and adds: 'Pooh and double-pooh!' Then he too, with a ferocious fart, folds. Respect from Wolfgang Amadeus Mozart!

Last to act, or the pot is mine, is (appropriately enough) the supreme actor of the twentieth century. If anyone could simulate to maximum effect, you would think, it is he. He muses a while, still scanning my desperately twitchy visage, and finally says in a mildly aggressive, self-satisfied monotone, as if it were blindingly obvious: 'Raise!'

He doubles my bet.

That's all? Not much of a raise. It's thirty years since I wrote his biography, but I don't remember Laurence Olivier – Lord Olivier, to you and me – ever having played poker. He may well have risked the odd backstage hand with chums like Ralphy Richardson and Johnny Gielgud; but he knows nothing at all, I'm sure, about this level of game. He was even asking me dumb questions about bluff amid the small talk as we settled into our seats a few hours back. Olivier is most himself, what's more, when pretending to be someone else. When playing himself, as now, he is really not very convincing.

After appearing to think for an Oscar-winning pause, staring him down the while, I reply without (I am proud to report) the slightest quaver in my voice: 'All in!'

As I push my pile of chips into the centre of the table – the first 'shove' of the evening – Olivier suddenly looks revealingly downcast. Or is he now acting for real? Uneasily I remember that he won his own Oscars, for *Henry V* and *Hamlet*, when he had barely turned forty. Could I have misread him? Does he indeed have a king or an ace, and wanted to stop this hand right here?

No, it turns out. 'Fold,' he eventually shrugs, showing us all pocket nines.

The whole table exchange pained glances as I haul in the pot, with my wilfully infuriating mantra: 'Come to Grandpa!' (It used to be 'Come to Daddy!', but time's wingèd chariot has been moving on rather swiftly of late). So now I'm chip leader, maybe even table boss.

Rashly, no doubt, I feel like I've got the measure of these players. After all, I have written books about all of them; I probably know more about them, I reflect cockily, than they do themselves. And they know little or nothing of me. Most of them, after all, have actually been dead quite a while, which must surely give me something of an edge?

All but one, who is next to act. He's been acting pretty haughty all evening, as if put out to be here. Inspecting his hole cards rather clumsily, like a man used to others doing this sort of thing for him, he agonises in his oddly whiny voice, with its strangled vowel sounds, before wondering aloud: 'To bet or not to bet?'

His obsequious glance over to Shakespeare is met with a dark, disapproving glare. Charles, Prince of Wales turns away in embarrassment, and muses: 'Oh, this is simply *appalling* – even more agonising than that haunting passage in Berlioz's *Symphony Fantastique*.' Mozart looks puzzled. 'Or *Erbarme dich* from Bach's St Matthew Passion.' Now Mozart nods approvingly; that he appears to know.

'Put the clock on him,' I hear myself saying rather brusquely – which the floor manager, who bears an uncanny resemblance to the Grim Reaper, is summoned to explain to HRH. Evidently unused to being barked at by anyone, let alone told to get on with it, Charles sulkily just flat-calls.

Unhappily for them, if not for the rest of us, the draw for seats has placed the prince next to his ex-wife. With a withering sideways glance at him, Diana promptly triples his bet. She doesn't even check her hand before doing so. She knows what she's doing, this girl, I think as I promptly, discreetly, re-inspect my own while no one's looking. Yes, 7-2, as I had feared. Shakespeare calls; Mozart folds; Olivier calls; I shoot Diana an approving smile, and throw away my cards.

The turn brings a low spade, so no one can be pulling to a flush. With 5h-6c-10d-3s showing, a gutshot straight draw is possible, if a long shot. But this is scarcely the

World Series, where veteran pros can improvise moves which make such things look hauntingly plausible. These rank amateurs (among whom I count myself) can pull such things off only by dint of freakish luck. 'You know,' I hear Leigh Hunt saying beside me, 'the more I practise, the luckier I seem to get!'

He promptly re-raises. Poet, critic, editor, patron and friend of Keats and Shelley, Hunt was jailed in 1813 for insulting the then Prince of Wales, the Prince Regent who went on to become King George IV. An irate Charles seems aware of this. Can he have read my biography, *The Wit in the Dungeon* (the title conferred on Hunt by his sometime friend Byron), or is that kind of knowledge a standard slice of the royal DNA?

'You always were an irritating little man, Hunt,' he tells him testily, before nodding towards his cards, for his attendant footman to pass them back to the dealer.

And so to Diana, who pouts winsomely. 'Ay me,' she laments, 'what to do?' With a sigh, and another winning 'Ay, ay me', she flat-calls.

'The lady doth protest too much, methinks,' intones the Bard, and re-raises. The entire table folds, and he pulls in a hefty pot.

'What did you have?' Mozart saucily asks him.

'The rest,' replies Shakespeare, 'is silence.'

On my side of Charles, with Hunt safely between us, sits the mass poisoner Graham Young, whose trial in St Albans I covered as a rookie journalist on the local paper – gathering enough material for a true-crime book, later filmed as *The Young Poisoner's Handbook*. I'm mighty relieved not to be sitting next to him; this man could extract poison from a stone. That's why I declined all his many invitations to visit him in prison for a cup of tea. All evening I've been keeping a very close eye on the glass of vintage claret beside me.

During his trial the psychopathic Young – born the same year as me, so then twenty-four years old – sent me a note across the courtroom expressing the hope that my work would see him go down in criminal history as one of its most notorious serial killers, thus winning his rightful place in the Chamber of Horrors at Madame Tussauds.

Both wishes have long since been granted. So now, with a satanic smile, he seems ready to return the favour. Jerking his thumb in Charles's direction, while HRH is looking the other way, delivering more orders to his footman, Young taps his nose with his forefinger and whispers across Hunt: 'You're a republican, aren't you? I've read all your books . . .'

'Yes, but . . .'

'Is the monarchy *really* still going?' Hunt interrupts. 'The immortal Bard himself was a republican, weren't you, Will?' Hunt quotes *Julius Caesar*:

I had as lief not be
As live to be in awe
Of such a thing as I myself.

Shakespeare smiles indulgently, and Diana applauds with a grin while beside her Charles looks distinctly unamused. Young has meanwhile interposed his body between Hunt and the prince, so I can't see what he's up to. Still he has his back to me when suddenly it's my turn to act. Shakespeare has raised. 'A modest raise,' quoth he, 'perhaps even an ill-favoured raise, but mine own.'

Out of the corner of my eye I notice Charles sipping his martini. But I cannot let that distract me now. 'Call,' I eventually blurt, somewhat to my own surprise. The flop has brought 7c-9h-10h, and I have 4h-Jh. I badly need a heart, or an eight or a queen, but the turn brings the ace of clubs. Shakespeare bets the pot. He must have another ace, I decide, and/or a club or two.

In mid-conversation both Mozart and Olivier fold, the latter absurdly asking the former if he ever knew Peter Shaffer. All eyes are now on me.

While I sit motionless, deep in the tank, Shakespeare intones: 'γνῶθι σεαυτόν.'

The table is a sea of blank faces.

'Gnothi seauton,' I transliterate helpfully for them. '"Know thyself." The Delphic oracle. So much for Ben Jonson's taunt about "small Latin and less Greek"!'

'It's all Greek to me!' quips Olivier.

'Now you're quoting our friend here again,' I tell His Lordship. 'Also *Julius Caesar*. Casca to Cassius. Surely you remember that?'

'Never played Casca. I think, when playing Caesar, I was offstage at the time.'

'But Brutus ...'

'Oh, do get on with it,' Mozart intervenes. 'I have no idea what you two are on about. And we haven't got all ...' – he gestures to the expectant conductor behind him – 'all night!' The casino Big Band strikes up *Eine kleine Nachtmusik*.

'No music during play!' barks the floor manager.

'Oh, I was enjoying that,' laments the Bard. 'One of yours, Wolfgang?'

'Yes, indeed, one of his mighty output!' cries a late arrival who has finally turned up, it seems, just at the right moment. 'An honour to meet you, maestro. I'm a great admirer. My name is Pyotr Ilyich Tchaikovsky.' He pulls up a chair between Mozart and Olivier.

The band strikes up the *1812 Overture*, before being silenced again by the Grim Reaper. 'A pleasure to meet you all, whoever most of you may be!' smiles Tchaikovsky. 'This looks a bit like vint. I was a dab hand at that! Bit of an obsessive, actually.'

Again all the other players look flummoxed. 'A Russian variant of whist,' I fill them in. 'Pyotr here was obsessed with it. Cost him a lot of money, actually ...'

Everyone suddenly perks up. 'Are you ever going to play, Holden?' snaps Mozart. His Italian librettist Lorenze da Ponte, through whom I first met Amadeus, told me he could be like this. 'You're about as much use as da Ponte when that Jewish-born Catholic priest was down on his luck, playing his violin in his monk's habit in a Venetian brothel!'

'But he lived to be ninety, Wolfgang,' I can't resist replying. 'Emigrated to the new-born United States. Died in a place called New York.'

Mozart again points testily at the pot. Amid all this chatter, I'd quite forgotten the action is on me.

I flick away my cards. Shakespeare scoops in another handsome pot.

*

144

At this point Camilla, Duchess of Cornwall leads all the other molls back from their break in the bar. At the sight of Camilla, who brazenly flaunts her wedding ring, Diana seems ready to go on tilt; but her acute sense of public relations will surely come to her rescue. Anne Hathaway and Constanze Mozart embrace their husbands affectionately, but Vivien Leigh and Joan Plowright start a ferocious row behind Olivier, all but clawing each other's eyes out – to the point where the Grim Reaper is again obliged to intervene, moving them all to a safe distance.

'Thank God mine didn't turn up,' mutters Tchaikovsky, no doubt remembering his suicide attempt three weeks after marrying one of his students, in a vain attempt to hide the fact that he was gay. 'My poor Marianne will be sick, or busy with our ten children,' sighs Hunt. Neither of mine has shown, either, for all Cindy's delight in playing 'The Moll' in my book *Big Deal*. Just as well. With immortality at stake here, as the Reaper keeps reminding us, I've got to concentrate.

The next hand brings the first elimination. In prime position Shakespeare again raises before the flop – too much for Mozart, Tchaikovsky, Olivier and myself (another seven-deuce) – but Hunt decides to take him on. 'You are undoubtedly the finest writer who ever lived,' declares the Bard of Horsemonger Lane, 'but you're a really lousy poker-player, Will. Far too loose. No doubt bluffing half the time. But now you've met your match, O great one. All-in go I!'

'What the dickens?' harrumphs Olivier. Hunt shudders at the name, remembering how cruelly he was lampooned as Harold Skimpole in *Bleak House*.

'No, not *that* Dickens,' I reassure him, feeling for this vulnerable man's still raw sense of injustice. '*Merry Wives of Windsor*. Three hundred years before Jarndyce-v-Jarndyce and all that. The sixteenth-century Dickens was a maker of wooden bowls who just couldn't help losing money . . .'

Whoops. Not, perhaps, the perfect moment to draw that parallel. The Bard looks at me as if I'm giving him some sort of clue. Hunt is on my left, after all; can I have caught a glimpse of his hole cards? No, methinks – well, mehopes – that Will knows even I would never stoop so low. But he's definitely got some sort of vibe from my burst of Shakespeareana.

'Call!' he cries, and stands up, rolling over pocket kings.

'The game is up!' retorts Hunt – knowing he is quoting his opponent's *Cymbeline* – and flips pocket aces.

Oh no, we're not going to lose the Bard, are we? All my life I've ached for the chance to meet him, ask him a bottomless pit of questions. The Grim Reaper – for he himself steps in to deal such potentially terminal hands – burns the top card and rolls . . .

A-K-J. Hunt fist-pumps. Calmly, a resigned Shakespeare begins to gather up his ruff and quill pens. The turn brings an irrelevant deuce, the river . . . the quad king.

Hunt slumps back into his seat in disbelief. Even the Bard looks pretty startled, and makes his elegant way around the table past Charles and Di to commiserate on the bad beat of the evening. Poor Hunt: luck was never exactly, I reflect, his middle name. He shakes hands with Shakespeare, evidently used to this sort of thing, and declares: 'I leave you more in sorrow than in anger.'

'That's *Hamlet*!' cries Olivier.

'Yes,' replies Hunt. 'And now I am naught but that ghost ...' With which he bows to all and retires gracefully from the fray, heading straight for the free buffet.

Mozart looks baffled. Tchaikovsky's face shines with admiration. Charles and Di are still bickering. Graham Young gives me a sly look. Says Olivier of Hunt, with due solemnity: 'Nothing in his game became him like the leaving it.'

As Shakespeare resumes his seat, hauling in the pot of the night, the whole table around him begins to talk at once – to the point where I can hear only snatches: 'He's vanished into thin air' ... 'played fast and loose' ... 'more sinned against than sinning' ... 'refused to budge an inch' ... 'insisted on fair play' ... 'a tower of strength' ... 'in a pickle' ... 'hoodwinked' ... 'tongue-tied' ... 'short shrift' ... 'cold comfort' ... 'too much of a good thing' ... 'seen better days' ... 'stood on ceremony' ... 'danced attendance upon him' ... 'in a fool's paradise' ... 'it was high time' ... 'the long and the short of it' ... 'he won't sleep a wink' ... 'knitted his brows' ... 'made a virtue of necessity' ... 'green-eyed jealousy' ... 'his wish was father to the thought' ... 'I laughed myself into stitches' ...

The Bard looks at me conspiratorially. I smile back warmly; yes, I know what he knows. As the Reaper's angry calls for silence finally calm the hubbub, there follows a moment of shaken calm, into which I announce to all and sundry: 'None of you knows it, but every word you just said comes from Shakespeare.'

Charles slumps in his seat.

'Surely,' says the Bard with a smile, 'it wasn't all *that* bad?'

Looking pleased with himself, Graham Young gets up and declares he must go to the bathroom.

'No!' I say in alarm. 'The poisoned cup. It is too late!'

'I know what you mean,' says Shakespeare, grimacing. 'Not one of my best lines. Actors tell me it is cringe-making to deliver. Too melodramatic. Stating the obvious. Not like me. Even worse than Lady Macbeth's "What, in *our* house?"'

'No!' I yell again. 'Young has slipped something into Charles's martini ...'

Paramedics are summoned, but it doesn't look good. As HRH is borne off on a stretcher, the deceased at the table start asking about the succession.

'It'll be my Will!' shrieks Diana. 'I must go and phone him ...'

Shakespeare looks perplexed.

As she departs, Di whispers into my ear: 'See you later in the Sinatra bar ...'

She never comes back. Nor does Young.

Suddenly we are down to five. The Grim Reaper is about to distribute black armbands, just in case, when news arrives that Charles has been resuscitated. Mozart and Tchaikovsky have declined them, anyway, saying they've no idea who Charles is, and they're getting rather bored. They've never played this game before, and still don't understand it.

'It takes a moment to learn,' I tell them unoriginally, 'and a lifetime to master.'

But no, it seems, these two would rather talk music. So off they go, too, taking the Big Band with them. The Reaper directs them towards the casino's showroom. Part of me wishes I could go with them; it sounds like a helluva floor-show.

As it is, Olivier and I look respectfully towards Shakespeare.

'When shall we three meet again?' asks Larry.

For once, I know whereof he speaks.

'When the hurly-burly's done,' I muse. 'When the battle's lost and won.'

'That,' we all say in unison, 'will be ere the set of sun.'

Which seems to settle that, so we hunker down to play on.

It doesn't take long to eliminate Larry, who has one last thing he wants to say before he leaves. 'I know most of your lines have passed into history, Will, but Charles there reminded me of a literary reference no one else has ever noticed.'

Olivier looks at me. 'You of all people know that, when Charles and Diana announced their engagement, they were asked on TV if they were in love. Diana promptly said "Of course!" and Charles said ...?'

'Whatever love means,' I sigh, wondering where he is going with this.

'Exactly,' says Larry. 'And do you know I said those very same words only some twenty-odd years before, as Archie Rice in *The Entertainer*? John Osborne?'

Shakespeare looks at me inquiringly.

'Significant mid-twentieth-century playwright,' I tell him. 'Pioneered what they called kitchen-sink drama. A bit like your tavern scenes. Falstaff and Mistress Quickly, Doll Tearsheet in the Boar's Head – that sort of thing. Slices of real life.'

Now he's getting interested. But again the Reaper intervenes.

'Gentlemen, we are now heads-up. There is no prize for second place. The winner will live for ever!'

Larry wants to stay and watch, but he is told that no spectators are allowed – apart from some guy called Faust, with whom the prize apparently involves some sort of pact. 'Ah, yes,' says Shakespeare, 'Kit Marlowe told me all about him.'

The Bard and I will now be escorted to a *salle privée* for the solemn denouement. So Olivier wishes us both luck, and reluctantly takes his leave – with a seriously redundant 'Exit pursued by bear!' We both groan.

'Of all men else, I have avoided thee,' I quip to Shakespeare.

'May I call you Will?' I ask him respectfully as we follow the Reaper into the casino's V-V-VIP zone.

'Feel free, Antonio,' he smiles graciously.

'Will, how did you learn to play poker so well? It wasn't even invented in your day . . .'

'Ahah!' says he. 'Have you never heard of primero?'

'I've heard of it – even seen paintings of some of your contemporaries playing it – not least Milord Burleigh – but I don't know much about it.'

'But you seem quite familiar with my work. Any references?'

'Well, of course, your Henry VIII plays primero with his brother-in-law, the Duke of Suffolk. And in *Merry Wives*, in the Garter Inn, Falstaff says "I never prospered since I forswore myself at primero". But ...'

'Do you remember that Lancelot Gobbo, in my *Merchant*, confides in his father that "For mine own part, as I have set up my rest to run away, so I will not rest till I have run some ground"?'

'Vaguely ... that line's usually cut these days ... but ...'

'To "set up your rest" was a gambler's manoeuvre in the Italian version of primero,' he continues. 'The groundlings loved that line!'

Will goes on to explain that primero originated in Europe at the beginning of the sixteenth century. The Tudors really took to it. Henry VIII's daughter Mary – that same 'Bloody Mary' who married the King of Spain, thus helping to popularise the game in England – was constantly diverting funds 'for the playe at cardes'. Elizabethan paintings show large piles of cash on the table, mostly gold and silver.

Will has even heard primero called 'the mother of poker', but he had never known what was meant by 'poker'. Until now. 'The playing cards were just as they are today, but longer and thinner, with plain white backs. Primero was played with only four cards in a hand, but all the principles – flush, straight, etc. – are exactly the same as poker. It didn't take me long to catch on!'

He stops and turns to me: 'You seem to know your *Cymbeline*. Remember what the First Lord says to the wretched Cloten, to which he replies: "It would make any man cold to lose"?'

This time, I'm stumped. So he helps me out: 'Your lordship is the most patient man in loss, the most coldest that ever turned up ace.'

The Bard himself was always a bit of a gambler, of course, in life as in art. I'm tempted to ask him if he's read *Big Deal*, but for once rein myself in. He tells me that versions of primero are still played today around central Europe, especially in Spain and Italy, under such names as *goffo* or *bambara*. But the original version he knew eventually gave way to a game called Trump. 'Especially in the New World,' he laughs. We both grimace. 'As for that hideous new coinage "Brexit" . . .'

'Come on, you two!' The Grim Reaper is again losing patience with our banter.

Well, it's not every day you get the chance to table-talk with the Swan of Avon – or indeed to meet the self-styled 'Doctor' Faust, who turns out to be the casino's owner, oozing hollow charm. He reminds me of Mozart's dastardly Don Giovanni.

'Viva la liberta!' I cry, but neither of them seems to get the reference. Beneath me, nevertheless, I can feel a heat as raging as the flames of hellfire. Under-floor heating, it strikes me, seems somewhat redundant here in 120-degree Vegas.

As Will and I settle down to our monumental heads-up, and I put on my best primero face, even I know which one of us deserves immortality – already, indeed, enjoys it – and for once it sure ain't me.

But I'm not going to throw this game, not even out of respect for my revered 'rude groom' of Stratford. Fiercely competitive as we both are, we play on deep into the night, to the point where I even forget about my date with Di.

'Diana?' says Will, when I mention it. 'To Di, to sleep, perchance to dream ...'

That last word finally jolts me awake. As always, the Bard has hit upon *le mot juste*. Dreaming – that's what I've been doing all this time, dammit, in spectacularly lurid fashion, not without troublingly egomaniac undertones. Aye, there's the rub.

As I begin to drift inexorably downwards, even the roar of infernal flames cannot drown out Will's touching farewell: 'We are such stuff as dreams are made on, and our little life is rounded with a sleep.'

Mrs Beast

from *The World's Wife*
by Carol Ann Duffy

These myths going round, these legends,
        fairytales,
I'll put them straight; so when you stare
Into my face – Helen's face, Cleopatra's,
Queen of Sheba's, Juliet's – then, deeper,
Gaze into my eyes – Nefertiti's, Mona Lisa's,
Garbo's eyes – think again. The Little
        Mermaid slit
Her shining, silver tail in two, rubbed salt
Into that stinking wound, got up and walked,
In agony, in fishnet tights, stood up and
        smiled, waltzed,
All for a Prince, a pretty boy, a charming one
Who'd dump her in the end, chuck her, throw
        her overboard.
I could have told her – look, love, I should
        know,

They're bastards when they're Princes.
What you want to do is find yourself a beast.
    The sex

Is better. Myself, I came to the House of the
    Beast
No longer a girl, knowing my own mind,
My own gold stashed in the bank,
My own black horse at the gates
Ready to carry me off at one wrong word,
One false move, one dirty look.
But the Beast fell to his knees at the door
To kiss my glove with his mongrel
    lips – good –
Showed by the tears in his bloodshot eyes
That he knew he was blessed – better –
Didn't try to conceal his erection,
Size of a mule's – best. And the Beast
Watched me open, decant and quaff
A bottle of Château Margaux '54,
The year of my birth, before he lifted a paw.

I'll tell you more. Stripped of his muslin shirt
And his corduroys, he steamed in his pelt,
Ugly as sin. He had the grunts, the groans, the
    yelps,
The breath of a goat. I had the language, girls.
The lady says Do this. Harder. The lady says
Do that. Faster. The lady says That's not
    where I meant.
At last it all made sense. The pig in my bed

Was invited. And if his snout and trotters
    fouled
My damask sheets, why, then, he'd wash
    them. Twice.
Meantime, here was his horrid leather tongue
To scour between my toes. Here
Were his hooked and yellowy claws to pick
    my nose,
If I wanted that. Or to scratch my back
Till it bled. Here was his bullock's head
To sing off-key all night where I couldn't hear.
Here was a bit of him like a horse, a ram,
An ape, a wolf, a dog, a donkey, dragon,
    dinosaur.

Need I say more? On my poker nights, the
    Beast
Kept out of sight. We were a hard school,
    tough as fuck,
All of us beautiful and rich – the Woman
Who Married a Minotaur, Goldilocks, the
    Bride
Of the Bearded Lesbian, Frau Yellow Dwarf,
    et Moi.
I watched those wonderful women shuffle and
    deal –
Five and Seven Card Stud, Sidewinder, Hold
    'Em, Draw –

I watched them bet and raise and call. One
    night,

A head-to-head between Frau Yellow Dwarf
    and Bearded's Bride
Was over the biggest pot I'd seen in my puff.
The Frau had the Queen of Clubs on the baize
And Bearded the Queen of Spades. Final card.
    Queen each.
Frau Yellow raised. Bearded raised.
    Goldilocks' eyes
Were glued to the pot as though porridge
    bubbled there.
The Minotaur's wife lit a stinking cheroot.
    Me,
I noticed the Frau's hand shook as she placed
    her chips.
Bearded raised her final time, then stared,
Stared so hard you felt your dress would melt
If she blinked. I held my breath. Frau Yellow
Swallowed hard, then called. Sure enough,
    Bearded flipped
Her Aces over; diamonds, hearts, the pubic
    Ace of Spades.
And that was a lesson learnt by all of us –
The drop-dead gorgeous Bride of the Bearded
    Lesbian didn't bluff.

But behind each player stood a line of ghosts
Unable to win. Eve, Ashputtel. Marilyn
    Monroe.
Rapunzel slashing wildly at her hair.
Bessie Smith unloved and down and out.
Bluebeard's wives, Henry VIII's, Snow White

Cursing the day she left the seven dwarfs,
    Diana,
Princess of Wales. The sheepish Beast came in
With a tray of schnapps at the end of the game
And we stood for the toast – *Fay Wray* –
Then tossed our fiery drinks to the back of
    our crimson throats.
Bad girls. Serious ladies. Mourning our dead.

So I was hard on the Beast, win or lose,
When I got upstairs, those tragic girls in my
    head,
Turfing him out of bed; standing alone
On the balcony, the night so cold I could taste
    the stars
On the tip of my tongue. And I made a prayer –
Thumbing my pearls, the tears of Mary, one
    by one,
Like a rosary – words for the lost, the captive
    beautiful,
The wives, those less fortunate than we.
The moon was a hand-mirror breathed on by
    a Queen.
My breath was a chiffon scarf for an elegant
    ghost.
I turned to go back inside. Bring me the Beast
    for the night.
Bring me the wine-cellar key. Let the less-
    loving one be me.

A Devil In New Jersey

by Michael Craig

I.

Lenore was a prisoner of Atlantic City. For two days, confined to her hotel room, her world had shrunk to a handful of text messages from a professional poker player named Jonah Ashburn.

Her relationship with Jonah defied easy description. She had been referred to him by a mid-sized LA law firm for whom she freelanced occasionally. For the firm, it was a chance to offload a few of their more unusual cases to a lawyer with expert-level forensic accounting skills at a bargain rate. But for Lenore? Well, she could tell her mother – and occasionally herself – that she was still actually practising law.

In this instance the client, a payroll-services company, faced a common problem but of unusual scope. A former customer had ceased operations, leaving it with authority over a bank account on which it had written a few unclaimed cheques. In this instance, however, the chequing account had a balance of $443,000 – the amount of three cheques issued to but never cashed by a man named Jonah Ashburn. The address Ashburn had provided belonged to a long-shuttered Bell Gardens card room. However, the most recent cheques had been returned as undeliverable.

Lenore accepted the assignment. Eventually, she found Jonah living in Las Vegas in an estate-style home in a neighbourhood favoured by senior casino executives and entertainers. He was easy to locate but difficult to find, as he rarely stayed in one place for very long.

Jonah seemed vaguely appreciative of the information but genuinely unconcerned that he had been dodging someone's attempt to pay him $443,000. After spending an hour together in his house, during which he casually mentioned that he had not opened his mail in over a year, Lenore could not tell if he was flirting with her or offering her employment. He was a mess – an oblivious and charming mess, but still a mess – and she had avoided messy situations ever since she'd accepted the suspension of her law licence some seven years prior. She was, however, mildly intrigued.

By the end of that evening, Lenore had agreed to help Jonah straighten out his finances, including what he dismissively referred to as 'a possible tax thing'. She took up his offer to stay in his guesthouse during the job, on the condition their relationship remained strictly professional.

'I'm away almost all the time,' he told her.

'Those aren't the times I'm worried about.'

He made her a promise, though she sensed he was also taking this as a challenge.

II.

That 'possible tax thing' turned out to be imminent criminal charges for tax evasion. He had ignored communications from the IRS for so long that the US Attorney assigned the case actually laughed at her when she asked whether they could negotiate the matter.

Lenore had spent most of the last six months recreating Jonah's wins and losses, preparing bulletproof tax returns, forcing Jonah to segregate the funds necessary to pay those taxes (and those incurred in earning the money he would be using), and persuading him to agree to make immediate payment of 150 per cent of what he owed to make the whole matter go away. Lenore reactivated her network of Washington contacts, and convinced a senior enforcement officer in the Treasury Department to take the deal. All that remained was getting Jonah to a meeting with the IRS in Washington, DC to formalise it.

Four days before their scheduled departure, Jonah announced he was leaving immediately for Atlantic City. To his surprise, Lenore took up his standing offer to come along. He even agreed to her conditions: separate travel and accommodations in Atlantic City, contact during the game, and his presence on the Sunday 5.50 p.m. flight from Philadelphia International to Reagan National.

III.

Resolving tax problems of this gravity would be a significant accomplishment. Lenore felt justifiably proud of her work, though that feeling had been evaporating with each passing hour. After scouring the casino-resort to find Jonah on her arrival on Thursday, she discovered he had fled to a hotel suite – he never told her which one – to play an ultra-high-stakes poker game. Even though the casino had a large poker room, this game was strictly private.

Jonah's opponent wanted to play heads up. To further speed the action, he insisted that he and Jonah deal themselves, constantly shuffling cards. A third person attended the game, shuffling additional decks, so each new hand could begin as the previous hand ended. Jonah had put up with this particular opponent's many eccentricities in private games over the previous two years: meeting on short notice in hotel rooms in different cities, frequent changes in games and rules, marathon sessions without breaks, demanding to raise the already astronomical stakes, crude conversation, foul manners and disrobing during the game, not to mention some occasional cheating.

Even though Jonah's opponent had never played a hand of poker in public, he was a legend in poker rooms around the world. Because this high-roller trusted no one (and was trusted by no one), he refused to play with casino chips, private chips, markers, a scorecard, or even cash. All transactions had to be conducted immediately, on demand, in gold. Consequently, all those players speculating about his origins, identity, and whereabouts nicknamed him 'Goldfucker'. Jonah, however, referred to him only as 'The Beast'.

IV.

Other than one short phone call, all Lenore's contact with Jonah since arriving in Atlantic City had been by text. Appearing at random intervals around the clock between late Thursday night and Saturday afternoon, Jonah's texts read like ransom notes:

DOWN 60 OZ-FAST!!!!!! (Friday, 12.08 a.m.)

Based on her general knowledge of the then-current price of gold – and she dared not ask Jonah any details, like where he got what must have been hundreds of ounces of gold that he had to bring to the game or how he transported it – he had quickly lost an amount approaching six figures. But from her work on Jonah's finances, that was not alarming.

Throughout Friday, she received sporadic messages about his deepening losses. She could do little but sit in her room and stare at her phone. She was starting to feel about her phone the way she did about Atlantic City.

Lenore hated Atlantic City, and not just for its tacky veneer, squalor, and stench of losing. A decade earlier, when she was a career-obsessed lawyer with a large DC law firm, she was in an emotional relationship with a man she met for weekends in Atlantic City.

He was older, a former Congressman, and then a lobbyist and DC power player. He was also a client of the firm. She knew this was an ethical violation and a firing offence. She faked naivety but ended up fooling only herself. Too late to save either her career or her feelings, she discovered he was married.

V.

DOWN 390 OZ-SUGGESTIONS?????? (Friday, 11.28 p.m.)

That text riveted her attention, based both on the amount (indicating a loss of nearly half a million dollars) and the six question marks at the end, which could be interpreted as an invitation to reply. Before she could consider how to respond, she was startled by her ringtone.

'I've only got ten pounds left. I told him my friend has another five hundred ounces.'

'Me?'

'If we have to, do you know where we can get more gold?'

Before she could inquire further, he made the point moot by hanging up.

It took Lenore three hours to fall asleep after that. During that time, she had gotten subsequent texts that Jonah had started a comeback (FINELY WINNING POTZ-180 OZ, Saturday, 1.18 a.m.) and the Beast had raised the stakes. (HES RAZING STAKES TO 4-8 OZ-OK, Saturday, 2.11 a.m.)

Good news for Jonah, though it did nothing to quell her growing sense of dread.

Once again, she was miserable in Atlantic City. Again,

she was here with a client. Again, it was complicated. And she still hated the place.

VI.

She slept late on Saturday, waking up to the sound of another text message.

BIG TURNAROUD +30 OZ!!!!!! (Saturday, 12.13 p.m.)

'Congrats!' she typed back. 'Ahead almost $40,000. Impressive!'

For the first time in their relationship, Jonah immediately responded to a text from Lenore.

?????? HOW MANY LBS PUR OZ

She quickly texted, 'That's ounces per pound. Sixteen.'

I MEANT LBS ... +30 LBS

Lenore could fake only so much insouciance. Scrolling through the texts, she realised that meant he had turned around a half-million-dollar loss into over a million-dollar win in just twelve hours.

VII.

At exactly 8 p.m. on Saturday, Lenore found Jonah waiting at the entrance of Le Gautier. His hair was still damp from a recent shower. He wore a fresh shirt and a sheepish smile. He looked like a schoolboy on Picture Day. It was also the only time she could remember him appearing when and where he had promised.

When she looked closer, she momentarily forgot how exhausting the last few days had been for her. Jonah was unshaven, his eyes unfocused. As he leant forward to greet her with a hug, she felt his unsteadiness. She noticed the casino gift shop tag dangling from a sleeve of the shirt. He had not slept since she last saw him on Thursday.

The maître d' led them through the darkened restaurant, along a path formed by two rows of tea candles. The path led to their table. They were the only diners in the room.

The meal was unbelievable. Lenore had travelled throughout the world, often with people who took pride in introducing her to amazing restaurants. Le Gautier could compete with any dining experience. That such a place existed in Atlantic City amazed her most of all. Le Gautier's full staff attended to them. Each course was paired with a superb wine.

The absence of their host, along with the opulence, aroused Lenore's curiosity. Jonah ate and drank everything the waiters put in front of him, including several glasses each from four bottles of wine.

'You better watch out,' Lenore warned. 'This could be his strategy: Get you drunk so he has a better chance of winning his money back.'

Jonah took a deep drink from his wine glass. 'Hey, it might work. Probably has a better chance than anything he's tried so far.'

When waiters wheeled a pair of dessert-laden trolleys behind the sommelier, Lenore somehow knew the Beast had arrived.

'I hope you're enjoying dinner at Le *Gutter*.' The Beast had a short, broad face, a wide gap-toothed grin, and coarse, curly hair covering his head and face.

He pulled up an adjacent chair. 'You like that?' he asked Jonah, who had just tasted the dessert wine.

'Yes, very sweet. Reminds me of what they served on Passover at my grandparents'.'

'Manischewitz?' Lenore giggled.

The Beast roared. 'I hope you'll like it a little more than that. This is Château d'Yquem, the only Premier Cru Superior Sauterne. This is my favourite vintage,' he said, blithely drinking from the bottle. 'It's from 1990. I've been buying it up all over the world.'

'Well, tastes as good as new,' Jonah said, lifting his glass before draining it.

Then the Beast was gone, and he took Jonah with him. He found Jonah a willing participant when he suggested that they 'test the dice' before going back upstairs to play poker.

The Beast's last words were, 'Stay and finish dessert, sweetie. I ordered it all so have as much as you want. You could stand to put on a couple pounds.'

A half-hour later, Lenore walked along the edge of the packed casino. Across the floor, she could see Jonah and the Beast playing craps. A lively, noisy crowd surrounded them. The Beast cackled, throwing around chips, shouting out his bets, and guzzling the last of the Château d'Yquem.

She kept walking towards the elevator. She was nervous about returning to Washington and making sure she and Jonah resolved his tax problems with the IRS. Although she was happy to be slipping out of Atlantic City without incident, she could admit that, from this perspective, the town wasn't quite the undisguised hellhole of her memories. In fact, the casino seemed like a pretty nice place to be on a Saturday night.

VIII.

On Sunday morning, Lenore sent Jonah several texts outlining their plans for leaving town and staying overnight in Washington. When he failed to respond, she tried without success to get some exercise. The resort's 'Spa Elegance' was closed. Running on the Boardwalk was out of the question. The sky, which she had not seen since Thursday, appeared angry and grey. It was cold outside and the hard rain looked ready to turn to snow.

At least she would get some sort of exercise walking the edges of the casino while looking for a decent cup of coffee. When Lenore walked past the poker room, she snapped out of her torpor. There was Jonah sitting in a game.

He was not in a hotel suite.

He was not playing the Beast.

He was not answering her texts.

He was not on his way to Washington, DC for a vitally important meeting with the IRS, a meeting Lenore had succeeded in orchestrating after six months of expert work on his tax problems.

Instead, Jonah was playing a hand of poker with a table full of people who looked like shipwreck survivors.

170

Lenore walked into the poker room, which was mostly empty. Jonah noticed her approach as he threw away his cards. He stood up.

'Lenore,' he said, waving casually, 'how's it going?'

Her perturbed expression was not difficult to read.

'I've got good news and more good news.' Without waiting for Lenore to reply, he added, 'You don't have to worry about the game with the Beast getting in the way of our tax meeting tomorrow. We can leave for DC any time you want.'

'What's the other good news?'

'I got a tip on another great game. Michael Jordan's game is going again in North Carolina. It's a very reliable tip and I can lock up a seat. But only if I can get to Charlotte. But we gotta go to DC, right? Take care of taxes and such.'

'What's going on here, Jonah? Where's the *Beast*?'

A few of the formerly comatose players at the table lifted their heads. Jonah ducked under the rail, grabbed Lenore by the arm, and walked her towards the entrance of the poker room.

'Don't refer to him out loud! There was an incident while we were playing craps, and he got arrested. They finally let me go at about five. It was too early to wake you so I sat down in the game here. It's not even a very good game.'

'What did he get arrested for?'

'He gave a cocktail waitress the finger. The bad part is that he's not allowed in Atlantic City any more. I heard his host tell him he's banned from this property for life. That was before the police even showed up.'

'That seems pretty extreme for giving somebody the finger.'

Jonah leant close and whispered. 'He gave it to her in the vagina.'

IX.

They agreed to meet in fifteen minutes in the lobby. Lenore did not want to let Jonah out of her sight, but she had to get her bag and clear her head. She had too many questions to think straight, and so far none of Jonah's answers added up. Other than his acknowledgement that they would proceed to their meeting in Washington, none of it made sense.

That was at noon. It had taken them five miserable hours to get to Philadelphia International Airport. During that time, they had been harassed by a succession of hotel employees, security guards, and people offering them rides who – most likely for good reason – were not authorised to provide such services. This included the Beast himself. In addition to carpet-bombing Lenore with text messages, she thought she saw him ride slowly by while they were being chased from the property as Jonah dragged a broken suitcase loaded with sixty pounds of gold through the snow. At least she thought it was the Beast. Who else would be riding in a gold limousine with vanity '9999' plates, painted with images of nude women, covered only by strategically billowing scarves?

Even though Jonah wore no coat in a snowstorm and was burdened by a load of over $1,000,000 in gold bullion, he seemed unaffected by the inconveniences. If anything, that bothered Lenore more.

When they were finally on the way to the airport, Jonah's only concern seemed to be with staring at his cell phone and sharing trivia about the Michael Jordan game developing in Charlotte. 'The group wants to play a lot of triple-draw games: Badugi, Badacy, Badeucy, Deuce-to-Seven. Triple-draw: the favourite form of poker for players in the mood to gamble.'

'How are you getting text messages about the game on your phone? You told me last night you lost your phone.' That was how the Beast had gotten Lenore's phone number.

'I lost *that* one,' Jonah emphasised. 'I still have the one where I get tips on good games.' He held up a phone, which had a piece of masking tape on the back, on which was scrawled 'TIPS'. Indeed, the drawstring sack between them in the back seat, which Lenore had earlier noticed swinging from the handle of Jonah's suitcase, had several phones inside. She glanced at the bag, and saw similar pieces of tape on the collection of decrepit cell phones. 'POKER ROOM'. 'J'. 'LA MIKE'. 'LEIF'. And one that said 'LIZZ'.

Jonah saw that phone at the same moment. He chuckled. 'Some of these are pretty old.'

X.

The weather had delayed flights out of Philadelphia International Airport. Even though the airport was packed with angry, miserable people, Jonah seemed oblivious to the chaos around him. He certainly didn't comprehend the issues arising from carrying sixty pounds of gold through an airport security X-ray machine. An hour earlier, while Jonah dozed in the car, Lenore had called the TSA.

It was a calculated risk. She thought if they wanted to make it out of town any time soon, it would be better to alert the authorities, offer no other information, and make sure Jonah paid the IRS their share. They were, after all, on the way to settle his taxes. She didn't spend all this effort so he could commit a fresh set of offences.

A group of TSA agents, along with some other state and federal law enforcement personnel, escorted them to a private screening room and peppered them with questions. She had told Jonah to say nothing and, on this occasion, he deferred to her. Everyone was polite and, after a few minutes, there was nothing left to do but to get their identification and let them proceed to their flight.

Lenore handed over her passport, noticing that a TSA agent copied the information before handing it back. Jonah started fishing through his pockets. Finally, he pulled a wad of folded papers from his back pocket and placed it on the table.

'What is this?' a TSA agent asked. The tone was slightly less courteous, though Lenore was about to ask the same question, and probably in a harsher tone.

'This is a photocopy of my passport.'

One of the agents unfolded the weathered papers and took some notes.

'See, when I came back into the United States from Thailand last December,' he pointed to the back of one of the pages, 'one of the guys at LAX, I think from Immigration, had a problem and took my passport. They said it wasn't valid. See, I had a valid passport, but I lost it. I found this one, which I had lost earlier, and used it because I was in a hurry.

'The man said he had to take it because it wasn't valid. I didn't want to give it up because, obviously, it's an issue when you don't have your passport. We talked about it for a long time and, finally, I said, "Just give me a *copy* of my passport back. And write your name and phone number on it in case someone needs to contact you about it." You can call him to confirm it.'

The three TSA agents looked uncomfortably at each other. After what seemed an eternity, one of them asked, 'Do you have some other form of government-issued identification?'

Jonah shook his head and removed from a back pocket a thick stack of cards held together by a rubber band. Credit cards, business cards, scraps of paper with phone numbers, one card with a lipstick print and a phone number, some valet parking stubs, and player cards from more than twenty casinos.

Lenore whispered, 'What about your driver's licence?'

'Oh, that's a whole other problem. My Nevada driver's licence expired or got lost. So I contacted the DMV to renew or replace it. They told me to go to one of their offices in Las Vegas, which I did. After waiting in line, the person there told me that someone in California had stolen my identity – not in so many words, but they used my name, said they had moved to California, and applied for a California driver's licence in that name. California told this to Nevada, and Nevada cancelled my driver's licence. Then they told me I had to go to the main office in Carson City to straighten it out. From Las Vegas, I either have to fly there' – he gestured, indicating the obvious problem of flying without ID – 'or make a six-hour *drive*.'

Fifteen minutes later, Jonah and Lenore stood on the strip of pavement outside the airport where they had been an hour before, watching buses, vans, cars, and taxis drop off passengers. A detail of Philadelphia airport police officers followed them to the nearest exit from the terminal, two of whom continued staring at them from the other side of the sliding-glass doors.

XI.

Jonah never apologised for the debacle at security, but he did promise to fix it. 'We're going to make that IRS meeting. I know what I'm doing.'

It was distressingly clear that Jonah did *not* know what he was doing when he leapt up from the bags to wave towards a car approaching the kerb. It was that gold limousine adorned with paintings of naked women.

The Beast.

'Well, isn't this a great break?' Jonah asked as he hauled their bags into the back of the car. Lenore stared at him, and then at the squat silhouette in the back of the limo, saying nothing.

'The Beast is taking care of everything,' Jonah said.

'He's giving us a lift to the private airport in Millville where he's got his plane. I'll charter us a plane to DC from there. I know how important that IRS meeting is. We'll be in DC tonight. I don't care what it costs.'

Jonah got in behind the driver, sitting next to the Beast. Lenore stepped among the men's splayed legs and the garbage on the floor to the space opposite Jonah.

After she settled in, the Beast leant forward, waved a paw, and said, 'Good to see you again, doll. Glad to help out. Seems we're on a real adventure here, huh?'

She sank back in the seat, exhausted. She dozed off for bits of the hour drive to Millville Airport. Some of the conversation between Jonah and their host could have been part of a dream, but she had experienced enough during this ride-along with Jonah to know better.

Beast: 'Unless you want to continue our game tonight, I think I'm going to fly to Charlotte and give that Michael Jordan game a look-see. Listen, what do I owe you for getting me in the game? You want a piece? A flat fee?'

Jonah: 'Nah. I'm glad it worked out.'

Beast: 'What about you? I wouldn't be in this game if it wasn't for you.'

Jonah: 'I've got this meeting with Lenore. It's important to her – and me. Taxes, you know.'

Beast: 'Yeah, taxes suck. But you're going to show up after the meeting at least, right?'

Jonah: 'I suppose. If it's still going. If I can get there. If there's still a seat.'

Beast: 'I'll have my plane fly to DC and pick you up. Wait. How about this? Why don't we all go to Charlotte in my plane? Tonight. Now. We can play in the Michael Jordan game, and then my plane will drop you off in DC in the morning.'

Jonah: 'That might work, but I don't know if we' (gesturing in Lenore's direction) 'can take a chance on cutting it that close.'

Beast: 'Can't you just write a cheque and make this disappear?'

Jonah: 'Is that what you'd do?'

Beast: 'I've never paid taxes so I don't know what I'd do. But I'd start by telling the government to suck my sweaty, uncircumcised dick. And I wouldn't need a fuckin' meeting in fuckin' Washington to give them that message. But you just won a fuck-ton of my money, so what do I know, right?'

The Beast kept hammering away at Jonah how simple it would be if they all flew to Charlotte. 'We'll just lock up our seats. Give 'em a little smell of our money. Then you pop back to DC, circle-jerk with the IRS, and return to the game.'

'Theoretically, it seems like it could work out,' Jonah said.

'Everybody wins this way.' The Beast started laughing maniacally. 'God bless the IRS!'

XII.

The car stopped. Lenore opened her eyes. They were apparently at the airport, but not any part of an airport Lenore had ever seen. They were on the macadam, adjacent to a runway. A jet, clearly the Beast's, awaited. It was gold, painted with nude women, strategically covered by contrails, on the side.

The Beast stepped out first, bounding towards the aircraft. Jonah got out, waiting for Lenore. Reluctantly, she followed.

There was no terminal in sight, no office where someone would book a flight or rent a plane or whatever was involved in private air travel.

'So ...' Jonah began uncomfortably, 'what do you think? If we all go to Charlotte, we can skip the hassle and expense of chartering a plane. We can fly from there to DC late tonight or even early tomorrow morning.'

'Jonah, you're going to do what you want. If you come with me to this meeting, you have an almost unheard of opportunity to fix a situation that sends others to prison and haunts them financially for years to come.'

'And all that is important.' Jonah grabbed Lenore's arm, pulling her away, so the Beast wouldn't hear him. 'See, I just won a half-million dollars from this guy. It looks bad if I quit—'

'Quit? He got arrested and banned for life from the casino for committing sexual assault. You didn't quit the game.'

'Look, there's clearly a lot more money where that half-million came from. This guy is such a terrible poker player, you can't believe it. How about this? I bet you that I win $50,000 from him just while we're in his airplane. If I don't win $50,000 by the time we're wheels-down in Charlotte, I won't get off the plane. We'll fly straight on to DC.'

The Beast somehow heard and approached them, calling out, 'He's right. I don't know the first thing about Open-Faced Chinese Poker but I was going to propose playing him for $1,000 a point on the flight.'

Lenore held her ground. 'If I got on that plane with you, it would conflict with my professional responsibility, which now is solely to get you to that meeting with the IRS tomorrow morning.'

'You're right,' Jonah said. 'Of course you're right. You're looking out for my best interests and I appreciate that. Got to get to DC ASAP. That's the most important thing, right?'

The Beast, now standing across from Lenore and Jonah, chimed in. 'How about this? Jonah gets on the plane with me. We stop by the Charlotte game before he hops back on and meets you in DC. My driver will take you to DC right now. You'll be there in time to enjoy a leisurely evening at a fine hotel, Lenore, on me.' It was the only time the Beast called her by name, and it made her skin crawl.

The Beast started peeling from a huge wad of bills but Jonah pushed him away. 'I swear. I'll lock up my seat in the Jordan game. Play a little while, at most, and then fly to DC and meet you at the hotel. I'll even write the address of the meeting on my hand so, worst-case scenario, I go there directly from the airport tomorrow morning. But get me a separate room at the hotel – all business, right? I'll do everything humanly possible to get there tonight. Tomorrow morning at the absolute latest. Promise.'

The Beast added, 'I swear on my honour it will

happen. We'll move heaven and earth to get Jonah to your meeting.'

Lenore sighed, the decision having been made. 'Fine.'

Jonah said, 'This is a great plan.'

The Beast enthusiastically agreed. 'It'll be a real adventure.'

Jonah bear-hugged the suitcase full of gold and followed the Beast towards the plane. 'I'll see you in DC before you know it.'

XIII.

Lenore stood outside the limousine as Jonah and the Beast walked towards the waiting jet. Jonah appeared overburdened with baggage, despite travelling with no possessions but the clothes on his back.

A door to the jet popped open and a stairway descended. Jonah dragged the suitcase behind him. At the top of the steps, he tried to wave back at Lenore but his hands were full. It came out as a shoulder shrug, concluded with a lopsided grin.

A flight attendant pulled up the stairway and closed the plane door. The limousine driver asked Lenore, 'Am I driving you to DC? It's about three hours, four if we run into traffic in Newark or Baltimore.'

'No,' Lenore said as she ducked into the back seat of the limo, shovelling away the litter on the floor at her feet: food wrappers, newspapers, a bath towel, water bottles, drink cups. 'Take me back to Philadelphia International.'

*

Her phone buzzed from inside her purse. It was a text from an unknown number, though the sender's identity was obvious.

SEE U IN DC 2MORROW, YEA?

For once, Lenore did not respond to Jonah. Instead, when she stepped out of the limousine at Philadelphia International, she dropped her phone in the first trashcan she saw, and flew home.

And on the Eighth Day

by Shelley Rubenstein

The story, names, characters, and incidents portrayed in this piece are all true. Any resemblance to actual persons, living or dead (especially dead), places, or actual events is entirely intentional.

An abhorrent roar emanated from the Superior's office. It was a sound of rage like no other, staggered intermittently with violent thudding and crashing noises. It was only when Isidore heard the words, 'It's rigged! It's all rigged!' that it became apparent to what this was referring.

'Great timing,' he sighed, clumsily attempting to mould his trembling hand into a fist. Slowly and purposefully, he primed it into position, a fraction away from the most foreboding of doors. Just as he'd garnered the necessary momentum to bring knuckle to gopher wood – a perennial favourite in these parts – he heard another almighty roar. The Almighty's roar, to be precise. The Good Lord was pissed off.

The job had really started to get to God over the last century or so. He sorely needed an outlet, a diversion to provide a little escapism from the daily grind. Because He could never be wholly off duty, He wanted this pastime to function as a channel whereby He could walk among His children unnoticed. If He truly experienced what it felt like to be a mere mortal, without them becoming aware of His identity, then it surely would help Him become a better Omnipotent One.

Thus, contrary to popular belief, poker was not invented in New Orleans, Persia, or France. Mankind does love to take credit for everything. No, poker originated in The Heavens during a lull, post-Creation, post-Flood, and amid a brief period of harmony. One Sunday evening, several centuries ago, God decided to invite some of the gang over to His place to test drive a new card game He'd been working on. He also had a cracking recipe for guacamole He wanted to try out. This became the first home game in history.

He'd striven to create a platform where everyone would have parity – saints and sinners, angels and demons, even men and women. They'd leave their baggage and millennia-old disputes at the door. If, throughout the course of the game, ancient quarrels should incidentally be resolved as enemies were converted into comrades, then job done.

As the genesis of poker evolved, God found it fascinating to observe how each player's endemic character traits were unwittingly brought to the forefront. They seemed incapable of concealing their true feelings when involved in a big hand. Even though this was managed with ease in everyday life after death, they were rendered powerless at obscuring their vulnerabilities.

And it was good that the game of poker frequently acted as a microcosm of society, aiding The Lord to do His work.

God considered poker to be a great success, a leveller – a chance to unwind and be like one of the guys. After the weekly game, He felt His batteries recharged, ready once more to face the onslaught of another week reigning over man and beast which, quite frankly, was getting to be exhausting and a tad repetitive.

The Sunday night game quickly became the highlight of God's week. He'd devised a rotating list of players so no one felt left out. For it's important to note that, even though this was His night off, He was inherently benevolent, and keen to set a good example to others on the off-chance that poker caught on.

There was one name, though, that was a firm fixture on the guest list: Barry. God loved playing with Barry. He felt like Barry was the only one who really got Him. Barry was certainly the only one who never threw the game if he thought God would get mad at him if he bust Him out. If anything, he strove to suck out on God wherever possible. Barry had, let's call it, a 'playful' nature. You might know Barry by one of his many other sobriquets – King of Babylon, Abaddon, Evil One, and the one he favoured most, Satan. His true name though, largely because God knew it really wound him up, was Barry, for this was deemed the most diabolical of all monikers.

It was Barry who'd started the craze for bringing card protectors and lucky charms to the poker table. He'd regularly try to big up his evil by placing a mini fire-breathing demon atop his cards, psyching out the other players. He used this demon to encourage his opponents to worship at the altar of Beelzebub, yet another ridiculous name he was trying to popularise. Unfortunately, this failed to intimidate anyone and merely elicited ridicule. It did, however, galvanise their enthusiasm to address him as Barry, or, to really pique him, they'd address him by the loathsome hypocorism, Bazzer, wherever possible. And so, from the offset, he'd be on tilt. And hilarious it was to behold.

The other core members of the Sunday night crew pretty much proved God's theory of playing to type, their personalities oozing into every hand. Noah constantly overplayed pairs; Abraham would rather sacrifice his own hand lest he beat God; and Jonah's attempts at bluffing were cringe-worthy. He found the women were the trickiest to play. With their fair and calm matriarchal demeanours, Sarah and Esther were consistently the big winners. They were also the most pleasant to be around, should they hit a losing streak.

God always made sure there was balance between the genders. It bothered Him greatly that the game on earth in the present day had such a low ratio of female players.

That didn't mean to say it wasn't tricky getting women along to the game even back then, and He often had to invite Eve along to make up the numbers. Annoyingly, if Eve was playing, that meant He had to invite Adam, which inevitably led to constant bickering between the two as she couldn't stop herself from using her feminine wiles in the most audacious fashion.

The Sunday night game continued for many years, but God's enjoyment was curbed as He became aware that the others had a predilection for soft-playing against Him. He missed the gratification one feels when victory is earned by the refined skills of the experienced card sharp. He'd explained repeatedly that this was the one time and place everyone should treat Him like an equal, but He couldn't blame them for their apprehension. Sure, He had been known to get a bit smitey when riled, but that was all in the past.

Following the success of poker and its many variations in the 1990s, God graduated poker from 'bricks and mortar' to the online platform and thus internet poker was born. It was the perfect device! It brought together His people from all over the earth, among whom He could sit without any awareness of who this mystery player really was. It wasn't long before even He forgot who He was at times. He truly relished those moments when He didn't have to behave with the lofty sense of decorum one would naturally expect from The Creator.

O how much pleasure He derived from witnessing

players from various nations putting aside prejudices and befriending one another. His belief in poker's ability to act as a conduit for peace-making grew, as His flock would organically sit down together over a game of cards and play it out. He wanted to spread this message and increase poker's popularity and decided to implement a cunning plan.

In 2003, God chose an accountant from Tennessee, who led a simple, honest existence. He helped this man soar to victory in the World Series of Poker (WSOP), winning a life-changing purse of $2,500,000 in the process.

He groaned wearily at the countless comments remarking, 'What an astonishing coincidence it is that a man whose surname is Moneymaker should win such a vast amount of cash!' He agreed that would be an astonishing coincidence, but it was all part of His grand design. He'd really pared down the histrionics since the Burning Bush days, but He'd clearly gone too far the other way with such subversive tactics. All He yearned to achieve was to convey the message that, with a little faith, great rewards would be reaped.

Not to be disheartened, He tried again a few years later. This time, He appointed a rather sweet but misunderstood chap with a name evoking images of untold riches. In 2006, Jamie Gold defied the odds to pick up the record-breaking first prize of $12,000,000. God was positive that the humans couldn't fail to comprehend the directive this time. Not only did they miss the point, but the plan ended up spectacularly backfiring as man's greed and bickering over filthy lucre reared its ugly head.

More irritating even than this was how insufferably smug it made Barry, as he considered the fallout from Gold's win to be a personal victory.

Still The Lord persevered, for He was merciful and patient even when mankind proved to be blatant dumbasses. He continued to finesse the online game. But my, these humans could be brutal; their anonymous personas seemingly giving licence to unleash the worst in them. He was amazed at how swiftly they scaled the heights of offensiveness with negligible encouragement to merit such venom. Sometimes, it took all of His might to restrain Himself not to inflict one of the really bad plagues on them right then and there. But, just as He wavered, He'd recall the pledge He'd made on the inception of internet poker: that His godly status was to be left behind at the log-in stage. It was the only way this experiment could work. It was also imperative that He could never be accused of abusing His powers at the poker table, nor of having access to a super-user account. To ensure the authenticity of the implementation of these assurances, He'd appointed the impartial Elevated Grand Committee (EGC) to govern all facets of the online game.

If additional proof were needed of God's 'normal' status while playing online, you only had to look at His recent hand history. Time after time, He'd been rivered in the most unceremonious of ways. Subsequently, it was true that He'd developed some anger issues from internet poker, which caused bouts of sulking unbecoming of The Master of the Universe, but ... He was working on it. He

189

too, like His children, was a constant work in progress. He looked at the screen with abhorrence. Oh no, it was happening again!

Another blood-curdling cry of anger was heard from behind the door. Isidore was grateful that he no longer had any blood to curdle nor bowels to evacuate, for this sound was one of pure fury.

Despite his departure from earth in the year 636, Isidore of Seville was still on a probationary period in the celestial zone. It took an awfully long time to get things approved around here – which, in the grand scheme of eternity, wasn't really that long at all. A mere 962 years had passed before Pope Clement VIII canonised Isidore in 1598. This promotion had been contentious at the time, as rumour had it Clement decreed this canonisation after pulling a series of all-nighters, making the clarity of his decision-making abilities somewhat dubious. Allegedly, he was the first Pope to have imbibed coffee, and he got a little carried away by the feeling it brought forth within. He could barely sign the paperwork, his hand was shaking so much. On such caffeine-buzzing occasions, he had a tendency to agree to a whole lot of random stuff and his charges tended to sneak in the occasional document to sign that Clement would ordinarily discard. Controversy aside, though, Isidore had more than proven his merit over the centuries.

He'd continued to work studiously, steering mankind forward in all matters technological. To reward him for these pioneering inroads, Pope John Paul II decreed Isidore Patron Saint of the Internet in 1997. As ever, remaining consistent in the subject of elongated trial periods, the Vatican had yet to deem him worthy enough to make it official.

Back to the matter at hand; Isidore was here today – and he dry-retched (no innards) every time he thought about it – upon orders from the EGC. After many hours of discussion, they'd voted unanimously that The Almighty could no longer get away with exploiting His position online. Isidore had been given the daunting task of reprimanding God. No one of his status had ever done this before, because, well, it's God, isn't it? You don't tell Him off, it doesn't work like that.

The EGC had selected Isidore for the job because he was one of God's own personal recruits and, therefore, it was hoped He would look upon him favourably. Since undertaking the role, Isidore had been fairly prolific in his achievements. He was rather proud of Twitter, although it wasn't deemed a universal success and many sniped that it was 'like the Tower of Babel all over again'.

Isidore followed this up with Tumblr, Instagram and Snapchat, but God's disdain for all of these was apparent. His real bugbear was humankind's propensity for taking selfies and other such displays of egotism. Although He was flattered as man was created in His image, He would seethe, 'I did not design lips solely for the purposes of pouting.'

Another cacophonous din jolted Isidore back to his objective. This was swiftly followed by a familiar loud and distinctive crashing noise. '*Caray!*' gasped Isidore, then,

'Ay,' after a painful current ran through his essence. '*Lo siento*,' he said to no one in particular, knowing his apology would be heard. After all this time, he still resorted to cuss words in his native tongue during times of crisis. Hence the interminable limbo. With that thought, he finally understood why his title as Patron Saint of the Internet had yet to be made official by the current Pope. And in that moment of comprehension and humility, he edged a little bit closer and a warm glow exuded from his being. Isidore inhaled and braced himself once more. This time, he would knock, and no fear of what was occurring on the other side of the imposing heavenly door would deter him.

'Oh, do stop loitering outside like a petrified school-child and come in!' boomed God. Isidore should have anticipated that He knew of his whereabouts at all times, even more so when at such close proximity.

'Ah, Isidore, how lovely to see you. Pray tell, what is the purpose of this visit?' He knew, He had to. Isidore was about to answer when God interjected.

'Tell me, when was your last good idea, Isidore?'

'I think Isipedia was a big success, my Lord. It was a continuation of my work on earth, picking up where the *Etymologiae* left off—'

'Except it's not called that though, is it?'

'No,' he said dejectedly, 'you thought Wikipedia was a catchier name, as you were listening to a lot of hip hop and hanging out with Biggie and Tupac at the time.'

Isidore recognised God's tactics and that He was playing for time. For a supreme deity, He could be extremely transparent. Slowly and nervously, Isidore continued.

'My Lord, I've come to discuss a delicate matter with you. It's about your online chat etiquette ...'

'I see ... do go on, Isidore of Seville.' He hated it when God used his full name, it meant He was really mad at him. Plus He was using His extra-scary Old Testament voice for added intimidation.

'Well, you see, Heavenly Father, I'm afraid you've exceeded the warnings and, erm, it's been decided by the EGC, following some hugely inappropriate comments you made to fellow participants during the online tournament last night, that you're ... to ... receive ... achatban—'

'What's "achatban"? Is it a frequent player points reward?' He asked excitedly. 'Did I win a prize, Isi?' God could be such a fucker sometimes. He was toying with him and revelling in it with the most ungodly demeanour.

'No, Great One,' replied Isidore, adding, 'The Greatest There Is and Ever Shall Be' for good measure and protocol. 'You have been penalised with a – chat – ban ... for three months,' Isidore said meekly, confident with that declaration that he would never inherit the earth.

And so it came to pass that God was miffed.

Silence. Big, sinister, ominous silence. And then it also came to pass that Isidore was appreciative that he no longer had a urinary tract, nor wore pants, for they would undoubtedly be soaked through at this point. Fortunately, though, God's a big chatter and was rubbish at sustaining the silent treatment for very long.

'You, a mere messenger, are informing *me*, The

Creator of everyone and everything, of what I can and cannot do?'

'O Kind, Calm and Benevolent Divine One, I'm so very sorry, but this has been decreed in accordance with Your Holiness's commandments and your wish to be treated like everyone else at the poker table.' God looked sheepish, which bolstered Isidore's confidence. 'My Lord, some of the things you wrote in the chat box contained words of such blasphemy, banished on this very plane by your pure and pious self.'

'Enough!' God shouted. Seeing the look of fear in Isidore's eyes, God took pity on him. He attempted to calm down, using some techniques learned from His mindfulness coach. Taking a deep breath, He began to recite the names of the WSOP champions: 'Johnny Moss,' – he omitted Amarillo Slim because he had committed heinous crimes for which he had yet to repent – 'Puggy Pearson, Sailor Roberts, Doyle Brunson, Bobby Baldwin, Hal Fowler, Stu Ungar – Oh, Stu ...' How he loved Stuart Erroll Ungar. Such a charismatic, generous, lost soul. He'd put a little bit of His own poker prowess into Stu, but it didn't help him in the end. He ached over His precious children and felt their pain. Isidore jolted Him out of these thoughts.

'My Lord, there's something else.'

He glowered at Isidore. Even though He really liked messing with him, because He was The Almighty, and it was one of the benefits of the gig, He remembered that this wasn't the internet and therefore not how one actually behaves IRL.

'Yes, my child,' He said, the compassion returning to

His voice. He did sneak in a hint of sarcasm, though, because God can be playful too.

Crap, He was going to kill him (again) with kindness. Isidore didn't know which God he preferred.

'Well, dear Merciful One,' he said, as he looked over at the debris smouldering on the floor, 'I'm afraid that I was also sent to inform you by the Upper Heavens IT Department that if you smashed up any more laptops, you wouldn't be getting a replacement.'

God stared incredulously at Isidore, who was close to tears of both trepidation and genuine empathy for his Creator's agony. Poker was His game, He loved it, and He didn't want to become like the unfortunate people in the USA who'd been banned from playing in their home territories. And not just because some of them were terrible human beings.

'But Isidore,' The Lord beseeched, 'you wouldn't believe what just happened! Some muppet fish' (God was allowed to call people this since He'd created muppets and fish and loved them both) 'decided to call my raise, holding jack-deuce off-suit ...'

Isidore switched off. He couldn't bear to listen to any more of God's tedious bad beat stories. 'O Divine One, you said yourself with such wisdom that wanton destruction does not solve problems.' Isidore shut up at this point for he knew he was now pushing his luck.

'You are right, my child,' God said resignedly. 'I appreciate how courageous you were for being the one to confront me with this devastating news.' God looked towards Isidore and with a coquettish tilt of His head, He continued, 'Starting from now. No more smashing of laptops.' Isidore could swear God fluttered his eye-lashes at him as He said this. What was going on? Was God pulling an Eve and trying to flirt His way out of this?

'I'm afraid that,' he said, pointing at the smoking mess of shattered computer, 'was your last chance, my Lord. You've maxed out your insurance claims.'

Creator stared hard at createe, and createe quaked in his turn.

'You know, Isidore, when my people screw up repeatedly, I give them chance after chance. Do I not deserve the same clemency?'

God had a point. He really was very gifted at nego-tiations and it was apparent that He was going to be intransigent on this point.

'Rules may be rules, Isidore of Seville, but take a look at the small print.'

Isidore looked bemused as a parchment scroll mirac-ulously (AKA normal for these parts) and conveniently appeared before him, unfurling until it reached the clause in question: 'In the event that His Holiness, The Lord, who created you and all your loved ones, selflessly ded-icating Himself to your happiness, becomes a little too mortal while He metaphorically walks among His crea-tures ...' Isidore was about to comment on how overly wordy and clumsily written this document was, until God's ire shook the room. '*Continue!*'

Sensing that really scary Wrathful Bible God could surface at any moment, he tried his hardest to keep the sneer from his voice and the stammering to a minimum. '... and the self-important and somewhat up-themselves Committee have the temerity to deem Him in need of penurious treatment, then God, your Father and, lest you forget, The Creator, has the right to challenge the bearer of this beastly news to a game of heads up, which said bearer is compelled to accept. And it shall be decreed that the victor of this momentous game shall be allowed to keep His internet and computer privileges.'

Although Isidore was the first to commend God on His many fine qualities, he was rather insulted by the cockiness of the author of this excruciating, maundering caveat. He was a little hurt that God would presume that He would have an easy victory over him, just because He was the All Knowing One – or, as He liked to remind everyone, 'the original Big Slick'. Wasn't that the whole point of poker and its *raison d'être*? That anyone, from any walk of life, had an equal chance of winning.

'Gosh, your wisdom exceeds expectation, my Lord. As ever, You are full of surprises.'

Oh dear, he had abandoned any attempt at hiding the contempt in his voice. God rubbed His hands together with delight, confident of success. Isidore wasn't suggesting that God had been neglecting him of late, for one could never doubt He was always there when you needed Him. It was more a case of the ever-expanding population and pre-apocalyptic problems on earth taking up increasing amounts of His time. That, and the fact He was currently giddy with insufferable childish glee at how smart He was for introducing risible contract clauses for every possible circumstance. His thoughts were so preoccupied with strategising His heads up game, He'd forgotten about Isidore's lonely period and how he'd resolved it.

After a long period of isolation and introspection, Isidore decided that, in order to make the most of eternity, he should probably get out more. In the late 1950s, a spate of social clubs were set up in the upper levels to encourage mingling. Although he was a little apprehensive, having been used to his own company for several hundred years, Isidore decided it would do him good to join a heavenly group where he might make some new friends. It was during a meeting of the 'Holy Smokes' cigar club that he met the recently deceased Herb, who was to become his dearest friend. They had so much in common – their main shared passion being the dissemination of information. They were big fans of each other's writing and, inspired by reading one of Herb's books, Isidore honed some pretty impressive card-playing skills.

Herb began his career as a government telegrapher and code clerk, priming him for the job of cryptological officer for the American Expeditionary Forces during World War I. He had a natural aptitude for code-breaking which he rapidly developed. One of his greatest achievements was the successful cracking of the Japanese codes shortly after the war, when he'd been relocated to New York. Following the winding-down of his career in this field, Herb dedicated his time to one of his favourite passions. In 1957, he published a book that would remain a bible for the game of poker for decades to come. Isidore was inordinately grateful that he could say his closest confidant, Herbert Osborn Yardley, the esteemed author of *The Education of a Poker Player*, was his personal poker coach. The game was very much on.

And it was with great gusto that God spake those immortal words: 'Let there be poker!'

Table Manners

by Neil Pearson

'I'm the only person here I don't recognise.'

Nice opener: notes of humility, showy aftertaste. Self-deprecating humour inviting scrutiny from fellow diners, who are now considering whether the glimpse of intelligence just shown was calculated or inadvertent.

  Nice opener.

Mark's starter was served. Since receiving tonight's supper invitation Mark had given a lot of thought to how best to comport himself in the rarefied company he would be keeping. The evening had now arrived, and he'd come to few conclusions. He did know he must *speak*. Speaking was, after all, what had secured him the invitation in the first place: what he'd said at the most recent company convention, and the conviction with which he'd said it. And he must speak *early*. Say something while the first course was still on the table, something which would command his fellow guests' attention, something which would demand some sort of response. Nothing too outspoken, nothing he'd have to defend all night, but a mildly diverting talking point of some kind. He knew that if he didn't chip in early it would become increasingly difficult as the evening wore on to contribute meaningfully to any conversation taking place around him. Most of his dining companions had the social ease that comes of shared history; he knew no one, except by sight. Early participation would be essential. The fellow diners he'd chatted to at the convention would expect him to be talkative: they'd seen his presentations there, seen him pitch with conviction and humour and zeal. It was that bullishness, uncharacteristic for Mark and which he had dredged from somewhere that day, that had put him right at the centre of things. At first it had merely sparked the usual clamour of argument and counter-argument, claim and counter-claim, but as the day wore on and he'd continued to stand his ground he had watched his colleagues slowly quieten, take him to task less often, ask fewer questions, give him a respectful, largely uninterrupted hearing, until eventually – and to his own quiet amazement – a general acceptance seemed to spread among those few who had stayed late into the evening that he really might be on to something. It was around that time that some really quite senior employees – one or two directors, even – had started to gather while pretending not to, had stood quietly at the back and eavesdropped, had said hello. And then one of the directors, at the very end of the evening and finding Mark within hailing distance, had turned abruptly away from the employee who had been boring her and had made a beeline for him, had *spoken* to him, had mentioned a quiet dinner a few days from now. *Very informal, just a small get-together for supper, supper and a few drinks. Mostly social, of course, but we'll throw some ideas about, talk a little about the future of the company. We'd love to hear more about where you see us going. Can you make it? Do come – it would be so good to have you along. Always nice to welcome a new face.* Finally! God knows it had been a long time coming. But these were busy, important people: they weren't having supper for his benefit. Middle-management employees received invitations like this all the time, but few received more than one. So he would need traction early on. He would need to identify a friendly face somewhere, someone he could use to help him unclench, help him speak with the voice that had got him invited here in the first place. Which was why he'd sent up the flare.

'I'm the only person here I don't recognise.'

'I still feel like that. Most of us do.'

The friendly face was sitting immediately to Mark's left: it belonged to a gangly young American with a refined East Coast accent and an unrefined dress sense, who had lately become something of a regular fixture in the company's in-house magazine. Mark knew that some of his fellow diners could be tight-lipped to a fault; he'd hoped for a chatterer nearby. The rest of the guests, waited on by a liveried staff with the near-invisibility common to the best of the profession, were settling to their food: deploying their napery, appraising their appetisers, listening. Mostly listening. Mark felt their interest, wondered what he should do with it, wondered what he'd said to excite so much of it. He looked to his left for guidance, but the friendly face's attention was now fixed on the terrine in front of him, and he was clearly disinclined to say more. *'I still feel like that. Most of us do.'* Hardly chatty, now Mark thought about it. Perhaps not even friendly. *I've been here before, many times. These people who are unnerving you are friends of mine.* Mark was aware he was over-thinking this. All East Coast had said was: 'I still feel like that. Most of us do.'

'SPEAK FOR YOURSELF, COLLEGE BOY. JESUS.'

The head of the company's Russian office, sitting four seats down from Mark, would speak infrequently this evening – infrequently, but always at very high volume. He may have thought it necessary to shout so that the table could hear what he was saying through the greatcoat, muffler and ear-flapped headgear which, for reasons best known to himself, he had declined to leave in the cloakroom. (He didn't stay long, and to judge from his behaviour he'd never intended to.)

No one seemed surprised by his rudeness or his decibel count, most seemed quietly amused. No one around the table spoke. Instead they all looked to Mark for a reaction. He tried to look unruffled, but after a pause whose length told a different story, he smiled faintly, let it go, and turned his attention to his food. East Coast, by now almost finished with his starter, also thought better of trying to exchange pleasantries with a grumpy Russian at this stage of the evening, and said nothing further. Mark's ice-breaking attempt was over almost before it had started, and the attention of the table moved on.

It hadn't always been like this. Before moving to his present employers – God, three years ago now – Mark had felt valued at work, valued and listened to. He was a big fish back then. He still *felt* like the big fish now, but at this bigger, hungrier company feeling like the big fish didn't give him the same satisfaction somehow, and certainly didn't translate into results. He'd become disheartened and enervated by his inability to cut through this company's workforce, to rise through them, to shine. He knew he should work on reinvigorating himself, try to cultivate a more front-foot attitude to work, but never having felt that change was necessary before he was unsure how to begin. He felt his failure most acutely at the regular staff get-togethers. The conventions: part social, part professional events where colleagues would throw out ideas, exchange information, and talk long into the night about business projections and company strategy. Mark had never warmed to these hot-desking free-for-alls, and could never put his finger on why. It certainly wasn't the fault of his colleagues. They were always *delighted* to see him, welcoming and talkative, and always genuinely sorry to see him go. But he rarely stayed long, even though he always regretted leaving these things the moment he was out on the street. It was strange behaviour in someone who was still so keen to impress, but he'd never examined it, and unexamined the behaviour had curdled into habit.

Mark worked quietly on his steak, listening to the table talk swirl around him. Two guests at the far end of the table were dominating proceedings at present: a bluff, friendly man of Middle Eastern origin, a respected stalwart of the company who was universally liked, and a very young-looking girl with an accent he couldn't place, the outlandishness of whose views was in direct inverse ratio to the quiet politeness with which she expressed them. Others were occasionally offering up a point of view or raising a question, but for the most part the table was happy just to listen to a conversation which showed promising signs of escalating at any moment into an entertaining row. A few minutes ago the man known as one of the industry's most original and far-sighted thinkers had begun to give the table an outline of his ideas for the company's direction in the coming year. He had often done this, and was used to being given the floor when he did. But tonight he'd barely begun when the young-looking girl seated across from him started asking him questions. They were fairly basic questions at first, questions about figures and forecasts and bases for projections, and the man, decently and patiently, took pains to answer them fully, but this brought him no respite. The girl continued to fire questions, questions which were rapidly becoming (at least to Mark) more and more cryptic, questions about prototypes and paradigms, conjectures regarding (Mark thought he'd heard this right) the Trondheim Model. When the man asked the girl as politely as he could manage to save her questions for now, and to accept the underlying truth of what he was saying, it was quickly made clear to him that he had misread her.

'"*Truth is neither objectivity nor the balanced view; truth is a selfless subjectivity.*" *Knut Hamsun.*'

Having thought about this for some time, and having failed (quite understandably, thought the table) to come up with any cogent response, the man gave a tight smile, pushed back his fringe, plate and chair, in that order, and left the room. At first Mark assumed he'd gone to the bathroom, or maybe stepped outside in an attempt to calm down and avoid a scene. But twenty minutes passed, during which the girl helped herself to the food the man had left on his plate, apparently oblivious to the bemused bafflement she had brought to proceedings.

Now certain the man would not be returning that evening, Mark's attention returned to his steak as he tried to piece together what had happened. The girl's interjections had been grating, more like heckling than questioning. What she had said had certainly commanded attention, and yet seemed to have no basis in any accepted understanding of how the company worked, or how strategy was conceived and put into practice, or how you should talk to people. Excusing her on the grounds of her extreme youth merely made people wonder what she was doing there in the first place, and why she wasn't getting on with her homework under a One Direction poster. But whatever it was she'd done, and why ever she'd done it, she now had the attention of the table. Those present with long, long company service seemed to see in her something of the Corporation's future. What that something was was way beyond Mark's field of vision. He had listened carefully, he'd understood every word the girl had said. Every word, but not a single sentence. And as for his own contributions, he realised he had barely spoken for the first two courses, and also realised that nothing now happening around him was making him feel any more talkative. He felt some time ago that he'd run out of things to say, and now he had the unnerving feeling that he was also running out of things to think. He was relapsing into his old ways, he could feel it. The change in him, the change which had got him invited here, was going to prove nothing more than a blip.

Senior management had never looked at him twice before tonight. They'd never looked at him *once*, not once in the three years he'd spent with the company. He'd shared a convention room with most of them often enough at company events, but then the entire workforce did that: the corporation's open-plan, open-access ethos was designed precisely to give staff access to senior management. Access, but not acquaintance. With so many on its payroll, with so many ambitious and imaginative employees looking to shine, the halls in which these in-house bunfights were held were usually cavernous and packed. No matter how physically proximate people were at these brainstorming sessions, these 'Festivals of Ideas', the accustomed distance between executive and staff was never seriously compromised. Middle management made representations, canvassed opinion, gathered support. Innovation was applauded, the occasional promotion was bestowed. But the make-up of the boardroom never changed.

If he was honest with himself (and his breakthrough had, finally, encouraged him to be more honest with himself) he'd never completely settled to this job. He'd taken the position, had grabbed it with both hands, because it played so obviously to what he identified as his strengths: independent thought, understanding of people, radical thinking. He'd long been an ideas man.

208

But in this changed, more challenging environment, though ideas came to him as freely as they ever did, most now seemed to shrivel under the scrutiny of his new and shrewder colleagues. The reason might have been flawed thinking, of course. It might have been that in this new, more pugnacious environment he lacked the necessary interpersonal skills to present ideas to their best advantage. He could never decide. But whatever the reason, at too many of these company get-togethers he'd see his strategy proposals, which he would table with his accustomed professionalism and quiet conviction, received with the scarcely concealed aversion – and occasionally the scorn – of his fellow workers. Mark would be subjected to a fusillade of questions – obvious questions, now they were put to him. His interrogators would be all smiles while cross-examining him as if sure they had missed something obvious that Mark would now point out to them. But they hadn't missed anything. He had. The questions, asked by one, endorsed by all, and unconvincingly answered, would induce a perceptible shift in Mark's demeanour. Chastened, he would contribute less and less to the business of the meeting, and later opinions or suggestions tabled by him would fail to resonate simply because of their source. Very occasionally he'd make a forceful point, an *undeniable* point. But it would be an obvious one, a point self-evident to the others, and would in no way rehabilitate him. Before long the discussion would be bypassing him entirely. He would listen for a while, looking on attentively and nodding in all the right places, but the sense of dislocation would grow and grow until, after a few further contributions which Mark knew were inane even before he'd made them, he would make some excuse and nip away early.

But at this last convention, things had been different. His growing doubt that this company was where his future lay seemed to fire in him the confidence and determination not to be so quickly undermined in the face of others' lukewarm reception of his proposed corporate strategies. Faced with the usual querying this time he'd remained firm, realising that, just as he was, others around the table were looking to get their ideas heard and accepted ahead of all others – it was in their interest to disparage his own contributions, regardless of merit. So this time he'd remained firm, prompting an immediate change in the attitude of those around him. They listened, took note, reflected. Those not directly involved in any current conversation no longer gossiped idly with each other, but looked on and took note also. There was a change in the temperature of the meeting, and a change in Mark's place in it. Heartened, he contributed more. Occasionally he would overreach himself, offering only half-formed opinion rather than a thoroughly considered view. But even then, his colleagues listened. And when once in a while someone found the nerve to suggest that what he was saying, though admirable in its aims, was perhaps not immediately achievable, Mark would concede the point with such good grace and humour that the meeting would be united not as before, in an unspoken but palpable conviction that Mark had been over-promoted, but in envious admiration of someone capable of such farsightedness, unafraid of the possibility of failure or ridicule.

Even his most gnomic theorising was listened to in respectful silence, and punctuated by solemn nods. Mark only had to speak for the meeting to turn to him as a body. He would make a joke; they would laugh. He would make a poor joke; they would laugh at that one too. Contributions from elsewhere became more tentative. Early contributors had melted away and were replaced by different voices, with different points of view. Mark had looked up, the first time for some time. He recognised one or two faces from meetings gone by, but was startled to see a member of the Executive sitting in, listening more than speaking, quietly bringing herself up to speed with the conversation she'd joined. Seeing a Director listening so intently to their deliberations seemed to unnerve most of Mark's colleagues; one by one they began to lose their thread and clam up. Presently the floor was left almost entirely to Mark – still assured, still voluble – and the Director, who without becoming exactly chatty had now begun to make a little small talk with him. One by one others had said goodnight and made for home. At last, Mark had found himself in an all but empty hall, with an embossed invitation to supper in his pocket.

It was a blip. His assertiveness, inventiveness, his confidence in the face of naysayers. It was a blip. Mark saw that now as he sat alone at his end of the table, chasing a small piece of sorbet around his plate with the last shards of a wafer, apparently mute. All evening he'd felt like a ten-year-old who'd been invited to sit with the grown-ups: thrilled at first but quickly bored, unable to make sense of the conversation around him, uncomfortable when looked at, agonised by attempts to include him, feeling time stretch away while he waited and waited to be allowed down from the table. People had left before him, but they seemed to have achieved more. They'd made interesting, intelligent presentations, had had spirited exchanges with one another across the table, had told each other jokes. (One of Mark's few contributions to the evening had been a joke. He'd bungled the set-up, realised too late that everyone had heard it, and never got as far as the punchline.) Mark had sat and watched while, one by one, other guests had followed the lead of the irascible Russian and the affronted Middle Easterner and departed early. With nothing occurring to him to say, and with nothing left to eat, Mark rose from the table and politely thanked his hosts for inviting him. There were cursory nods and tight smiles in acknowledgement, mostly from the serving staff, but the muted, earnest conversation at the far end of the table didn't miss a beat. It was taking place between the young woman (who had scarcely paused for breath all night) and the company's Shanghai Operations Manager, one of the only guests whose questions she'd seemed to find worthy of serious consideration all evening. They talked as both rivals and friends, and would continue to talk long into the night, finishing each other's sentences, anticipating each other's positions, disagreeing on almost everything, but mutually respectful. Both knew their conversation would continue for a long time to come, wherever they left it at the end of supper. Both seemed strangely glad of it, and both knew the other felt that way. Setting their course for what would prove a long association, both talked, but neither said.

212

Mark understood none of this. He left them talking, collected his things from the cloakroom, let himself out, and pedalled his way home on the long deserted road which tracked the shoreline of the fjord.

He Played For His Wife

by David Curtis

'For my sins, I suppose it must have been, I lived once in
Egypt,' said the grey-haired young-looking man in the
club smoking room.

And if Egypt on the other side of the world is anything
like the southern part of Illinois, I can readily understand
how the children of Israel found the wilderness prefera-
ble. As I remember the story, though, in Pharaoh's realm
they had only one plague at a time, whereas in southern
Illinois ... however, there may be a better condition of
things there now, so there's nothing to gain by recalling
our experiences. I sincerely hope things are better, but
I scarcely think I have curiosity enough to go back and
find out. In our village, for I was a part of it, and a part
of it was mine, about the same conditions obtained as in
all the other small settlements within a hundred miles.
We had a railroad station and two trains a day. We had
a post office and one mail a day. We had a general store
and a blacksmith's shop and a tavern, and we had a few

215

private residences. If there was anything else of importance, excepting the farmers' wagons, that came in with
loads that were too heavy for the horses, and too often
went back with loads that burdened the farmers, the
details have escaped my mind. It was a typical southern
Illinois village.

Small as it was, there were two social sets in town.
The married men lived in their own houses, and their
wives visited one another and had their small festivities
from time to time in the most serene indifference to the
fact that there were other human beings around. And
these others, that is the unmarried men, lived at the
tavern, or hotel, as we preferred to call it, equally indifferent to the occurrence of social functions to which we
were not bidden. If, as occasionally happened, one of
the married men broke loose for a night or two, and
spent his spare time and money at the hotel, he was
tolerated, but no more. We felt sorry for him when we
thought of his return home, but we had no yearnings
towards reciprocity in his effort to break down the
barriers. In our set there was, it is true, one married
woman, but she did not count. At least we thought so
till the trouble came.

She was the landlord's wife. Old Stein, as we called him,
though he was not over forty, was a placid, easy-going
German, who kept the hotel fairly up to the standard of
the country, and I think a trifle above it, but he hadn't
energy enough, apparently, to make any strenuous effort
to improve things. What was good enough for his boarders was good enough for him, and we were demoralised

enough by the climate, or whatever it is that tends to the deterioration of mankind thereabout, to make no demand for unusual luxury. As far as we ever noticed, he had no remarkable affection for his wife, but seemed rather too indifferent to her very pronounced hunger for admiration.

She was a born flirt, but though she carried her flirtations with anybody who would flirt with her much nearer to the danger line than would be tolerated in a more strait-laced community, it was the general opinion among the boarders that there was no real evil in her and, moreover, that she was fully capable of taking care of herself in almost any emergency. So, though she would not have been recognised as respectable by any other married woman in town, a fact that troubled her not, she was considered all right by our set, and we looked upon her as a good fellow rather than as a woman bound by the ordinary rules of propriety. She was a German by descent, and Stein was German by birth, but Lena was perhaps too thoroughly Americanised in a poor school.

Naturally trouble came of it. We were accustomed, as the people in most small Western towns were accustomed some years ago, to receiving occasionally a visit from what we used to call a 'cross-roads gambler'. These worthies are perhaps the least useful and most 'ornery' specimens of humanity to be found in North America. They are professionals without the skill or nerve they need to enable them to hold their own among other professionals. Knowing just enough to cheat, but not enough to cheat deftly, they travel about the country, usually alone, but sometimes in pairs, stopping in the smallest settlements for a day or a week at a time, looking for victims. No game is too small for them, though they will play heavily at times, but they manage to live on their little skill by worming their way into friendly games of poker, such as are played all over the country, but perhaps more openly in the West than in the East.

When Dick Bradley happened along our way and stopped over at our town, we had, though we did not realise it immediately, all the elements of a drama right at hand. It was not long before the drama was enacted, and perhaps it was just as well that we were not a little farther west, for there might have been considerable shooting in the last act. As it was we had a duel, but that was fought with the pasteboards instead of revolvers, and the difference was supposed to be settled by a freeze-out in the great American game.

Bradley was an ordinary cross-roads gambler, and nothing more. He was a little handsomer than the usual run of men, and he dressed rather better than custom demanded in that part of the country. Moreover, he had a free-and-easy way with him; it was a part of his stock in trade that was attractive to anybody, and I suppose especially so to a woman like Lena. At all events he hadn't been with us twenty-four hours before there was a violent flirtation going on between the two. We all considered that natural enough, and supposing we knew the woman thoroughly well, we thought no harm of it at first. Stein took no notice of it apparently, and as it was a matter that concerned no one else so closely as it did him, none of us felt called on to say anything.

Somewhat to our surprise, however, Bradley stayed on for more than a week. It wasn't his regular business that kept him, for though we played poker every night, as a matter of course, in the back room of the hotel, and though he got into the game, equally as a matter of course, he didn't make enough out of it to make it an object to stay. There were some of us who understood the game and the ordinary tricks of crooked players as well as he did, and he was not long in finding out that he had to play square if he played at all. So, as we never played for big money, the prospect was a poor one for him. Still he stayed. After a few days we all, excepting Stein, began to see that he was staying entirely on Lena's account. He was a bit cautious at first; more so than she was, but seeing that Stein made no objection to anything she did, but gave her a perfectly free foot, the gambler grew bolder and bolder, until there was no longer any possibility of remaining blind to the fact that a scandal impended. Some of us talked it over very quietly and carefully, but it was agreed that no one ought to interfere, since Stein did not see fit to do so.

We had begun to think that Stein was absolutely indifferent and to regard him with considerable contempt, when one evening he undeceived us, and gave us a great surprise by his manner of doing it. It was early in the evening, and, though we had gathered perhaps a dozen of us in the card room, we had not yet begun playing when Stein came in, and, after fidgeting around for a minute or two in a manner quite unlike his usual phlegmatic way, spoke suddenly to Bradley.

'Look here, Bradley,' he said in his broken English, 'I must settle things with you. I have talked things over with my wife, Lena, already, and she says she will go away with you. If she goes this world is no good to me any more, and you and I must settle if she goes or if she stays. I would kill you, but it would be foolishness to try that, for I am not a fighting man and you always carry your gun. Now, what shall we do? Will you go away and leave me my Lena, or will she go with you?'

The poor German seemed not to understand in the least what an amazing sort of a speech this was. His voice trembled with his strong emotion, and there were tears in his eyes. The rest of us were struck dumb. I don't know what the other fellows thought, but I know that there came to me a sort of hungry longing to organise a tar-and-feather party, with Dick Bradley as the principal guest. And, despite my contemptuous pity for the husband who showed so little manhood, I made up my mind that there was going to be fair play, anyhow.

Bradley was fairly staggered. He flushed and stammered, and, I think, was for a moment about to say that he would go; but he pulled himself together, and seemed to remember that as a bad man he had a reputation to sustain. At length he said:

'It's pretty hard to tell what to do, Stein. I'd be willing to fight you for the woman if you wanted to do that, but, as you don't, I suppose she'd better settle it herself.'

'No,' said the landlord. 'She is foolish with you now, and she would have no sense about it. You and I will settle it now. And what will you do? Will you go away and leave us?'

Bradley looked around, as if to see what the crowd thought about it, and perceiving at a glance that our sympathies were all with the other man, he replied: 'Well, if you won't fight, supposing we settle it with the cards. I'll play you a freeze-out, $1,000 against your wife. What do you say?'

'I say no,' said Stein again, and we began almost to respect him. 'I will not play my wife against your money, but I will play you a freeze-out for $1,000, my money against yours, and if you lose, you will go away. And if I lose, I will go away, and she may do what she likes. Only you will play a square game.'

'You bet, it'll be a square game,' said Jack Peters, the biggest man and the best card player in the party. 'I don't like your proposition, but that's your business and not mine. But if you're going to play, Stein, you may be perfectly sure that Bradley won't try any cross-roads tricks in this freeze-out.'

Bradley seated himself at the card table and said: 'Get out your cards.' At the same time he pulled out his wad and counted off the thousand. Stein got the cards and chips, and, each man taking chips to represent his pile, the money was laid at one side. It did not seem like an even contest, for Stein was not a good player. I was delighted to notice, however, after they were fairly well going, that Stein was the cooler of the two. Bradley, I suppose, was a bit rattled by the consciousness that we were watching his play suspiciously.

Bradley tried at first to force the play, and once or twice caught Stein for considerable money, but the game went on for perhaps twenty minutes without anything like a decisive result. Suddenly, as Stein was about to cut the cards, Jack Peters exclaimed:

'Shuffle 'em, Stein!'

'Can't Stein play his own game?' asked Bradley.

'I reckon he can,' said Peters, 'but in case the cards should happen to be stacked against him, and I found it out, there'd be a lynching right here in this town tonight. I don't want that to happen, so I thought I'd make sure.'

It was an unfair trick, for Bradley had not stacked the cards. He hadn't dared to. But Peters told me afterwards that he did it to 'throw a scare' into Bradley if he could. He succeeded, for the gambler lost his nerve when he looked around once more, while Stein remained as cool as before. He nodded and shuffled the cards and the game went on.

The end came suddenly. It was a flush against a full, and Stein held the full and swept the board. There was a moment's silence, and then Bradley said with a short laugh:

'Well, I've lost, and I'll leave town on the morning train. That'll do, I suppose, won't it?'

'Yes, that'll do,' said Stein, gravely. He had won in the outrageous contest, and I expected to see him greatly elated, but instead he seemed curiously depressed. And as the situation was decidedly embarrassing for all hands we went to bed uncommonly early that night, so that everybody was up in time next morning to see Bradley go on the early train as he had agreed to do.

'Well, yes,' said the grey-haired young-looking man, in

222

answer to a question, 'that is the end of the story, as far as the poker part of it goes. Of course there was this sequel. It was inevitable, I suppose. Lena followed Bradley a day or two afterwards, and Stein drank himself to death.'

The Upper Hand

by Grant Gillespie

Celia woke abruptly to the shrill sound of wailing.

She had endured a difficult home labour and had fallen into such an exhausted sleep that she'd momentarily forgotten about the birth. As she wearily lifted her baby to her breast, she became aware of two things: her husband was no longer in bed, and she could smell smoke. Surely even the feckless Frank couldn't be burning leaves at this hour?

It was then she realised that the smoke was coming from inside the house.

Clutching her newborn, Celia rushed onto the landing. A fire was hungrily engulfing the stairwell. She flew from room to room and shook awake her five other children. After swiftly considering her options, she hauled open the dumb waiter, pulled out a pile of laundry, and bundled Bryony, her eldest, inside.

'Be brave,' she said, before the child could object. 'I'm going to lower you to the kitchen. Bang once if it's safe and keep banging if it isn't.'

Then, using all her reserves of strength, Celia gradually let out the rope and operated the pulley. The moment the cage landed, a solitary 'bang' came echoing up the shaft, so she raised the wooden frame and slowly lowered down two more of her brood, then the next two. With no other alternative available, Celia – still clutching her baby – jumped out from the window, landing bruised – but miraculously not broken – on a bush of red-flowering rhododendrons that bordered the lawn.

It was while she was clambering painfully to her feet that she saw Frank running away down the street. She needed no further proof. Her weak-willed husband had attempted to wipe out his growing gambling debts and his growing family in one scorching sweep.

'In this, as in everything,' Celia murmured, 'he has failed miserably.'

'Don't have my boy arrested. Think of me!' her mother-in-law said, having employed every other plea for clemency. 'You have your children for comfort,' she told Celia with a slight pinch of her arm. 'I, poor soul that I am, lost all Frank's siblings in their first year … Oh, the good Lord giveth and he also taketh away …'

But, despite her mother-in-law's protestations, Celia felt no inclination to encumber her homicidal husband's passage to prison.

While she planned her next move, Celia and her children stayed with her sister, Ella. 'We're on our uppers,' she told her. 'How am I supposed to support them?'

'Children don't need riches,' the childless Ella said, offering a rallying smile. 'Time is all a child wants.'

'Yes,' Celia agreed, 'but they want all of it.'

When the couple were first married, thanks to Celia's inheritance, they were able to afford the assistance of several domestics. Now, thanks to Frank – whose fertility was not matched by his accomplishments – she had nothing.

'I wouldn't have minded his gambling,' she told her sister, 'if he'd been remotely accomplished, but what he lacked in skill, he made up for in sheer recklessness.'

'It is a pity,' Ella said, 'that women aren't afforded the opportunity to gamble. You would certainly have doubled your fortunes by now, what with your good luck and your cleverness.'

Celia wasn't convinced. Had she been blessed with good luck she would never have met Frank; had she been clever, she would never have agreed to marry him.

She made fervent inquiries about employment, petitioning even her most casual acquaintances, but her endeavours were met with no success. Then a letter arrived from overseas from an estranged uncle on her father's side, offering her a post in his Manhattan hotel.

'I can provide room and board for yourself alone,' he wrote, 'not for your children, but, should you work hard and live frugally, you should be able to send funds home for their upkeep.'

He also enclosed a cheque for First Class passage. 'As you are now using your maiden name – my family name – don't think of travelling Second Class and pocketing the difference. You need to be seen as a lady even if you are to work as a secretary.'

'Ella ...' Celia prompted, 'you said that all children want is "time" and you have plenty of that, certainly enough to care for the two littlest. They're no trouble ...' she fibbed. 'No trouble at all.'

'But I have my charity work!'

'Charity begins at home,' Celia reminded her, 'and, it seems, I no longer have one.'

It was an argument impossible to refute.

Celia then approached two spinster sisters – old friends of the family – who lived on Pennard golf course, asking if they'd harbour her eldest boy, Harry, and his brother, Bert.

'They can sing and dance for you in the evenings,' she promised, having never once seen them do either. That deal struck, she only had three children left to un-bosom. She took them to her mother-in-law's and, when she opened the door, Celia bustled them in – without invitation – beckoning the driver to follow with their cases.

'It would have been courteous,' the old woman said, 'to have—'

'I'm leaving for New York,' Celia interrupted.

Her mother-in-law eyed the luggage. 'And taking away my grandchildren?'

'Oh, no, they're staying ... with you,' Celia told her. 'But—'

'Poor soul that you are, you lost three of your own, but now you're recompensed with three more! It appears the Lord taketh away ... but occasionally he giveth back.'

And, with that, she embraced her children, instructing them, without meaning it, to behave for their grand-mother and, fighting back tears, fled down the steps to the waiting cab.

Though Celia was tempted to buy a Second Class ticket, or even Steerage, she followed her uncle's instructions and booked First. Besides, she told herself, if labour lay behind her on this continent and labour lay ahead on the other, she could at least cross between the two in style.

Boarding in Southampton, she was struck by the ship's splendour but, edging past her fellow passengers as they waved cheerful and tearful goodbyes to their loved ones, she was haunted by the absence of her own. She inhaled a deep breath of salt-sea air and, locating a steward, asked to be shown directly to her cabin.

When evening fell, Celia rallied herself and dressed for dinner. She selected an evening dress – that she hadn't had the opportunity to wear in years – and added a few simple pieces of costume jewellery, the only items that Frank hadn't been able to pawn.

The cavernous dining room, which looked as if it had been carved out of wedding-cake icing, had a balcony at one end where an orchestra played. Celia found herself in the exalted company of the liner's Commander, sporting a moustache that dominated his entire face; a thin-nosed man of the cloth; and a woman called Dorothea de Vere. Dorothea was also travelling alone, and Celia quickly decided that she was not only fiendishly bookish, but also witty and bold.

'It seems,' Dorothea whispered, 'that our little

gathering is divided neatly into two halves; we are the new world, and they,' she said, nodding towards the men who were deep in a conversation about Catholicism, 'are the very, very old.' And Celia laughed appreciatively.

'Did we miss something amusing?' the priest asked, his head turning sharply like a heron's.

'Almost certainly,' Dorothea told him with a seraphic smile.

The clergyman narrowed his eyes a fraction, then turned to the Commander to air his grievances concerning the smoking room.

'In inclement weather like this, it is the only place where a gentleman may, with any satisfaction, indulge in smoking a cigar and—'

'That doesn't seem very fair,' Dorothea interjected. 'What about us gentlewomen? Where is our designated smoking room?'

The vicar looked aghast. 'Do you smoke?'

'I do not,' Dorothea said, 'but that doesn't mean I should not be afforded the opportunity.'

'What I want to know,' said Celia, emboldened by her new friend's candour, 'is why gentlemen need to secure themselves a room so firmly immune from feminine intrusion. Are we ladies so very threatening?'

'I'm relieved to hear you don't indulge in smoking,' the vicar said to Dorothea, overlooking Celia's provocation. 'I always think that women who smoke have dubious morals.'

'I smoke,' Celia lied, boldly holding the vicar's eye till he turned away to readdress the Commander.

'What outrages me, Captain, is that the tables are

monopolised, not by gentlemen, but by,' he paused to inhale the word, 'gamblers. And not desiring to come into contact with men of this sort, I was compelled to go back on deck, my evening and my cigar entirely ruined.'

'How very tragic,' Celia said, taking a small sip of wine.

'Indeed!' the priest agreed, and he gestured with his sherry glass at a grinning, red-haired man at an adjoining table. 'He's the ringleader. He's from some God-forsaken place like Texas, I imagine.'

'Mr Brown,' the Commander said. 'I believe he's from the West.'

'Oh, the pioneer spirit!' Dorothea exclaimed, with evident admiration.

The Commander went on to explain that the gamblers' sole objective in crossing the ocean was to infiltrate a class of gentlemen players whom, under ordinary circumstances, they would never meet.

'Mr Brown and his ilk affect their clothes and manners,' he told them, 'so as to resemble men of refinement,' adding, 'obviously the American kind – and we Europeans are quickly and easily deceived.'

'I was not deceived!' the priest said, irritably.

Dorothea tried to change the subject, but Celia was intrigued. She inquired of the Commander if he had any jurisdiction in these matters and he was forced to admit that he was afforded no authority whatsoever to prohibit gambling on his ship.

'I did have a small placard mounted on the wall. Perhaps you saw it? "Gentlemen are respectfully requested not to play poker for high stakes."'

'I saw it!' the priest bristled. 'I pointed it out to our Mr Brown over there, but he told me that as he wasn't a "gentleman", the rule didn't apply to him and then he suggested I stick the sign up in my rectory ...'

Dorothea guffawed.

'What on earth is amusing about that?' the clergyman demanded indignantly. But, before he could expose himself to further ridicule, the Commander leant in to whisper a few words of explanation in his ear and, as the priest listened, his cheeks turned a distinct shade of puce and he began to sputter involuntarily like a kettle.

Celia glanced discreetly at the blithe Mr Brown, who immediately caught her eye and raised his glass. She raised an eyebrow in reply and turned away. So that was why he appeared so insouciant, she thought to herself. It was not in the company's interests to abolish gambling; the smoking room would certainly be furnished with an unending supply of wines and liquors that were not included in the price of passage and – if Frank and his cronies were anything to go by – men who played poker also drank, and copiously too.

'If you wish,' the Commander was saying to the vicar, 'to lodge a formal complaint concerning Mr Brown, I can arrange for the detective, Mr Marron, to meet me at quarantine.'

'Consider my complaint lodged!' the vicar declared, and he folded his hands together and glared at Mr Brown with peevish satisfaction.

'I've just remembered,' Celia said, already rising from the table, 'I packed playing cards in my luggage ... Dorothea, could I tempt you to a game of whist?'

'Splendid!' Dorothea exclaimed. 'I'll just nip to my cabin,' she said, adding with an exaggerated wink, 'to fetch my purse!'

'Do excuse us,' Celia said to the gentlemen. 'And thank you, your conversation has been most ... inspiring.'

The priest's expression – as she'd anticipated – was a grimace of perfect disgust, but when the Commander rose to give her a small, formal bow, she was gratified to catch a discreet, moustache-shrouded grin.

The new friends made for one of the First Class lounges where they easily recruited a couple of ladies to make up their whist party. Though Dorothea was not as accomplished as Celia, she was undeniably shrewd and, without much difficulty, they won twelve out of their thirteen tricks. A small crowd of spectators had gathered and another pair of enthusiastic ladies immediately asked to play. By the time they'd won this game, they had generated so much excitement that Celia – feigning reluctance at first – agreed to organise a tournament.

Before they commenced, Celia took Dorothea to one side and acquainted her with a few of the more ethically debatable practices of the game, or, as she delicately put it, 'the more nuanced language of whist'.

'If a player discards a high card followed by a low card of the same suit,' she explained, 'they are inviting their partner to lead with a trump.'

'Isn't that somewhat an unfair advantage?' Dorothea asked, adding, 'Not that I'm objecting.'

'It isn't an advantage if our adversaries have taken the time to master the rules ... and are observant.'

Dorothea tried to apply her new knowledge, but she soon grew inattentive and, though Celia knew it was unscrupulous, she resorted to giving her friend the occasional surreptitious nod or prod, strictly as guidance. When the tournament was over and they'd been declared the undisputed victors, Celia set about dividing up their winnings.

'Keep it. You earned it!' Dorothea insisted. 'When my husband died, I found myself richer than I could ever have imagined ... in more ways than one. Besides,' she said, lowering her voice conspiratorially, 'don't be offended, but that paste and glass jewellery of yours really is in need of replacing.'

Celia wasn't offended and accepted Dorothea's pot without further protestation. She would wire the bulk of it home for her children. Her only reservation was that she hadn't relished winning money from her fellow women. She doubted, however, that she'd experience the same discomfort when it came to men.

By the following morning, Celia had concocted a plan. Now all she needed was to find the instrument to put it into practice. As it was raining heavily, she made a circuitous perambulation around the deck's interior.

'I've been looking for you,' the Commander said, intercepting her.

'Oh yes?'

'What with the weather being so intemperate, it struck me as rather discriminatory our not providing a smoking room for the ladies.'

He lowered his voice and told her that she'd have to

keep it 'on the q.t.' but there was a private antechamber off said room that was usually reserved for the aristocracy and, as there wasn't anyone of that particular milieu on the voyage, he suggested temporarily elevating Celia's status to that of a Duchess.

'I've always thought,' Celia said, 'it would be churlish to turn down a title,' and, when she added the word 'Captain', she saw his moustache ripple in gratitude. And so it was settled and, after promising to notify the necessary stewards, the Commander took a low bow and her leave.

Resuming her seemingly directionless stroll, Celia entered one of the lounges. It was there that she spotted the red-haired poker player. He was sitting at a discreet table, barricaded in by an array of aspidistras one might have found in an old-fashioned drawing room.

'Mr Brown?' she said, making an approach.

'Guilty!' the man replied with easy charm.

'It has come to my attention,' she began, settling herself in the chair opposite, 'that you are a man who enjoys a wager at cards.'

'Really?' Mr Brown said, affecting gentlemanly outrage. 'May I ask who's levelling this slander at me?'

'I'll come to that,' Celia told him calmly, 'but first I have a proposition for you.'

Intrigued, Mr Brown leant in. Celia, keeping her proverbial cards close to her chest, explained that she possessed pertinent intelligence that would prevent Mr Brown from running into difficulties when he reached New York. In exchange for this information, she had two requests.

'You mean demands.'

'I would hardly call them that ... You see, I find I've grown tired of whist and bridge,' she told him, 'so I'd be obliged if you'd teach me how to play a man's game. Let's say ... poker.'

'I like your pluck, Missy, but knowing how to play poker and being able to play it are two distinctly separate skills.'

Celia smiled. 'If you assist me with the former, Mr Brown, I trust that, with practice, I shall actualise the latter.'

Mr Brown pressed to know her second 'demand' and to deliver up her 'pertinent intelligence', but Celia refused to be coerced.

'As I am sure you know,' she said, drawing a notebook and deck of cards from her purse, 'a good player never reveals his – or, in my case, her – hand until the game is quite over.'

A steward escorted Celia to her private antechamber. It was sumptuously decorated and had three round tables perfectly suited for the playing of cards.

'Kindly remove two of these, and I shall need no more than six chairs.'

'Of course, Your Grace,' the steward said, with a suitably servile smile.

'I'll be receiving guests,' she told him, casually. 'Please ensure their glasses are always brim-full. I'll be drinking gin and tonic. If I ask you to "hold the lime", I mean "hold the gin".' And to seal the deal, she tipped the man, heavily, from her previous night's winnings.

When the room was arranged to her design, she took out her cards and a freshly bought packet of Lucky Strikes, placing them squarely on the table. Never having smoked before, she thought it prudent to practise before anyone arrived. She was not a natural smoker; the colour drained from her face, her stomach heaved, and her head spun. Concluding that she did not need to be seen smoking, and that evidence that she had smoked would suffice, she lit two more cigarettes and watched them burn down.

At nine o'clock there was a knock on the door and Mr Brown's florid face appeared.

'Evening, Missy.'

'Duchess!'

'Sorry, Duchess.' He asked if she was ready for battle and, after taking a slow sip of her gin, she declared that she was.

'You guarantee,' he said, 'that if I keep my word, you'll keep yours?'

'Of course. Women, unlike men, invariably set some store by the promises they make. Now, remember, if I touch my ear, substantially raise the bet. I'll reimburse you for any losses incurred.'

'Yes,' Mr Brown agreed. 'You will.'

Half an hour later, five men, including Mr Brown, joined Celia in her enclave. She didn't bother to learn their names; she didn't plan to keep their acquaintance for long.

'The Duchess is intrigued by the game of poker,' Mr Brown told the assembly, 'though she only knows the rules of five-card stud ... if no one has any objections.'

The gentlemen collectively grinned and none of them put up any objections.

'Pity me if I play poorly,' Celia begged, 'but don't pity me with your stakes. I assure you, I have money to lose ... And the drinks are on me.'

The men laughed, making encouraging, patronising remarks; the cards were dealt, and the game commenced.

Celia was careful never to lead the betting. If she had a favourable hand, she simply touched her ear and let Mr Brown raise on her behalf. Then, on the subsequent round, as arranged, her accomplice would fold and Celia would opt to stay in, 'just to learn'.

'Oh, have I won again?' she'd ask, artlessly.

'Yes, you have!' came the men's replies. 'Well done, little lady.'

'Beginner's luck,' she'd insist ... every time.

Whenever the cards Celia had showing implied a winning hand, but her hole card hid a losing one, she would pose a seemingly innocent question to the table:

'Am I right in thinking a flush is all cards of the same suit?' or, 'In a straight, can an ace be either high or low?' and she watched her opposition politely fold. She was also careful, as her tutor had advised, not to win every round.

Mr Brown had taught her well, but Celia didn't feel inclined to cover his losses any more than was strictly necessary, and so, after an hour of play, she wrinkled her nose at him – her signal that she no longer required his collaboration – and, obediently, he excused himself from the game.

Inevitably, by close of play, Celia was up, and by a princely sum of two hundred pounds. She considered quitting while she was ahead, but she had her children to think of and so, as she had rather enjoyed sharpening her wits on these dull whetstones, she asked Mr Brown to provide a nightly supply of lambs to her sacrificial parlour.

On the third evening, however, Celia became too emboldened. She played rashly and it cost her every penny she had carefully accrued.

'Oh Dorothea,' she lamented. 'I behaved like that cocksure cretin, my husband, and wantonly abandoned logic for luck.'

Dorothea shook her head. 'This is nothing more than a temporary setback and you have learned an invaluable lesson. When we women lose our cool, we lose our advantage.' She took Celia's hand and, when she released it, a roll of notes curled up in her palm like a stack of fortune fish.

'I couldn't—' Celia began.

'You must,' Dorothea interrupted. 'As Croesus' widow I am fortunate; I'll never have to rely on patriarchal patronage again. Please me by beating these men at their own game.'

'I'll pay you back,' Celia told her, her eyes misty with emotion.

'My dear,' Dorothea smiled, 'of that I have no doubt.'

Celia decided it would be pertinent to further enlist Mr Brown's services.

'You must teach me,' she instructed him, 'the art, if you will, of double-dealing.'

Her mentor duly obliged and, by the next evening, she was able to deftly glance at the underside of each card that she dealt and, when the round was over, and she retrieved the spent hands, she slyly secreted a few choice cards to utilise herself. Unbeknownst to Mr Brown, she'd put another measure in place to ensure her success; she had marked the backs of the kings and aces, making almost imperceptible grooves and crosses with her fingernail. This way, she could more easily deduce her opponents' hands ... or bluff with importunity about her own.

Celia continued to lose the occasional game – now by strategy not stupidity – and by the time the liner docked in Manhattan, she had not only recouped all her losses and paid back Dorothea, she found herself well over a thousand pounds the richer.

Celia was happy to fulfil her promise to Mr Brown and she smuggled him through quarantine as her manservant – easy to achieve now that she was a known Duchess – thereby evading the waiting detective, Mr Marron.

When they'd safely set foot on terra firma, Mr Brown asked Celia what she planned to do next.

'Firstly,' she told him, 'I'll write two cheques; one to reimburse my uncle, since I no longer need his offer of employ, and another, larger one, to send home to my family.'

'And then?'

'Lunch with Dorothea.'

'What I mean is,' Mr Brown said, somewhat impatiently, 'what will you do with the rest of your life? Will you stay in New York?'

'Oh no. I think another trip is in order,' she told him

with a sprightly smile. 'I have heard that the West Indies are very fine at this time of year.'

'Duchess . . .' Mr Brown said with a tug of his thick red fringe, 'would you like your manservant to accompany you? We make a good team, you and I.'

Celia hesitated.

'It's an interesting and a tempting proposition, but from now on,' she told him, 'I fully intend to govern myself.'

By her fiftieth birthday, Celia was one of only two women who owned a Las Vegas casino. She named it The Pioneer Spirit, in tribute to Dorothea de Vere. The two friends had grown inseparable over the years and, after several prolonged trips, Dorothea took up permanent residence in The Pioneer Hotel.

In a town like Las Vegas there were, of course, rumours that Dorothea and Celia – who had declined many offers of marriage – were lovers, but they refused to deny them or fan the flames. They simply smiled and held their heads up high as they promenaded, arm-in-arm, along the Strip.

Celia's children, now grown up, often came to stay. She remained closest to her youngest, Pamela Grace, whose infant wailing had saved them all from certain immolation.

'Tell me again how you two met,' Pamela Grace said, as the three women sipped their dry Martinis.

Dorothea smiled, wistfully.

'She was on her maiden voyage. It was also,' she said with a sniff and a swift stir of her silver cocktail stick, 'where she met Mr Brown.'

'Did you ever see him again?' Pamela Grace inquired, with a twinkling curiosity.

'Once or twice,' Celia said, 'though we never acknowledged one another. I'm told he was involved in some brawl en route to New Orleans. The Captain locked him in the detention hospital and had him arrested the minute they docked.'

'Poor man,' said Pamela Grace.

'Not poor,' Celia corrected. 'He was very, very rich. He just never learned when to cut his losses.'

The detective, Mr Marron, caught all of Celia's fellow sharks in the end. For years, he had made it his sole purpose to apprehend 'The Duchess' too, but he could never find anyone to testify against her. The men she played fell into two neat categories: those who couldn't credit a woman with being a professional gambler and those who wouldn't admit they'd been outsmarted by one.

Celia lit a Lucky Strike – she had long since acquired a taste for cigarettes – and took a moment to admire a new ring – a ring that would never be pawned.

'I'm sure Dorothea will agree,' Celia said to her daughter, with a slow, appreciative smile, 'that it just goes to show, a woman can – against the most unfavourable odds – always assume the upper hand.'

Victoria

by Tena Štivičić

'We knew it was going to happen,' Leah said unhelpfully, followed by nothing. No plan, no suggestion, no course of action. She was impatient, almost out of the door when Hana got off the phone. Not a good time for this conversation.

Hana stood there, staring into a spot, worries agonisingly multiplying behind her eyes. It was going to take a long time to untangle them, relieve them of the explosive power they had when they came all at the same time, like an avalanche. They both stood there, Leah eager to go, not daring to say, I have to go. Hana, hoping that Leah would stay, already sensing the fury, which would hit her when she doesn't stay.

'Hana, darling, we knew it was going to happen. It's not that much of a surprise. We'll deal with it.'

'We'll never find anything this good at this price. And moving just bleeds money. We'll have to use our savings. Our savings, which are for ...' She stopped herself before finishing the thought. Leah knows what they're for. She knows all this. 'There's no time to start saving all over again. That's the thing. Biologically speaking, there's no time.'

'Look, those two are not necessarily related ... anyway it's a longer conversation and—'

'You have to go—'

'Well ... I do have to go ... The tournament starts at two, as you well know.'

Hana thought of herself as a tolerant person. She prided herself in not judging and she felt that if judgement did occur but was quashed before it could hit the object of judgement, then that was tolerance of an even higher order.

Other people judge. People back home judge. Sometimes they have a look about them, something resembling pity. She hates pity. She always hated pity. The look they give her, sometimes, is the somewhat uncomfortable look of not wanting to be the one to break it to her that she is living in a problem relationship. And if she were to try to volunteer an explanation that it wasn't actually anything like what they think, it would appear a little too defensive, given that nobody asked. Oh, fuck them. Fuck them and their small-mindedness. Which she left behind, anyway, a long time ago.

What had just happened was one of those moments when one, not small, but manageable piece of news landed on top of a delicately balanced heap of concern and resentment, toppling the whole thing into the abyss. One can't be expected not to resort to some unreasonable arguments in such situations. So she didn't mean it, really, when she said that her mother was right all along.

'A bit of a leap, don't you think?!'

What Hana's mother said, on a visit a while ago and sort of en passant, was that people who don't go to bed together don't make babies. She said it, despite it being glaringly inapposite. Despite the fact that no amount of shared bedtime between two wombs, a situation by then accepted as the permanent state of things, was going to make a baby. But a universal truth confirmed by years of life experience should not let something so profane as a biological technicality undermine it. She said it, because some people are just talented that way, able to string together words so elegantly loaded with meaning beyond what they first seem.

The people who go to bed at a reasonable hour and sleep, next to their partner, when the world is meant to be sleeping, have a decent chance of having a solid, healthy, sound life. With perhaps a house of their own and some children in it. Perhaps free of such disturbing phone calls as the one they just received from the landlord informing them the time had finally come and the house was set for demolition under the new construction plans for the neighbourhood.

On the other hand, the people who spend their nights playing poker at the computer, in dark rooms, unable to break away from the strings of blue screen lights like some helpless alien abductees, while their partners sleep alone – those people are screwed. And it would come as no surprise to her mother that such people would put what they call a hobby (but is more likely an addiction) before staying at home and talking through a situation of genuinely existential proportions with their partner.

The fact that Hana's parents had been going to bed together for forty-two years – you could hear the click of their bedside lamps going out with freakish synchronicity – and yet were no strangers to ample amounts of marital misery, didn't come to mind quickly enough for Hana. They did, after all, have a house, two children, a dog and plenty of empty space, which could be filled with grandchildren.

No matter how rationally Hana explained things, it would never quite stop hanging in the air, her sharing a life with a gambler. More importantly this fact was somehow going to affect the most momentous next step of her life, having children. Technically it didn't apply, because the act of conception would take place elsewhere, away from both their bodies. But it sort of applied in the way intimacy worked, in the way people are with each other. That was the crux of it, the bloody 'sort of' that had things both applying and not applying to their situation; all of that was causing Hana a lot of grief. So when she said to Leah, in the heat of the moment, 'my mother was right all along', she used these factually inaccurate words to express a wealth of things that were bothering her, but managing to convey hardly any of it.

'I'm only trying to say that—'

'Because whatever wisdom comes from the woman who calls me Dead-eyes is, you understand, not going to leave me best disposed for the argument we're about to plunge into.'

'Glass-eyed. She calls you Glass-eyed. Only sometimes. That's very different.'

'Oh. I do apologise.'

'You deliberately won't understand the subtext of what I'm—'

'What your mother said clearly indicates that neither she, nor your dad for that matter, ever accepted who you are. And they certainly never accepted me.'

'It's not fair what you expect of her. She just thought it was a little too much.'

'Which bit?'

'You know perfectly well which bit.'

'Your mother thinks I turned you. Though, in fact, your track record is far longer than mine. Now, having already inflicted my lesbianism on you, she would prefer it if I were a doctor or a lawyer rather than a part-time radio producer and film-maker, with something wholesome like gardening as a hobby, rather than poker, which is I believe the bit that's a little too much. It's really quite shockingly blinkered, believing that her daughter, even if lesbian, should be financially looked after by her partner, even if also lesbian.'

'As per usual, you're twisting things. You know how unfair it is to use your superior arguing powers against me—'

'Well, permit me to descend to your level – my parents are not exactly ecstatic with an Eastern European daughter-in-law. They, too, think I could have done better. They think any woman would be lucky to have me and they were hoping for someone with at least an OBE. Which, granted, reveals them as royalists, but at least they're not homophobic . . .'

'I know what you're doing. You never say Eastern

European except to deliberately annoy me. Not even your parents say that because they know how reductive and false and—'

'That's right, they don't. Because they're also not xenophobic.'

'They served borsch three times before they worked out it was a traditional dish about four hundred miles away from my country.'

'Well, that's patronising, perhaps colonialist at worst, but not xenophobic.'

'I hate beetroot.'

'Whereas your father thinks I have funny feet.'

'Not because you're black.'

'He didn't say it. That doesn't mean he didn't think it.'

'Leah, please don't make me justify my politically incorrect, embarrassing parents, who don't know better than to . . . you know this . . . Why are we arguing about our p—'

'I do know that, and as I said, I have elevated myself to the Zen plane of not caring, until you come out with such things as "my mum was right all along".'

Obviously Leah was right. It was only at moments of great insecurity that Hana felt so benevolent towards her parents' reactionary worldview.

But she did feel increasingly they were like a comedy couple, with overtones of the grotesque. Their overwhelming otherness, now soon to be rooflessness. The song had always annoyed her, how could a room without a roof possibly be happy? It was only at these low moments that she let her convictions wobble and the judgement seep in.

'There's a difference between a parent wanting their child to be kept by a partner and not wanting their child to end up homeless because their partner is a gambler.'

'I couldn't agree more. But if we can just clarify – when we say gambler do we mean me? And how is the house we're about to lose in any way connected to poker?'

'It's not that,' – Hana started slowly, with a lot of effort – 'it's that you leaving to play in a tournament ... I mean, given the situation, at a time when we should be working through this unsettling news is ... an indication of priorities ... which show to me that ... in terms of far reaching consequences—'

'You know, in film-making there's a rule that if you can't say what your story is about in one sentence, there's something wrong with your story.'

Hana looked away.

Leah exhaled, shifting gears.

'Have I ever put you or you and me and our livelihood in jeopardy?'

'No ...'

'Have I ever been reckless in any way that caused you any harm or damage?'

'You haven't but—'

'Have I not in fact been supplementing our relatively irregular income with regular cash injections of winnings?'

'They're not regular, Leah, for fuck's sake. You can't use the word regular with something that largely relies on the luck of the draw.'

'It doesn't largely rely on the – it largely relies on skill!

Another thing your family don't understand. They think I go and hit keys on fruit machines like some monkey.'

'Leah. Can we drop my parents from this? Please. It's ... I'm just ... frustrated ... because ... because ... we're waiting ... we're waiting to start our lives ... and to ... You know what I mean ... to have a family ... We're running out of time ... and ... Look outside. Just see what the skyline looks like. Remember what it was like six, seven years ago?'

Over the course of a few years, the skyline had in Hana's mind become a metaphor for everything that was wrong with their lives. While Leah spent her days away from the house, in breakfast, brunch, lunch, cocktail hour and dinner meetings, recording features, in the edit, always on the move, always with people, Hana sat at home. She wrote articles for a number of independent international media outlets, which seemed to get their funding cut with eerie predictability, shortly after Hana joined the team. She wrote staring from the ground floor of their house at the increasingly oppressive Islington skyline, peppered with cranes and tall, lean luxury tower blocks, feeling physically squashed by the inevitable super-state future of this city.

It was a stroke of luck she'd found this tiny house seven years ago when she and Leah decided to live together. Squeezed between a row of terraced Georgian houses and a housing estate, it was somehow overlooked and left in peace by a number of architectural generations adding to the landscape. The owner said, with how things were going, it wouldn't be long before he had to sell and the house was torn down. Which was fine because Hana and

Leah were going to be off to bigger and better places in life before that happened. Seven years on, it had finally happened; the house would be torn down. The neighbourhood was unrecognisable. And Hana and Leah were still in exactly the same place.

Their world was the world of freelance artists, of writers and entertainers. The kind of people who used to be drawn to London from every corner of the world. But these days the super-state does not look kindly on their existence. The super-state pities them on a good day, crushes them on a bad day and mocks them on an average Tuesday. The super-state is annoyed that they insist on occupying square footage where luxury towers for absent owners might be built and is in the long game of squeezing them out. It feels, as it has felt for a while, that the threads by which they cling to their chosen lifestyle are thinning. Because their world is also not a world of young aspiring wannabes with a naïve glint in their eye. These are people in their late thirties, forties, fifties. They own no properties, they have no savings, they have no mortgages, they don't receive a pay cheque every month. They typically have no children, having postponed starting a family until after the big break. They are ostriches. The world around them is manifestly changing, with ever-diminishing windows of opportunity.

'We're not reckless,' Hana thinks to herself, 'Leah isn't actually reckless at all. We are trying to live responsibly to the best of our abilities. It's only that our abilities are antiquated.'

Opportunities present themselves occasionally, bright, hot and ephemeral, like matches on a windy night. But even occasionally hefty fees will never afford them a steady decent life in the super-state, a house, school fees, private healthcare when the NHS is finally dismantled. Still, they can't stop trying. Because they have at best passed the middle of their lives. What else are they going to do? They are under-qualified and too old even to be receptionists and bartenders.

They are often in debt, often unemployed for months, their prospects are not improving and they are getting older. At times when there is no work, Hana draws up the bridge, reads books and this takes her down a rabbit hole of existential despair. Leah usually plays poker. At those times, it's not just a pastime. It actually seems like a more solid source of income. And how could Hana, with her meagre earnings, help but be complicit in it? Help but herself rejoice when the money is won and grumble when it's lost? But the tunnel is starting to seem circular. The precarious, non-conformist life used to be exciting. Now, with those sinister cranes looming just outside her door, she feels smaller, weaker and less visible by the day.

She isn't even sure, when she peers very deep into her soul, whether this desire to have children, which grips her like some sort of a heart condition, restricting her breath, is real or it's simply her mind grasping for a change.

'Have I ever neglected you – have I ever put playing first, before your needs?'

'Just now.'

'Oh, Hana, honestly …'

'You know what I hate the most?'

'There's quite a list, I couldn't say for sure—'

252

'Condescension.'

'Ah, yes. I knew that one would come up.'

'The banality of my pain, how tiring it is for you ...'

'Banality of your pain? Do you hear yourself? I asked you if you wanted to do anything this weekend. You said you had no plans. You know how much money is at stake in this tournament—'

'Forgive me for managing my expectations ...'

Leah took a second to let that go and take a patient breath.

'You said you didn't mind.'

'I don't mind! I don't mind! Don't make me into some kind of a controlling, uptight ... It's only in my world a biggish piece of news like this merits a conversation ... an immediate conversation ... and it trumps ... ah, fuck it, I feel stupid having to explain.'

'Please, don't sulk. We can have the conversation tomorrow. Everything will still be there. We can examine all the implications, put it in perspective with literally everything that's bothering you.'

'Please don't patronise me.'

'Jesus ...'

'Yeah, Jesus is the right person to invoke.'

'What do you want?'

'Nothing. Just go. Just go. It's OK. Go.'

Leah left. Hana cried. They were tears of self-contempt. Because it was exactly what her mum used to do. Say it was OK, then feel mortally wounded if the truth had not been recognised. Say, just go, thinking, please stay.

Here comes another night of procrastinating. Her

willpower collapsing under what suddenly seemed like a complete lack of options. Going over her past choices. Beating herself over the head for being so laissez-faire about life. Believing that things sort themselves out. But not if you're foreign. Not if you're gay. Not if you're a woman. Honestly, shouldn't she be entitled to some sort of a grant just by the number of boxes she ticked?

Before Leah, she gave men what she thought was a good old go. Two in a row. Perhaps she should have at least got pregnant by one of them. It was the second of the two that took her to that party, where she wandered into the poker room and saw Leah, the only woman at a table of men, and couldn't take her eyes off her. Leah looked focused, merciless and completely in control. She spoke little, in caustic one-liners, impeccably treading the fine line between witty and rude. When she looked up and held Hana's gaze for a lot longer than would have been expected, so long in fact that a couple of men turned round to look, Hana distinctly remembers thinking: 'Oh, fuck. Trouble ahead.'

Now, Leah mostly plays online. Until the early hours. Hana wakes up, middle of the night, alone in bed, checks her watch, rolls her eyes, goes to the bathroom, pops her head into the living room where her presence more often than not goes unnoticed. On the rare occasions Leah stirs and looks up, she meets her with a glass-eyed gaze of someone wired and entirely absent in spirit. Glass-eyes. She doesn't look focused and merciless, more like a rat in the lab, one of those ones who keep hitting the orgasm button instead of the food button and end up climaxing themselves to death.

'That's harsh,' Hana thinks, 'that's a really harsh thing to say about her. I must remember never to say it.'

She spends some time blaming herself for allowing her brain to spin in overtime and falls asleep vaguely grumpy about the day ahead.

'Wake up.'

'What?'

'Wake up.' Leah is sitting on the bed, wide-eyed and excited.

'What's the time?'

'Quarter past seven in the morning.'

'What . . . why?'

Two clear plastic bags are placed beside Hana on the bed. Clearing her eyes and her head, she can make out wads of twenty- and fifty-pound notes.

'Based on your latest estimate, this should cover three rounds of IVF,' Leah says and sits on the bed. 'Or two, plus a move.'

*

Extrapolating from the current political landscape of the world, Hana was explaining how people like her and Leah were running out of places to move to. Everywhere seemed to be closing in on itself. The people belonging to her extended family, now sat around her mother's dining room table, were people who never moved or considered moving, regardless of the tectonic shifts of the world around them. The thought hit her mid-sentence. They now understood her less than ever before and were possibly even more convinced that this girl liked to choose the trickiest paths in life. But somehow she felt herself speaking from another place. Not the deliberately antagonistic one of her early years away. Not the defensive, self-questioning one of recent years. She felt she talked about herself effortlessly. Though it could just be that all the actual focus was on the baby, snoozing and drooling as it was passed around the table. Leah stood by the door, trapped by two cousins who were repeatedly failing to successfully translate a punchline to a joke. She signalled with some horror that the baby was about to be fed a spoonful of cake.

'Please don't feed her cake, Auntie. She's only starting to eat solids, I'm not giving her any sugar,' Hana said.

'It's home-made pie. The apples are as natural as they can get. Not sprayed or anything. I have a guy. It's all health and love.'

'Nevertheless.'

'There, there, you come to your auntie, little thing. No apple pie,' the auntie tutted with indignation.

'You really shouldn't be dressing a little a girl in grey. She's going to be depressed.'

'What should I dress her in?'

'Happy colours. Red and pink. Girl colours. Like the dress I got her.'

'Sure.'

'Little Victoria. Little Victoria. Like the queen.'

'Well, actually,' – Hana smiled at her sleepy daughter in her grey baby suit – 'it's Victoria. Like the casino.'

Jimmy Ahearn's Last Hand

by Peter Alson

They came in right behind Stevie Freckles. Two big guys, one in a white sport coat, the other in a puce-coloured Dacron shirt. They must have been waiting for just the right moment; at any rate, they moved too fast for the door guy to react. Now they were in and it was too late to do anything about it.

Jimmy Ahearn was at one of the six tables in the small well-lit loft, playing $5–$10 hold'em, and though the sudden appearance of the intruders caught him off guard, his immediate take was that they weren't robbing the place. The rest of the room had gone from noisy to dead quiet in a matter of seconds.

'The boss around?' the guy in the white sport coat demanded gruffly of nobody in particular. Jimmy noticed that he was wearing white loafers to go along with the coat. Could these guys look more the part?

The kid at the door, Joey, didn't know what to do.

257

He glanced at Jimmy, who wondered if either of the two thugs saw the look.

What the fuck. It didn't matter.

'I'm the boss,' Jimmy said. 'What can I do for you?'

The two men turned in his direction. 'Like to have a word with you.'

Jimmy did a little shrug of his palms and got up. He motioned for them to follow him and headed back through the kitchen to the smoking room. He held the door for them, then stepped in himself. Two exhaust fans were going. A smoke eater overhead. The room still stank like a wet blanket in a flophouse.

'Let me guess,' Jimmy said. 'You didn't come here looking for a game.'

The one in the sport coat smiled, wagged a scolding finger. Of the two, he was apparently the point man. Up close, you could see pockmark scars of long-ago acne on his face. His eyes were dull but not stupid. 'I'm Dominic. This is Anthony. We're here to offer our services.'

'Is that right?' Jimmy said.

Dominic nodded, lighting up a Parliament. 'We hear you're doing pretty good. We want to make sure that continues.'

Anthony suddenly picked up a chair by the legs and swung it like a baseball bat into the window of the smoking-room door. There was a loud thud and the Plexiglas pane cracked although it didn't come out.

Anthony started winding up for another swing.

'All right, all right, I get the picture,' Jimmy said.

Anthony swung the chair again despite Jimmy's plea

258

and this time the pane popped out, crashing to the floor on the other side of the door.

'Jesus,' Jimmy said.

'That's a shame,' Dominic said.

'Let me guess. You'll make sure nothing like this happens in the future.'

'It's good you understand.'

'Thing is, it's not me alone,' Jimmy said. 'I got a partner.'

'Sure. You need a couple of days to think things through. I understand,' Dominic said. He dropped his half-smoked cigarette on the floor and rubbed it out with his heel. 'We'll be back.'

After they left, Jimmy stayed in the smoking room a few moments to collect his thoughts. Then he called Ray Howie. Two years earlier, Ray had approached Jimmy about starting up a room. They'd known each other for years as players.

Ray was a solid guy, a contractor who'd made a bundle flipping properties in the Hamptons, and now in his mid-forties was basically retired. He was a winning poker player himself, though not on Jimmy's level.

Jimmy was considered by many regs and pros to be one of the top two or three players in the city, legendary for his ability to sniff out bullshit and weakness and make crazy calls and impossible folds. He was pushing fifty himself when Ray came along with the idea of starting a place. Jimmy's two kids were in middle school. The games in New York had gotten tougher, young sharp kids from the finance world and the Ivy League, combined with the higher rakes, cutting into his edge. On top of that, even great players could go through down times, and Jimmy was a realist – especially with college tuitions on the horizon.

Ray said he'd put up the bulk of the start-up costs, the build-out of the space, tables, chairs, cards, chips, flat-screen televisions. All Jimmy had to do for his half was contribute ten per cent of the capital, bring in players and be the public face. Two years later, with half a million in profits stashed away in a half-dozen safe deposit boxes, Jimmy felt like it was the smartest thing he'd ever done.

Now this.

'I'll ask around,' Ray said. 'See what I can find out about our friends.'

'Miserable fucking lowlife parasites.'

Ray looked at the business card Jimmy had gotten from the guy. The name Dominic Pagano was written in the middle. On each corner in embossed letters was the following: No Home, No Phone, No Job, No Number.

'He's got a sense of humour anyway,' Ray said.

'Yeah, a real wiseguy.'

Next day, Jimmy met Ray at the club in the afternoon before the doors opened. A couple of the dealers were there already, cleaning up from the night before, taking out bags of garbage, stocking the refrigerator with bottles of water and soda, sorting decks.

'Let's go sit in the smoking room,' Jimmy said.

When Ray saw the temporary plywood over the window, he shook his head.

They sat down on the built-in banquette. 'So what'd you find out?' Jimmy asked.

Ray drummed his hands on his thighs. 'They're small-timers. But they like to drop names. Joey Salzano for one.'

'Joey Onions? Jesus.'

'Yeah, but that's like me saying I got the US Government behind me because I pay taxes.'

'You don't pay taxes.'

'Point is they might give Salzano a piece of whatever they're doing, but that doesn't mean he's *behind* them.'

'But he might be?'

Ray turned up his palms. Jimmy had always found Ray to be careful and meticulous in his approach to both poker and business. He knew people on both sides of the street, and had enough juice that they'd been able to operate up till now without any interference. It was Ray who'd brought in Captain Mike, an ex-NYPD cop. In exchange for promising to tip them to any activity at the local precinct, Mike got back every dime of rake he paid. And since he was there most days, it amounted to a lot, maybe twenty grand over the course of the year. So far, Mike hadn't sounded any alarms, and the cops had stayed out of their hair. This was something different.

'So what's our plan?' Jimmy said.

'Why don't we see how much they want.'

'Really? There's a number you'd be good with?'

'What are we gonna do, Jimmy?'

'Tell 'em to go fuck themselves?'

'Yeah, we could do that.'

'But?'

'It might be easier to play ball, is all.'

261

'Fuckin' vultures.'

'I know, I know.'

At home, Jimmy spent the afternoon in the kitchen. He liked to cook. His wife, Rosemary, said he brought the same intensity to cooking that he brought to poker. He found working in the kitchen relaxing, another way to occupy himself and not obsess about moves he had made or hadn't made in his last session. When Rosemary had first started dating him, he'd bent her ear recounting hands he'd won and lost, amusing her with his descriptions of the crazy degens who inhabited the clubs. By the time they got married, the poker talk was old hat and she made fun of him and gave him the business whenever he started in. 'Yeah, I know,' she'd say, 'and then you raised, and like an idiot he called, and of course hit his three-outer on the river cuz he's just a dumb luckbox. And that's why I can't buy a new couch this week.'

He no longer talked to her about poker or what happened at the club. For her part, though she had made her peace with what he did, she was happier not hearing about it. These days, at home at least, he was all about sous vide and powdered olive oil and blowtorching steaks. Benji and Chloe, eleven and twelve respectively, tolerated his more ambitious experiments but the two tweens made no secret of preferring the simple pastas and meatloafs their mother made and were grateful that their father was working at the club and unable to cook most nights during the week. *Seriously, Dad, bourbon pecan chicken? Are we even allowed to have alcohol?*

Both kids went to public school. It had been good

enough for Jimmy, growing up in Brooklyn, but Rosie thought they should at least think about private school when it came time for the next phase. 'It's not like we can't afford it,' she said.

Jimmy didn't argue it though it kind of ticked him off that his wife refused to acknowledge the uncertainty of their future. He wanted to say, 'Don't you understand? I'm in a business where you have to plan for a rainy day – maybe even a rainy rest of your life?'

Once, he thought poker would last forever. Couldn't imagine that changing. There'd always be juicy games he could beat. Lately, though, he found himself afraid of being left behind. For a guy who'd always made his living taking risks, it was a funny way to be thinking. Maybe the illusion of stability he'd found with the club was making him soft. He worried about that.

Five days after their initial visit, Dominic and Anthony returned. This time they rang the bell like anyone else. After being called over to look at the security monitor, Jimmy told the door guy to buzz them in.

Again, Jimmy walked the two men back to the smoking room. As he ushered them through the door, he decided that Anthony purposely bought shirts that were a couple of sizes too small to make himself appear bigger. Like the Hulk, he could probably split apart the seams just by flexing.

'So you had a chance to talk things over with your partner?' Dominic said.

'I have.'

'And?'

'We'll listen to your offer.'

'Like I told you, we know you been doing pretty good. We did some calculations. Based on what we came up with, we think fifty per cent of the net is fair.'

'What, fifty per cent! Are you fucking kidding me?'

'Do we look like we're kidding? Anthony, you want to show him if we're kidding or not?'

Anthony moved very close to Jimmy, backing him up against the wall. He put a massive hand on Jimmy's shoulder and squeezed so hard Jimmy had to say, 'Hey hey.'

'That's OK, Anthony,' Dominic said.

The big man stopped squeezing but stayed in Jimmy's face, staring him down with his dead shark grey eyes.

'Look,' Jimmy said. 'You guys come here—' He tried to move to one side as he talked but Anthony moved with him.

Dominic nodded and Anthony backed off. 'You come to this place that my partner and I built up from nothing, and you demand half of it. Just like that. Like it's your birthright. So that's a little hard for me to digest. Half. I mean if that's not negotiable, we may just decide to close our doors.'

'I really doubt that,' Dominic said. 'You made at least three hundred gees last year, personally. You going to walk away from that?'

'It would be a hundred and fifty,' Jimmy said.

'What?'

'If we give you half, I'd only be walking away from a hundred and fifty.'

'So raise the rake. Squeeze a little more out of the players. You work it right, you won't make a penny less.'

264

'You don't think I'm being serious?'

'I think when you talk it over with your partner, you'll see the light.'

'The guy hit you?' Ray asked.

'He got up in my face. He didn't actually hit me. Although I've got his fingerprints on my shoulder.'

Ray frowned. They were sitting at the bar of the Hungry Giant, across the street from the club. 'You mean it about walking away?'

'What do you think?'

'I don't know. I can't read you.'

'You never could.'

'You bluffing them?'

'They think I am.'

'The guy has a point though. We could take more out of the game. Put in another table. Figure out ways to increase the gross. It doesn't have to affect our bottom line.'

'I want to be able to live with myself.'

'Even if it means going back to grinding?'

'I just want to be able to live with myself.'

Jimmy never told Rosie what was going on. He knew she'd freak. The truth was, he was afraid. Of Dominic and Anthony, but also of the alternative, of going back to poker without a net. Sure, he had a bigger bankroll now and was better equipped to weather the variance. But he'd gotten used to a stable income. He worried that he didn't have the nerve for the swings any more.

It was true what they said about getting older. He was

forty-eight and he felt like he was seventy. His world had shrunk. His balls had shrivelled. He didn't like what he saw when he looked in the mirror. Some of the clarity and sharpness had drained from his blue eyes, which now projected a slightly rheumy milkiness. His earlobes appeared suddenly pendulous. His eyebrows seemed to be disappearing. He'd even noticed a patch of grey in his pubes. Fuck, could anything be more depressing than that?

Ray kept making the case that dealing with mob shake-down artists was the price of doing business, that they had actually been lucky to have operated free and clear so long and they should be grateful for that. But Jimmy couldn't stomach it. Not on such usurious terms, not when dealing with a pair of such unbending do-nothing bloodsuckers. Without even another sitdown, he closed up shop, turned off the lights, told his dealers and floor people and cocktail waitresses that he and Ray were suspending operations, maybe for good.

Then, less than a week later, coming out of his apartment building on Prince Street, he saw the two bozos waiting for him, leaning against a parked car, looking like cartoon versions of themselves. His heart rate spiked though outwardly he remained calm.

'We seem to have had a misunderstanding,' Dominic said.

'How's that?' Jimmy muttered, continuing to walk, glad that the street was crowded in the late morning.

'You didn't inform us what your plans for the club were.' Dominic fell into step beside him, with Anthony trailing behind.

'Is that right? I thought I was pretty clear. I told you that I'd rather shut down than give you half.'

'And I suggested how you might maintain your rate of profit by making a few adjustments to the way you were running things.'

'Yeah. Except that doesn't work for me.'

'You'd really rather go out of business than accommodate us?'

'Apparently I would.'

Jimmy turned into the Apple store and the two men followed. He thanked the helpful salesperson who approached them, saying that he knew where he was going, and he made a beeline for a polished waist-high wooden table that had speaker systems for iPhones. He pushed a button on one and the sound came on, playing some pop song he'd heard but didn't know the name of.

'Not bad quality,' he said. 'For something so small.'

'Look, maybe we can work something out that's more agreeable to you,' Dominic offered.

Jimmy laughed – not because he was surprised, the opposite actually. It was mostly just a question now of how far he could push this. 'Like what?' he said.

'Like we'll reduce our take to a third.'

Jimmy stopped an Apple salesperson and told her that he wished to purchase the Bose sound dock he'd been looking at. As she punched in the order on her iPhone, Jimmy could sense Dominic's agitation. Jimmy handed her his credit card and signed the screen with his finger.

'All right, twenty-five per cent,' Dominic said. 'But that's as low as we go, and you don't say nothing to nobody.'

*

Ray was dying. 'You didn't stop there? You got 'em all the way down to twenty? Fuckin' A, Jimmy, who's better than you?'

'I think I might have pushed it to fifteen, I don't know. But if I had, Anthony woulda busted out of his shirt and Dominic might have popped a blood vessel in his forehead.'

Ray and Jimmy reopened the club a week later. After a slow first couple of days, word got around and before you knew it the room was packed again.

From a financial perspective, they did better than ever. Though he refused to raise the rake, Jimmy introduced a $10–$25 game that proved extremely profitable for the house – as well as for him. Sitting in on the game regularly, he beat it for near two hundred grand over the course of the year. On top of the three hundred he cleared from his share of the business, it was his best year ever.

Somehow it didn't matter. Just knowing that Dominic and Anthony were getting a piece of things – no matter how small – ruined it for him. He felt compromised. Diminished. No longer his own man. So after the holidays were over, a year after things had changed, he told Ray that he had decided to sell his piece.

Ray tried to talk him out of it of course. He certainly didn't intend to buy Jimmy out himself. Besides, if Jimmy left, who was going to run the place?

As it turned out, one of the floor guys, Larry the Pirate, was dying for the chance. He didn't have the upfront cash, but he agreed to pay Jimmy three hundred grand on a three-year instalment plan, and that was that. Jimmy was done.

For the next several months, he went back to being a player, going to various games around the city three or four nights a week. But it wasn't like it used to be. He didn't have the same hunger for the game that he had once had. He wound up spending too much time at home, driving Rosie and the kids nuts with his pent-up, unfocused energy. One day, while Rosie sat at the kitchen island, sipping a glass of Verdicchio, watching him shell and devein shrimp for a paella, she said, 'Why don't you start a restaurant? You know you want to.'

'A million reasons,' he said. 'For one thing, I'd never be home—'

'Yeah?' She looked at him, clearly not perceiving that as a problem.

He continued, ignoring the jibe. 'And for another, eight out of ten restaurants that open in New York fail ...'

'Uh huh.'

'That isn't enough? The fact that I'd be in a foul mood all the time and probably take it out on you?'

'Which would be different how, exactly?'

'Funny. Look, I know you think I'm good in the kitchen, but what if I'm not? I mean what if I'm just OK?'

'Then you'll have tried something. So what?'

It wasn't as if they had never had this conversation before. It was just that this time he couldn't seem to get it out of his head afterwards. It nagged at him for days, then weeks. He took it up with Ray when they met for lunch at the Hungry Giant one afternoon.

'She's right,' Ray said. 'You should try it. I'll even put my money where my mouth is.'

And so it was that Jimmy Ahearn, with the backing of

his good friend Ray Howie and several other poker pro friends, opened a home-style café and restaurant called Ahearn's Folly in the neighbourhood near their Prince Street apartment. And while it wasn't the huge success he hoped, it was also, against the odds, not a failure. In time, the Folly, as he called it, even became something of a local favourite, proving appealing even to his picky-eater children and their new private school friends, who took to hanging out there after school, much to Jimmy's and Rosemary's delight.

The day they showed up, Jimmy was in the kitchen, chopping vegetables for a stew. One of the waiters came in, a bit nervous, saying, 'There's a couple of guys out there say they know you.'

Jimmy stepped from the kitchen, wiping his hands on his apron. The two men looked up as he approached, Dominic in a flowered shirt and brown leather jacket, Anthony in a shamrock green velour tracksuit with white stripes down the sleeves.

He had never kidded himself that this day wouldn't come. In many ways, the restaurant business wasn't so very different from the poker club business except that it operated out in the open and legally.

'Nice place, Jimmy.' They were standing just inside the glass door entrance, Dominic looking around, nodding in an appreciative way at the white-painted brick, the tasteful black-and-white photographs.

'I like to think so,' Jimmy said.

'You know why we're here, right?'

'I got a pretty good idea.'

'Look at him, Anthony. He's starting to get nervous.'

The two men laughed.

Jimmy regarded them uncertainly.

'Relax,' Dominic said. 'We're just yanking your chain. We happened to be in the neighbourhood and thought we'd stop in, see how you're doing.'

'He don't believe you,' Anthony said.

'Why should he?'

'Why shouldna he?'

'The truth is,' Dominic said, looking Jimmy square in the eye, 'if not for us, he probably never woulda opened this fuckin' joint in the first place, am I right, Jimmy?'

Jimmy smiled. It was hard to deny the truth of that. In a funny way, he realised, he owed these two mooks a debt of gratitude.

'You're fuckin' right I'm right,' Dominic said. He picked up a menu from the rack near the door. 'So tell me, what's good here, anyway?'

'Loads of things,' Jimmy said. 'The special's a very nice lime-chilli marinated swordfish . . .' A thought occurred to him. 'But tomorrow, tomorrow is my personal favourite – bourbon pecan chicken. You guys really oughtta come back for the bourbon pecan chicken. As my special guests, of course. Assuming, that is, that we're still open tomorrow . . .'

Although he said this in a joking way and with the confidence that it would be taken in that spirit, it was also possible he meant it.

With Jimmy Ahearn there was always that chance.

271

Author biographies

Co-author of *One of a Kind*, a biography of Stu Ungar (2006), **Peter Alson** has written three other non-fiction works, including *Take Me To The River* (2007). His forthcoming novel, *The Lucky and the Good*, is set in the world of New York underground poker.

Author of the poker classic *The Biggest Game in Town* (1983), the poet, critic and novelist **Al Alvarez** also published *Poker: Bets, Bluffs, and Bad Beats* (2001) among many other books on a wide range of subjects including an autobiography, *Where Did It All Go Right?* (1999).

Co-founder of the Hendon Mob, **Barny Boatman** is a highly successful professional poker player, winner of many tournaments including two World Series of Poker bracelets.

New Yorker **David Curtis**'s *Queer Luck: Poker Stories from the New York Sun* was originally published by Brentano's of New York in 1899.

Author of *The Professor, the Banker, and the Suicide King: Inside the Richest Poker Game of All Time* (2005), **Michael Craig** was also blogger for the FullTilt poker website and edited its strategy guides.

The British poet laureate **Carol Ann Duffy** has published more than thirty volumes of poetry as well as plays and books for children. She is Professor of Contemporary Poetry at Manchester Metropolitan University.

The American-born British author **David Flusfeder** has written seven novels, including *The Gift* and, most recently, *John the Pupil*. He was poker columnist for the *Sunday Telegraph*, and edited the IFP handbook *The Rules of Poker*.

Grant Gillespie is an actor, novelist and screenwriter. He published his debut novel, *The Cuckoo Boy*, in 2010. He has also appeared in numerous TV and film roles.

Co-editor **Anthony Holden** has written forty books including the poker classic *Big Deal* (1999) and its sequel *Bigger Deal* (2007), as well as two manuals, *All In* (2005) and *Holden on Hold'em* (2008). From 2009–13 he was the first President of the International Federation of Poker.

James McManus is the author of *Positively Fifth Street* (2003), *Cowboys Full* (2009), and *The Education of A Poker Player* (2015), a collection of short stories, among eight other works of fiction, non-fiction and poetry.

Oscar-nominated for his screenplay of Zoe Heller's novel *Notes on a Scandal* (2007), the playwright and director **Patrick Marber** made his debut with *Dealer's Choice* (1995) and has since written nine more plays, including *Don Juan in Soho* and *The Red Lion*.

The actor and antiquarian book dealer **Neil Pearson** has appeared in numerous TV and film roles, not least the Bridget Jones series, and wrote *Obelisk: A History of Jack Kahane and the Obelisk Press* (2007).

Winner of the 2003 Booker Prize for his first novel *Vernon God Little*, the Australian-born writer **D.B.C. Pierre** has since published four more novels and two collections of short stories.

The English actor, comedian and writer **Lucy Porter** has made numerous appearances on radio and TV, regularly performing live shows at the Edinburgh Festival and touring the UK with her one-woman shows.

Shelley Rubenstein is a writer, broadcaster and producer. She learned to play poker at the age of seven, and has hustled her way through life ever since. She features regularly on TV, as both player and pundit.

The writer and journalist **Grub Smith** has published two books, *Real Sex* and *Real Lover*, and hosted several TV travel series.

The works of the Croatian-born playwright **Tena Štivičić** have been performed in a dozen European countries, including *Fragile* (2005) in Slovenia, *3 Winters* (2014) at London's National Theatre and *Goldoni Terminus* at the 2007 Venice Biennale.

The Canadian-American actress and professional poker player **Jennifer Tilly**, who won the WSOP Ladies' No Limit Hold'em bracelet in 2005, has also appeared in numerous film and TV roles, winning an Oscar nomination in Woody Allen's *Bullets over Broadway* (1994). For ten years, she wrote a monthly poker column for *Bluff* magazine.

Acknowledgements

The kernel of the idea for this collection of stories first emerged while Anthony Holden was President of the International Federation of Poker. In partnership with Bobby Nayyar of Limehouse Books, IFP published *The Rules of Poker*, edited by David Flusfeder, in 2012; and the plan was to develop the idea of an anthology of new fiction on poker to follow that. When IFP, Anthony and Limehouse Books parted company, however, the idea was put on hold, until Anthony and Natalie decided that they must take it forward and make it happen. And now, at long last, here it is!

The editors would like to thank our esteemed colleagues at Simon & Schuster for all their encouragement, advice and enthusiasm while this project came together – in particular, Ian Marshall, Suzanne Baboneau and Ian Chapman for their invaluable support. We are indebted to Al and Anne Alvarez for their simpatico reading of the book, especially to Al for writing such an elegant Preface. We also offer warm thanks to David Headley and all at DHH literary agency. Most importantly, to all our excellent contributors, without whom ... we owe you a huge debt of gratitude for these wonderful stories and for all your hard work, patience and creative vigour throughout this labour of love. Each one of you did us proud and the result is a truly outstanding body of new writing on this most compelling of games.

Copyright and Credits